# DOES THE WOMAN OF MY DREAMS EXIST?

# Does The Woman Of My Dreams Exist?

Phillip Parcheminer

| Library of Congress Control Number: | | 2022918786 |
|---|---|---|
| ISBN: | Hardcover | 978-1-6698-5104-2 |
| | Softcover | 978-1-6698-5105-9 |
| | eBook | 978-1-6698-5106-6 |

Print information available on the last page.

Rev. date: 11/02/2022

**To order additional copies of this book, contact:**
Xlibris
844-714-8691
www.Xlibris.com
Orders@Xlibris.com
844717

# CONTENTS

# About The Book

Does the Woman of My Dreams exist? This is the question that I am asking the universe as I write my second book. I doubted the existence of the woman of my dreams when I started to write my second book. I doubted her existence because of how cruel the rest of the world could be to someone with social anxiety. I thought my years of being bullied were over before the writing of my second book. Then the bullying started all over again after I was somehow able to find the courage to let one of my angels know how I felt about her. This vilification led me into another pit of darkness. It had me believing it was wrong to love beautiful women. Yet my love for beautiful women was also the only thing to keep me alive.

# Does The Woman Of My Dreams Exist?

Will I ever meet a beautiful woman who has the social confidence to make the first move? Will I ever meet a beautiful woman who is able to defy the odds by approaching me first to let me know that she is interested? Will I ever meet a beautiful woman with the compassion to understand the weirdness of my anxiety? Will I ever meet a beautiful woman who is able to look past my love for beautiful women to see that there is only one woman of my dreams? Will I ever meet a beautiful woman who is able to accept the fact that I have never had a romantic relationship? Will I ever meet a beautiful woman who has any of the qualities that I am looking for in a beautiful woman who is also single when I finally do find her? Will I ever find a beautiful angel with any of these qualities who also loves the cold and is of the appropriate age?

These are the questions that I am asking the universe as I start to write my second book. However, the ultimate question I am asking the universe is, does the woman of my dreams exist?

I do not know if the woman of my dreams exists. I am not sure if there is a beautiful woman out there who is able to defy the odds of normal society to be the woman of my dreams. I hope she exists. However, the older I get, the more I am starting to worry that she might not exist. I am starting to doubt her existence because as I get older, I am finding it more difficult to find a beautiful woman who is both available and of the appropriate age. Thus I am starting to lose all hope that the woman of my dreams exists. My loss of hope is something that has me living life anxious and depressed because I fear my greatest fear will turn into my darkest reality.

My greatest fear has always been to grow old and alone without ever finding love. My greatest fear has always been that I might never feel the warmth and compassion of a beautiful woman. This fear is an all-consuming fear that has me lying awake at night, thinking about the emptiness that I feel from obsessing over all the beautiful angels who I will never be able to get.

My name is Phillip Parcheminer. I am a man without a voice who loves beautiful women. These are two things that I will never be able to change about myself. I do not care how much I wish I could tell a beautiful woman how I feel about her. This is, unfortunately, something that will never happen because I am always placing them upon these pedestals. Then once I place them upon these pedestals, they turn into an angel I will never be able to approach. I do not care how much I like them or how beautiful they are—I will never approach them because I start finding all these reasons why I could never be with them. They are too beautiful for me to ever have a chance with them. They probably have a boyfriend, or they are married. These are only two of my excuses for never being able to approach them. Sadly, these same excuses then lead me to living life isolated and alone while still obsessing over beautiful angels.

My obsession with my beautiful angels is something else about my life that will never change because of how I feel whenever I see a beautiful woman. I do not care how depressed I might get because I have never known the warmth of a beautiful woman. I do not care how gloomy and dark my reality might get because I fear I will grow old without ever finding love. I will always be inspired and energized by the beauty of beautiful women. There is nothing more inspiring than the sight of beautiful women. I will walk half an hour through the humidity and heat of ninety-degree weather for the chance of seeing a beautiful woman. I know I will not talk to her once I see her. However, this does not change the fact that I want to see her. I felt this when I decided to go to the library rather than stay at home to write one day.

I went to the library because it was Tuesday, and this was when one of my angels was working at the library. So I decided to suffer through the heat and humidity to see if I could be inspired by her while I was writing. Then when I got there, I saw an even more beautiful angel than I could have ever imagined, and I knew that I made the right decision when I decided to go to the library to see her.

This beautiful angel left the library soon after I got there. She was only there for about fifteen minutes before she left. However, while she was there I was able to get a good look at her while she was walking around looking for some books. There was even one point where she started to walk right beside me as she was looking for these books. I could not believe how close she was to me as she was looking for some books. I could not believe how beautiful this angel looked. This beautiful angel was a beautiful young brunette angel with a nice tan, wearing a pair of shorts and a green top that did not cover much at all. I could not stop thinking about this angel during those fifteen minutes she was at the library. Then when she was near me, I was feeling so anxious that I could not sit still or focus. She finally left, and my anxiety was overtaken by this dark depression since I'd lost any chance I had of being with her. I knew I could not be with her for so many reasons. She was half my age. She had a boyfriend. She probably was not thinking of me half as much as I was thinking of her. She might be uncomfortable with me looking at her so much. Yet the greatest obstacle that was standing between us ever being together was my debilitating social anxiety. I knew I could never socialize with this angel no matter how much I liked her due to my debilitating social anxiety.

My social anxiety has me believing that I will never be able to socialize with people because of my fear of humanity. My fear of humanity originated from my many years of being bullied during elementary and middle school. My years of being bullied were going to traumatize me for the rest of my life because I started to see everyone as a bully. I saw bald-headed, heavyset men as being bullies. I even started to refer to these men as Bluto, because they reminded me of Bluto from *Popeye*. I saw middle-aged women as being bullies because I saw them as the female versions of a Bluto. I saw young males as being bullies because they learned how to be bullies from their parents. I was even starting to see my angels as bullies because I believed they were quietly having others do the bullying for them. Yet I still wanted to see my angels since their beauty helped me deal with my fear of humanity.

My fear of humanity is the root cause of my social anxiety. My fear of humanity is inescapable. Thus my social anxiety is inescapable. My social anxiety has made it impossible for me to ever live a normal life. I fear I will never know the warmth and compassion of a beautiful woman because of my social anxiety. I fear I will never know what it is like to have a group of friends to socialize with because of my social anxiety. I fear I will never know what it is like to feel safe around men because of my social anxiety. I fear I might never feel comfortable around people at work because of my social anxiety. These fears are only a few of the many fears that I have to deal with everyday because of my social anxiety. This social anxiety has turned my existence into this dark reality from which I might never be able to escape.

I fear I will never escape the dark thoughts that have created this dark reality. I fear I might never escape the discomfort I feel from being obsessed with beautiful women. I fear I will never be able to escape the fear of being judged by men because of my obsessions. I fear I will never be able to escape the depressive thoughts I have of never having had a girlfriend. I fear I will never be able to escape the fear I have of being hurt by women if I approach them. These are the dark thoughts that plague my life. These are the dark thoughts I am unable to escape no matter how much I try to change them. These dark thoughts are the thoughts that keep me living a life isolated and alone. I live my life isolated and alone because I fear how others might react if they discover my dark thoughts. I especially fear what beautiful women might think. This is not to say that I do not care what others think because I do care. I have always been sensitive to what people think, be it a man or a woman, young or old. However, I have never cared more about what people think than what beautiful women may think. My sensitivity to what beautiful women think is ultimately what keeps me from ever approaching them. So I live life at my locations of inspiration, obsessing over them from a distance, writing about their inspiring beauty.

I love seeing beautiful women. I love the feeling I get every time I see a beautiful woman. There is nothing more inspirational than seeing a beautiful woman. This feeling I get from seeing a beautiful woman is the only reason I want to live at times. I have had moments when my existence has been so dark that I did not know how to keep going. Then I remembered how I felt when I saw one of my angels, and I was inspired to keep going. I felt inspired to keep going because of the hope of one day finding the woman of my dreams.

Does this woman of my dreams exist? Is there a beautiful woman out there who is able to defy the odds of normal society to make the first move? I do not know if this woman of my dreams exists. I hope that she exists. I hope to someday find this angel who is able to break the many walls of anxiety I have built. Unfortunately, the older I get, the more I am starting to fear that she might not exist because I am a man in his forties who has never dated. Yet if there is any hope of finding her, then I believe my spiritual journey will have been a journey worth traveling. I believe there is nothing more special in this world than finding the woman of my dreams.

My spiritual journey to the woman of my dreams started with the discovery of my beautiful blonde library angel. My spiritual journey started with me making a powerful decision to follow my obsession with her wherever it may lead. I had no clue where this journey was going to lead me when I started my obsession with her. I only knew that she was one of the most beautiful angels that I had ever seen and I had to see her angelic beauty again and again. So I started to spend all my time at the library trying to catch a glimpse of her angelic beauty. Then the more time I spent at the library, the more I had to find a way to pass my time while there. Journaling was going to be my way of passing my time while I went there to see her. I spent my time journaling about my fall into my pit of darkness, and her angelic beauty. I also was spending my time there journaling about my fear of humanity and my love for beautiful women. Mostly, I spent my time at the library journaling about how my beautiful blonde library angel was helping me find the courage and confidence to keep going since she was my symbol of hope.

I had lost all hope of ever being with a beautiful woman before my beautiful blonde library angel turned into my symbol of hope. I still do not know if the woman of my dreams exists. She might not exist. However, when I spent these two years at the library obsessing over this beautiful blonde library angel, she had me believing that she might exist. She had me believing that I might one day find my way to her with my passion for writing. I believed that if I wrote my books and got them published, then one day I might find my way to her. I knew that I could never be the initiator of a conversation with her because of my debilitating social anxiety. So I had to think outside the box and think of another way to be with the woman of my dreams. I started to believe that if I wrote and published my books, the woman of my dreams might be the initiator.

I believed I was never going to be able to get over my social anxiety to initiate a conversation with a beautiful woman. It made no difference how much I wished things could be different. It made no difference how beautiful I found my angels. I knew if they were expecting me to initiate a conversation with them, then nothing was ever going to happen with them.

I knew the hold that my debilitating social anxiety had over me and my life. I knew how much of a handicap it was to my life. I knew that this was a handicap I could never get over no matter how much I liked a woman. After all, if I was never able to say a word to my beautiful blonde library angel after two years of obsessing over her, what chance did I have with my other angels? So I was starting to believe that my passion for writing was the only path to the woman of my dreams. I believed that the only chance I was ever going to have with a beautiful woman was if I got my books published and she learned about me through my books. Then I was getting impatient with my spiritual journey. Thus I started to write them letters to tell them how I felt. Sadly, this was to be a costly mistake since it led me into another pit of darkness. This was going to lead me back to my belief that my only way of finding the one was if I wrote my books.

I did not know anything about social anxiety before my move to America. I was never bullied when I was French. I was never ridiculed for being shy or sensitive as a French child. I am not sure if this was because of my French culture or my French family. All I knew about "My Wonderful French Childhood" was that I was not ashamed of being me when I was French.

My French family and friends are gone. Some are, sadly, dead. Some have now moved away. Annabelle is now married and most likely has a family. So I know that she will never be the woman of my dreams. I also know that I will never be able to return to "My Wonderful French Childhood" even if I move back to France. I know this because I tried to return to it after high school, with no luck. I tried to recapture the magic of "My Wonderful French Childhood." Sadly, I was unsuccessful because my social anxiety was too ingrained into my being after high school. However, I did get some glimpses of the best years of my life when I returned to France. There were my talks with my French grandmother, and there was the magical day I spent with Annabelle walking around the traditional streets of Guingamp. This was such a magical day because I felt so comfortable socializing with Annabelle. Two hours felt like only five minutes.

My return trip to France was also filled with moments of me feeling socially uncomfortable. There were moments when I felt anxious talking to my French grandfather because I was not a child anymore. My French grandfather was my favorite grandparent as a child because of how we always joked around with each other. We still could joke around. However, once we were done joking, my social anxiety returned, and I got really uncomfortable with him because we had nothing to talk about with each other after we stopped joking. I was also never that comfortable socializing with any of my other family members.

Pierre-Yves was the only other family member I was socially comfortable around. Pierre-Yves was my best friend and my favorite of my four French cousins. I loved spending time with him because I was so socially comfortable with him. Also, some of my best memories from France were of us reading Uncle Scrooge French comic books together. Alas, I was, sadly, never as socially comfortable around the rest of my French family as I was with Pierre-Yves and my grandmother.

My moments of feeling socially anxious around my French family outnumbered my moments of social comfort. I was spending most of my time hidden away at home listening to French music when I returned to France. I was also watching French TV while at home. I remember there being this one French show that I loved to watch called *Hélène et Les Garcons*.

I was obsessed with this French show. I never missed an episode. This show was all about the romantic adventures of French teens while they went to school. So I guess this show was more of a French teen soap opera than anything else. I also loved this show for its music. The star of this French teen soap opera was also a singer, and this was the real draw to this show.

This was how I spent most of my time during my return trip to France. I was either watching French TV or listening to French music. My passion for French music is the only thing more powerful than my love for beautiful women. I love seeing beautiful women. However, there is nothing more powerful or inspirational than the sound of a beautiful French song. The feeling I get from hearing a beautiful French song is like medicine to my ears. At times, a French song is all that helps me deal with my fear of never being with the woman of my dreams.

"Espérer"! This is a French song written by Michel Sardou. This French song is without question the most inspirational French song I ever heard. The lyrics of this French song are word-for-word how I feel about my life. It is difficult for me to write about this song without translating the entire song. The first few lines of this French song are about being different from everyone else who believes. Another line is about the world not going your way and never having anyone to love other than your dark, empty nights. Then it gets into the chorus, which is all about hope. "Hope" is the English translation of *Espérer*. The chorus to this song is all about how we still have to have hope because the world is still beautiful. One line states that when a star burns out, the sky is still alive. It sings about how if the world scares you and keeps you silent, you must continue to have hope. You must continue to have hope because it is worth it. You must have hope since you are still alive even if you did not choose where or when. Finally, this inspirational song closes with another verse of the chorus about hope. Then it closes with the best line of the entire song: "La Response est en toi, la question est ailleurs." The English translation is, "The answer is in you, the question is elsewhere." This line is the best line of this song because I believe the answer to my life's questions is within me and not elsewhere. I believe the answer to the question of my book lies within me and my spiritual journey to the one.

My dream of moving to France was replaced by my dream of moving to Alaska. My dream of moving to France died once I learned everyone I loved was gone. I still loved France and its beautiful French language. However, I did not have to go to France to keep these memories alive anymore. I now keep my memories of France alive through my love of French music and my passion for writing. After my dream of moving to France died, Alaska was my new dream for my future. Alaska is where I see myself living when I see myself in my snowy log cabin. This dream of living in my snowy log cabin was my dream for my future when I wrote *The Beautiful Blonde Library Angel*. This is still one of my dreams for the future. However, this is not the only dream that I have for my future anymore. I now also dream of someday being a traveling writer because I do not feel safe where I live anymore. I lost my sense of safety here after I was bullied out of three of my locations of inspiration. These losses were devastating losses and led me to change my ways of obsessing over beautiful women. I still loved beautiful women and I will always love beautiful women. This is who I am, and this will never change. Sadly, the rest of the world was trying to tell me I was wrong for loving beautiful women so much, or at least for how I loved them. It was telling me I was wrong for being obsessed with the beauty of beautiful women because it was wrong to stare at them. Sadly, this was something that was difficult for me to accept since I loved looking at my angels.

I loved spending hours at my locations of inspiration staring at beautiful women. It inspired me so much to see beautiful women. The more beautiful the woman, the more inspired I was by their beauty. I found four great locations of inspiration since I started my spiritual journey to the woman of my dreams. There was the library where I first discovered my beautiful blonde library angel. There was my original French Bistro. There was a new French Bistro that I was going to because there were so many angels who worked and ate there. Finally, I had this coffee shop that I was going to because I lost both my French Bistros. I could not imagine life without my locations of inspiration. Then, one after another, I started to lose them.

The loss of my locations of inspiration led me into another pit of darkness. I could not believe how cruel this world could be to someone with social anxiety. I could not believe how I was being vilified simply for loving beautiful women. Yet it was, and there was absolutely nothing that I was able to do about it other than write through the pain I was feeling. Sadly, I lost almost all my angels of inspiration after I lost my locations of inspiration. I knew I could still turn to the beautiful angels at Bon Gout for inspiration because I was still working there. There was also still another angel of inspiration who was left—my beautiful blonde library angel.

# My Beautiful Blonde Library Angel

My beautiful blonde library angel will always be the most inspirational angel of my spiritual journey. I know I will always be able to return to my beautiful blonde library angel for inspiration since she was this perfect angel that never hurt me because I never approached her. So after my fall into another pit of darkness, I knew of only one angel I could turn to who could lead me out of my fall into another pit of darkness, and it was my beautiful blonde library angel. Thus I decided it was time for me to return to the roots of where it all began after I fell into my pit of darkness. I decided it was time for me to return to the library because I wanted to see if I could feel its magic again since I now knew that she was working close by. Unfortunately, having her close was not the same as having her there. So I decided to find a new place to write.

I decided to start going to this coffee shop that was literally right across the street from the bakery where she was working to start writing. I thought if I could not see her at least I could see where she was working as I was writing. I was thinking if I knew she was right across the street, then maybe I could at least feel her spiritual energy while I was writing. So I left the library, and I drove to this coffee shop that was literally only two minutes away. Then as I walked into this coffee shop, I knew I made the right decision because of how it looked inside. The inside of this coffee shop looked like the farmhouse where I lived before I moved to America. So I knew I made the right decision because of how this coffee shop reminded me of "My Wonderful French Childhood." This coffee shop was not very impressive from the outside, which was why I never went there before my fall into another pit of darkness. Yet I always knew about this coffee shop because before it was a coffee shop, it was a restaurant. I remember this restaurant because I loved their fish sandwiches and fries. Their fish sandwiches were something of a treat whenever I had something to celebrate. Another reason why I remembered this restaurant was because this was also the restaurant where I left this large tip.

I left this large tip because I was feeling so generous when I moved to Ohio. I was feeling so generous because this was when I got my first credit card and I wanted to tip people. I felt the need to tip people because of my social anxiety. I felt this was a way to get their attention without saying anything to them. I thought if I tipped the waitresses, then they might be impressed and say something to me about getting these large tips. Sadly, this never did happen because I left right after I tipped them, never to return because I feared them saying something. I was going from restaurant to restaurant making these large tips. Then this restaurant was the last restaurant where I left a waitress a large tip because my tipping was getting so out of control.

I learned that this restaurant where I made my last large tip closed soon after. I knew there was no linking the two. However, a part of me was starting to think that there was a link between me making this tip and the restaurant closing. These thoughts never went very far, though, since I forgot about this restaurant after it closed. I thought this restaurant was going to get demolished after it closed, so I never gave it a second thought. Then a few years later, I saw that it was now a jazz coffee shop. Yet I still never went there. It was not that I did not like jazz music, because I did love listening to Louis Armstrong. I loved listening to Louis Armstrong ever since Ken Burns introduced me to him. Ken Burns had a ten-hour jazz special that recounted the history of jazz music in America. There was not much that I remembered about this special other than it being my introduction to the great Louis Armstrong.

Louis Armstrong had such a beautiful and unique voice. I could not get enough of listening to his instrumental voice. His voice literally sounded like a trumpet. I believe that this was how he got his nickname Satchmo. It made no difference what kind of music I was listening to from Louis Armstrong because it was more about his voice and not the type of music.

Louis Armstrong was one of five artists I listened to whether I liked their music or not. Each of these artists had such a unique voice that I did not care about the music because I wanted to hear their voices. Rod

Stewart, Elvis Presley, Luther Vandross, and Pavarotti were the other four artists who I loved to listen to for their voices. I am not saying that I did not like their genre of music. I am only saying that I never liked their music as much as I liked listening to their voices. I was especially impressed with Rod Steward because when you listened to him, it sounded like he had strep throat. As much as I liked these artists' voices, though, I never spent much time listening to their music because I wanted to listen to other types of music more. Sadly, I knew I only had so much time everyday to listen to music, so I had to start to prioritize.

My first choice for the type of music that I wanted to listen to was always French music. I was listening to French music every chance that I got during the week because of how French music filled me with pride. I always felt a special source of pride in knowing and understanding French music. I always felt this was a secret source of pride I had that no one was ever going to know about unless they read my books. The only time during the week that I was not listening to French music was Saturday, because this was my Latin day. I never understood much of the lyrics to Spanish music since I did not know the language. I did know some Spanish because I took classes during college. However, I was not fluent so I was only able to understand a word here and there as I listened to Spanish music. Yet I still loved listening to Spanish music because it was so energizing and romantic. Mana, Enrique Iglesias, La Oreja de Van Gogh, Chayanne, and Shakira were a few of my favorite Latin singers. Spanish music and French music were my first choice of music to listen to during the week. Yet it was not the only music that I loved to listen to during the week. There were also moments when I loved to listen to American music. Some of my favorite American singers are Bon Jovi, Bryan Adams, Taylor Swift, Michael Jackson, and the great lyricist Avril Lavigne. I also listened to Shania Twain, Billy Joel, ABBA, Phil Collins, and Meat Loaf if I felt nostalgic. Then I also loved to listen to New Age music whenever I wanted to be enlightened. I especially loved listening to "Kokoro" by Kitaro because it was more of a musical experience than a song. Every time I heard its seven-minute guitar solo, it took me to another spiritual plane. So, I had to make sure I picked the right moments to hear this song because I did not want to be interrupted. So yes, I did like to listen to Louis Armstrong and jazz music. However, it was never a priority unless I wanted to listen to Louis Armstrong's instrumental voice. The only time when I attempted to listen to jazz music was Friday night since Friday nights always felt like jazz night.

I never went to this coffee shop once I thought it was a jazz coffee shop since I never really had a reason to go there before. I always had other places to go to for inspiration before I fell into another pit of darkness. First, there was this bookstore that I went to and the college campuses where I went to school before I was introduced to my beautiful blonde library angel. Once I was introduced to my beautiful blonde library angel, the library turned into my main source of inspiration for the first two years of my spiritual journey. Then my original French Bistro turned into another location of inspiration when I saw this beautiful black-haired angel. This beautiful black-haired angel was one of the most beautiful angels I ever saw since my beautiful blonde library angel. However, it was not only her beauty that drew me to her as I started going to my original French Bistro. It was more her personality that drew me to her because she was so friendly and outgoing. I will never forget how she was always saying hello to me when I went there to write. This beautiful black-haired angel was my first angel of inspiration outside of the library. Hence, she was my introduction to my original French Bistro.

I spent close to a year going back and forth between the library and my original French Bistro. I loved spending time at this French Bistro because there were so many beautiful angels inspiring me to write when I was there. First, there was this beautiful black-haired angel who introduced me to my original French Bistro. Then when she disappeared, I had to try and find other angels of inspiration to take her place. The first angel of inspiration that I found to take her place was going to be this beautiful blonde angel who worked there. This beautiful blonde was going to be an important angel once my beautiful blonde library angel left the library. She was going to be so important because she carried the torch for her once she finally left. There was this tall beautiful blonde angel who was very friendly. Yet I was never too inspired by her because she was too intimidating. There were these two beautiful deerlike angels that worked there who were also my angels of inspiration. One of them was this tall deerlike blonde angel who occasionally wore glasses. I remember the times she wore her glasses because these were the times when she was the most beautiful. Lastly, there was this beautiful tall ebony angel who also reminded me of a deer. This ebony deerlike angel started working at this French Bistro much later than the other angels. Yet this did not make her any less inspiring. I found her inspiring because she was so quiet and shy. I loved her timidity because it had me thinking that she might also have social anxiety. Then she was looking at me when I was looking at her, which had me thinking she might be interested. One day she even complimented me on my haircut. Sadly, nothing ever happened because of my social anxiety.

I knew I was going to keep going to the library to see my beautiful blonde library angel since she was still the most inspirational angel of my spiritual journey. I knew of only two things that might keep me from seeing her at the library. The first was if that dreaded day finally arrived when she quit working at the library forever. Then the second was if I was somehow able to finally find success as a published writer. I knew I had to find success as a published writer because I still believed that this was my only path to finding the woman of my dreams. I knew I was never going to meet the one if I had to socialize with her. I believed that my only path to ever finding the woman of my dreams was if I wrote my books and I got them published.

My passion for writing was still the only place where I could imagine myself having a chance with a beautiful woman. I knew I was never going to have success with one of my angels if they were waiting for me to socialize with them. So I knew that the only way I was ever going to be with the woman of my dreams was through my writing, or if she made the first move. I knew I was never going to make the first move because of my social anxiety. I knew that my social anxiety was still too much of a handicap for me to make the first move. However, I was also starting to see that I could socialize with a beautiful woman if I was comfortable with her. I knew that this was something that was possible because of my best friend, who was a woman. Before meeting my best friend, I never could have imagined feeling so comfortable with a woman. However, after meeting my best friend, this changed, and I believed that it was possible.

My best friend was a very unique individual. I never met another woman as socially confident as my best friend. I never met a beautiful woman as compassionate as my best friend. I never met a woman that I felt so socially comfortable with as my best friend. I never met a woman I could be so honest with as my best friend. I could tell my best friend almost anything, and she never judged me for what I said or what I believed. Thus I treasured my friendship with my best friend because I was hoping that over time, this might help me talk to women. Sadly, it did not because I realized that other women were not like my best friend. I realized that my best friend was a unique individual that could never be matched. Sadly, she was also a woman with a family of her own and responsibilities. Thus she was not going to have much time for me after we stopped working together. This was very disappointing because once I started to spend less time with her, I realized I still could not talk to any of my beautiful angels.

My best friend was special because she was the first beautiful woman who I could socialize with about my love for beautiful women. I was able to talk to her about my obsession with my beautiful blonde library angel because she had her own obsession. Sadly, I could not spend much time with her anymore because of her responsibilities. So I started to return to my obsession with beautiful women and to my beliefs that I could not talk to beautiful women. I returned to being invisible to beautiful women and to feeling empty inside once they were gone.

I believed that my obsession with beautiful women was all I was ever going to have because of my debilitating social anxiety. I could not talk to beautiful women because I lacked the confidence to talk to them. I lacked this confidence because I felt unworthy of ever being with a beautiful woman. There were so many reasons why I felt unworthy of ever being with a beautiful woman. I was still living with my mother. I never had a romantic relationship of any kind. I lacked the financial stability to support a beautiful woman if I could say something to her. I could not compete with the other men out there who also wanted to be with these beautiful women. These were only some of the reasons I had for never being able to approach a beautiful woman to let her know how I felt. These reasons were so powerful that I was never able to see my way past them. Then I saw my beautiful blonde library angel at the library, and all this changed. This changed as she turned into my symbol of hope for what I hoped to one day attain.

I never thought I was going to see my beautiful blonde library angel again once she stopped working at the library. I believed that once she stopped working at the library, she was going to move to New York to be a dancer. It was my belief that my beautiful blonde library angel had a dream of being a dancer because of this article I read. This article said she had won an award for dancing. So after reading this article, it was my belief that she was going to be moving to New York to be a dancer when she left the library. Then soon after she left the library, I learned that she started working at this bakery across the street from the library. I was so thrilled to learn that my beautiful blonde library angel had never left town. It did not matter that my beautiful blonde library angel was not working at the library anymore. It made no difference to me that I could not physically see her anymore. She was still the most inspirational angel of my spiritual journey. I never found an angel who was more inspirational than my beautiful blonde library angel. I may have found some angels who might have been as beautiful, or even more beautiful than her. However, I never found an angel who was more inspirational than my beautiful blonde library angel. I believe she will always be the most inspirational angel of my spiritual journey until I find the woman of my dreams. So after I learned that she never left town, all I wanted to do was go to see her angelic beauty once again. Unfortunately, I was going to find this difficult to do because I was afraid of making her uncomfortable. Yet I decided to still make an attempt at going to see her because I still wanted to see her angelic beauty.

I drove to the bakery with every intention of seeing her before therapy. I had to try because I wanted nothing more than to see my beautiful blonde library angel again. Then once I finally got to the bakery, I kept driving because I could not find the courage to see her. However, as I was driving to therapy, I decided to try one more time because this might be my only chance to see her since I was not sure what my therapist might say after I saw him. I hoped that he was going to encourage me to try to see her again. Yet I also knew he might try to discourage me since it might be wrong for me to go to see her at the bakery. Thus I had to make one last attempt at seeing her before therapy because it might be my only chance. Sadly, once I got there, she was not there. Thus I never got a chance to see her before therapy.

I will never forget my beautiful blonde library angel since I have all these reminders of her. I am reminded of her with my passion for writing as I write about my spiritual journey with her. I am reminded of her when I listen to music that reminds me of my spiritual journey with her. I am reminded of her when I look at the pictures that I found of her once I learned her name. These pictures are what help me to remember her angelic beauty after she left the library. I still look at her pictures whenever I want to be reminded of her angelic beauty. She was so special because I never approached her. I never believed I had a shot with her, so I knew that if I approached her, I might lose her as my perfect angel. I could not lose her as my perfect angel.

It was not only her beauty that turned her into a perfect angel. It was also her timing that made her into this perfect beautiful blonde angel.

This beautiful blonde library angel appeared in my life at a time when I lost all hope for a better future. I lost this hope because of the return of my migraines. The return of my migraines meant I had to let go of my dream of being a truck driver. After I lost my dream of being a truck driver, I fell into a pit of darkness because I was going to have to work with people again, which meant socializing with them again. I dreaded the idea of having to socialize with people again after I thought I had found an escape. I did not know how I was going to return to work when I knew I was so afraid of people. I felt trapped because I knew I had to make money, yet I could not work with people again. Then I remembered seeing my beautiful blonde library angel. Once I remembered seeing her, my obsession with her started, which gave birth to my passion for writing and my spiritual journey.

She remained at the library until I wrote *The Beautiful Blonde Library Angel.* She remained at the library until I published *The Beautiful Blonde Library Angel.* Thus, as beautiful as she was, it was more her timing that made her such a perfect angel. I am not saying that she was not beautiful. I still remember those brown eyes that complemented her golden blonde hair so well. I still remember those rosy cheeks with those bright white teeth whenever I saw her smile and giggle. I still remember that great athletic figure she had because she was an aspiring dancer. Mostly though, what I will never forget is her angelic face with that cute button nose. So no, I never could have imagined there being a more perfect angel than my beautiful blonde library angel. So when I learned that she was working at this bakery, I decided that it was enough to simply know that she was working at this bakery that was right across the street from the library.

I decided it was best that I never try to see her there since I did not want to make her uncomfortable. I decided that knowing she never left town was enough. Then I fell into another pit of darkness, and I knew of only one angel that could guide me out of my pit of darkness. I knew I had to return to the roots of where it all began. I knew I had to return to the library and to seeing the angelic beauty of my beautiful blonde library angel. Unfortunately, once I returned to the library, I never felt the same magic I felt when my beautiful blonde library angel was there. So I decided it was time for me to find a new location of inspiration, and I thought that this coffee shop across the street from where she was working might be it. Sadly, my time at this coffee shop was not going to last since they were going to banish me from going there. My banishment from this coffee shop was going to lead me into an even darker pit of darkness. Although for now, I felt this coffee shop might be my new location of inspiration. So I started to go there as much as possible as I fell into another pit of darkness. I went there to see the beautiful angels working there and to see where my beautiful blonde library angel was working. I believed that this might be my new routine while writing my second book. I thought I'd found my way back to my beautiful blonde library angel after the day I always dreaded finally arrived.

# The Day I Always Dreaded

The day I always dreaded finally arrived. I was devastated to learn that my beautiful blonde library angel was leaving the library. I was devastated to learn that my spiritual journey with her at the library might be over. I was not sure how to survive the loss of this beautiful angel that changed my life forever. I only knew that she was leaving the library, and there was nothing that I could do to keep this from happening. I was going to have to find a way to continue my spiritual journey without her, or so I thought. Once my beautiful blonde library angel left the library, I believed that this was it. I believed that she was going to disappear from my life, never to be seen again. I never imagined that one day I might see her again outside the library. Then a few months later, I learned that she had started to work at this bakery across the street from the library, and I knew my spiritual journey with her was not over.

My beautiful blonde library angel was the most important person in my life when I started my spiritual journey with her at the library. I could not stop going to the library to see her once I got my first glimpse of her beauty. Her beauty was simply too mesmerizing for me to forget once I got my first look at her. I tried to return to a sense of normalcy once I got my first look at her angelic beauty. However, I found this impossible to do because once I saw her angelic beauty, there was nothing else that occupied my mind. All I could think about after I saw her were those rosy cheeks and that cute button nose. All I could think about were her beautiful brown eyes and her golden blonde dark hair. All I could think about was her incredible physique because she was an aspiring dancer. Yet mostly, all

I could think about was how I felt that one hot Saturday when I saw her for the first time at the library. How could I possibly ever forget her signature scarlet-red lipstick and the bright white smile on that angelic face? It was impossible for me to forget about this beautiful blonde librarian after I first saw her at the library.

I never expected my beautiful blonde library angel to outlast all the library angels that worked there. I never expected her to be at the library until I wrote and published my first book about my two-and-a-half-year spiritual journey with her. However, she did outlast them and remained at the library until I published and wrote my first book. I could not believe how blessed I was to have had this angel as part of my life for two and a half years. Sadly, as blessed as I felt, I knew there was going to be a day when she was going to leave the library. I did not know when she was going to leave the library. I only knew that this day was fast approaching since she was probably ready to leave. So I tried to prepare for this day the best I could by searching for a new location of inspiration to go write at once she finally left the library forever.

It has been over two years since I last saw my beautiful blonde library angel at the library. I might not know the exact date of when she entered my life because I had no idea what she was going to mean to my life when I first saw her at the library. How could I have known that this blonde librarian with this angelic face was going to change my life forever? How was I to know that she was going to help me discover my passion for writing? I had no way of knowing either of these things when I first saw her at the library. I had no way of knowing that she was going to be one of the most important people in my life. I had no way of knowing that seeing her there for the first time was going to give birth to my spiritual journey. So no, I never knew the exact date of when she entered my life. However, the one date and time I could never forget was when she was going to leave the library forever. Tuesday, May 28th, 2019, at 7:50 p.m.

I could not have asked for a more perfect way to say goodbye to my beautiful blonde library angel than that inspirational Tuesday. My last day at the library with my beautiful blonde library angel did not start out perfectly because it was raining outside. I did not want to run through the rain to go to the library. Yet I also did not want to miss a chance of seeing her at the library if she was there. So I knew I had to make my way through the rain to see if she was there. Then when I finally got to the library, I saw that she was nowhere to be found. Not only was she not at the library, but none of my other angels were there either as I started to look around. So I was starting to think that this was going to be a very uninspiring day at the library. Then I was about ready to leave when I saw my beautiful blonde library angel at the registers. She remained at the library until 7:50 p.m. that day. So I had a wonderful four hours with her at the library, where she inspired me to create an entire chapter about my last day with her. More importantly, she looked the best I ever remembered her looking when I saw her there that Tuesday.

She was wearing these torn blue jeans and a black top with flowers where she was showing her shoulders. She was wearing her signature red lipstick that accentuated her angelic face with that cute button nose. Yet what I remember best about how she looked was her angelic face. Then there was the fact that she passed by me where I was sitting several times before she finally left the library forever. So I was able to get a good look at her before she finally left. Sadly, these four hours I spent with her were not perfect because I should have left the library earlier than I did. However, I stayed at the library because I wanted to try to listen to her theme song as I saw her there one last time. Unfortunately, it was ten minutes until closing time, and I was the only person left who was keeping them there. So I was feeling really anxious about still being there. Also, I noticed that she was nowhere to be found as I looked around the library. Thus I left the library feeling very disappointed. Yet this feeling of disappointment did not last because as I drove away from the library, I had this urge to go back to the library. I wanted to go back to the library to try to get one last glimpse of my angel. I was glad I turned around because I was able to get one last glimpse of her as she was leaving the library. This glimpse I got of her leaving the library was going to be the last glimpse I got of her that Tuesday.

My spiritual journey with my beautiful blonde library angel was unexpected. I never expected to see this blonde librarian at the library that one hot Saturday. I never expected her to be this angel that was going to change my life forever after I saw her at the library. Yet my beautiful blonde library did forever change my life because she led me to my passion for writing. Then my passion for writing gave birth to my spiritual journey to the woman of my dreams. I also never expected Tuesday to be the last time that I was ever going to see her at the library. I thought Friday, May 31st, 2019, was going to be the last time I was going to see her there.

Unfortunately, I was mistaken since she never did reappear to me when I went there that Friday.

These two and a half years with my beautiful blonde library angel were the best years of my life since my wonderful French childhood. I will remember this spiritual journey for the rest of my life because it is the story that inspired me to write my first two books. So from this day forward, she will live within these books about my spiritual journey to the woman of my dreams.

My first book is called *The Beautiful Blonde Library Angel.* I finally published my first book two years ago before she left the library. I was grateful that she remained at the library until I got my first book published. I never met an angel as inspirational as my beautiful blonde library angel. Unfortunately, I knew that it was only a matter of time before she left the library. I knew the day of her leaving the library forever was getting closer and closer. So I had to find some new angels of inspiration to carry the torch for her once she left. I knew that my spiritual journey to the woman of my dreams was still not over once she left since I was still alone. My ultimate goal was still to one day be with the woman of my dreams. I still had no idea if the woman of my dreams existed. Yet I still held out hope that one day I might find my way to her.

It was actually a blessing that my beautiful blonde library angel did not make her final appearance at the library that Friday. This turned out to be a blessing because once I realized she was never going to make a physical appearance, I started to feel her spiritual presence. This Friday started out with me having to accept that she was not going to appear to me at the library. I decided to not wait until that last hour because after five hours, she was probably not going to reappear to me that last hour. So I decided to leave the library at about five rather than wait that last hour before they closed. However, my time at the library was not a waste because while there, I went through a mental and spiritual transition. This mental and spiritual transition started out with me saying goodbye to her physical presence at the library. As the hours passed, I did not see my beautiful blonde library angel anywhere. I kept waiting and hoping she might make an appearance. Sadly, this never happened. So I started to realize that Tuesday, May 28th, 2019, was going to be my last chance to physically see her at the library. Then I started mentally preparing myself for her loss as my passion for writing once again helped me find a way to heal.

I am so grateful to my beautiful blonde library angel for her existence because I never could have discovered my passion for writing without her. My passion for writing also led me to another discovery that Friday. It led me to the power of her pictures as I realized she was not going to reappear. These pictures were something I treasured since they helped me to not forget her angelic beauty. As a matter of fact, I am looking at these pictures of her angelic beauty now while writing about the day I always dreaded finally arriving. It was not right away that I got these pictures of her angelic beauty, though, because it took me some time to learn her name. I was able to finally learn her name when I overheard her talking to one of the other library angels. I remember I was sitting there at one of the computers at the library with my back toward them as they were putting books away and talking. Normally, I will not eavesdrop because I do not really want reality to mix with my fantasy of my angels. However, this time I decided to eavesdrop because I loved how inspirational it felt to hear their voice. Also, I loved that they felt comfortable enough talking with me being right there. This was another thing I really loved about my beautiful blonde library angel. She never did shy away from my obsession with her.

I was glad I made the decision to eavesdrop that day because this decision I made was what led me to finding out her name. It was such a beautiful name. Then a few months after learning her name, I found pictures of her for when she finally left the library. I wanted a way to keep her physical beauty alive after the day I always dreaded finally arrived. Then I tried to find pictures of her by typing her name into the computer. Luckily, this was not difficult to find because she posted so many pictures of herself. I was thrilled to find these pictures because they were another tool to keep her memory alive. I had my passion for writing to keep her spiritual presence alive when I wrote about my spiritual journey. Then I had these pictures to keep her angelic beauty alive when I wanted to remember how beautiful she was when I went there to see her for inspiration. So I had a way to keep her spiritual and physical beauty alive. I was grateful that this spiritual journey had provided me with a way to keep her memory alive. I was especially grateful for this as the day I always dreaded finally arrived. I was also grateful I had all these other angels to carry the torch for her.

I had all these beautiful angels to carry the torch for my beautiful blonde library angel after she left the library. There were going to be these new angels who arrived once she left the library. I also had the beautiful angels at my French Bistro. Yet as great as these beautiful angels were, none were as special or as inspirational as my beautiful blonde library angel. My beautiful blonde library angel was so special because she introduced me to so many things. She introduced me to the power of being obsessed with beautiful women. She introduced me to my passion for writing. My passion for writing was to give birth to my spiritual journey to the woman of my dreams. She also introduced me to my passion for music. These were only some of the things I was introduced to after seeing my beautiful blonde library angel. So as I am saying goodbye to this beauty, I am not feeling that devastated by her loss. I am more grateful to her for appearing in my life when she did. I am grateful to her for having had two and a half years with her at the library. However, as grateful as I am to her for having been such an inspirational angel, I am looking forward to seeing where my spiritual journey will lead me now.

I am feeling this sense of excitement because my beautiful blonde library angel had a powerful hold over me during these years at the library. I have no regrets about my time spent with her because they were some of the best years of my life. However, now that I know she finally left the library, I am able to see where my spiritual journey will lead me after her. My hope is that my spiritual journey will lead me to find the woman of my dreams. My hope is that I will find out that one of these angels I am obsessed over is the woman of my dreams. Therefore, I am feeling both grateful and hopeful now that my beautiful blonde library angel left.

I first started to make the transition from the library to my original French Bistro with this beautiful black-haired angel who was working there. This beautiful black-haired angel was another beautiful angel that I was never going to forget. She was only at this French Bistro for about two months. Yet she was a very inspirational angel because she was the first angel of inspiration that I was going to find to help me continue my spiritual journey outside the library.

I was spending all my time at the library before I discovered this new angel at my original French Bistro. I never went anywhere else since all I needed when I started my spiritual journey to the woman of my dreams was my beautiful blonde library angel and all her friends. There were four other library angels who carried the torch for her when she was not working. There was this beautiful black-haired angel who was very beautiful. However, I do not remember much else about her since she was there for only a small amount of time. There was this beautiful Irish angel with freckles. She was the only beautiful angel who worked there during the day. There was the beautiful angel who I approached with a letter, which she never accepted. Annabelle 2, was what I started to call this angel because she reminded me of my French soulmate. I was devastated when she rejected me after I approached her with a letter, but then this devastation led me to find the power to heal from my passion for writing. Then there was this beautiful angel who played a musical instrument. I started to call her my beautiful creative library angel. Finally, there were these two beautiful angels that started to work there when my four other library angels started to gradually leave. First, there was a beautiful ebony library angel who liked to hide her beauty. Yet I knew that this angel was beautiful. However, her beauty was sadly always overshadowed by this other new beautiful library angel.

I thought that this new library angel that arrived at the library was going to be the beautiful library angel who was going to carry the torch for my beautiful blonde library angel. I even started to call her my fiery redhead because of her red hair and her beauty. I thought she might carry the torch for my original angel because of how I was introduced to her. I first saw my fiery redhead when I saw her walking toward me with my beautiful blonde library angel. I had no clue what they were talking about when I first saw them walking toward me at the library. I only knew that she was beautiful, and when I saw them together, it felt as if the torch was being passed to her. I was preparing myself for that dreaded day when my beautiful blonde library angel would be gone from the library forever. I knew she was not going to work at the library for the rest of her life. I knew that someday she was going to be gone from my life forever because she was only working there while she went to college. So when I saw this fiery redhead at the library, I thought the universe was telling me that she was going to be my new angel. Unfortunately, I soon found out I was wrong about her since she left right after my blonde angel.

My spiritual journey with my beautiful blonde library angel taught me all about the power of beautiful women. It taught me how inspiring they could be once I entered my world of isolation with them. I first started to enter my world of isolation with them when I made my decision to follow my obsession with my beautiful blonde library angel. I knew that I could not spend all of my time at the library simply staring at my beautiful blonde library angel. I knew I needed to find a way to pass my time while I was there to see her. So I started to journal about her beauty and my fall into my pit of darkness. Then I needed a way to block out humanity while there.

So I started to listen to my passion for music while I was at the library. The cold and my soda also helped to empower my world of isolation at the library. Once these five elements converged to create my world of isolation at the library, my spiritual journey was born.

The library was my only location of inspiration for two and a half years. My beautiful blonde library angel was all I needed at the start of my spiritual journey with her. Unfortunately, she was not always at the library. So I started to turn to the other library angels who worked there when she was not working. However, she was always the most powerful of all my angels of inspiration, which is why I called my first book The beautiful blonde library angel. Then, my beautiful blonde library angel left the library about two years ago. Once this dreaded day arrived, my fear was that my spiritual journey to the woman of my dreams might be over. Yet, it was not over. Instead, I was going to find out that once she left, my spiritual journey to the woman of my dreams was only starting because I was to find all these other angels of inspiration.

I lost the library as my location of inspiration when my beautiful blonde library angel stopped working there. I tried to return to the library to try to be inspired by this other angel who was now working there while I was taking a break from my new French Bistro. Unfortunately, I was not feeling the same inspiration I felt there with my beautiful blonde library angel. So, I knew the library had lost its magic. So I returned to my new French Bistro, and I said goodbye to the library again. I was never planning to return to the library once I thought it had lost its magic. Then I fell into a darker pit of darkness than I could have ever imagined, and I had to try to make my way back to the library since it was the only place that I felt safe again.

Does the woman of my dreams exist? I am starting to believe that the woman of my dreams does not exist. I am really starting to doubt that a beautiful woman exists who is able to break through all the walls I have built because of my fear of humanity and my social anxiety. Yet I still have a speck of hope that she might exist. Although I am starting to believe that I will have to expand my search for this woman by looking elsewhere. I am seriously starting to doubt I will ever find her where I live because I am haunted by so many dark memories there. Therefore, as I continue my search for the woman of my dreams, I must turn more to my writing. I still believe that my passion for writing will lead me to her. I still believe writing my books is my way to her. I first discovered my spiritual journey to the woman of my dreams five years ago as I started to follow my obsession with my beautiful blonde library angel. When I started my spiritual journey with her, I did not care what others thought about the weirdness of my anxiety. I did not care how people judged me for spending all my time at the library to catch a glimpse of her angelic beauty. All I cared about was catching a glimpse of her beauty because of how I felt when I saw her. So this was how my spiritual journey to the woman of my dreams started. It started with my obsession with a beautiful blonde library angel.

It has been five years since the start of my spiritual journey with this beautiful blonde library angel. It has been over two years since the dreaded day finally arrived. I could never see my beautiful blonde library angel at the library again. After the day I always dreaded finally arrived, my spiritual journey to finding the one had to continue with my search for a new angel of inspiration.

# MY SEARCH FOR A NEW ANGEL OF INSPIRATION

My search for a new angel of inspiration started with the loss of my beautiful blonde library angel. I was not sure how I was going to survive the loss of my beautiful blonde library angel. I was not sure how I was going to survive the loss of this angel that changed my life forever after she introduced me to my passion for writing. I only knew that I was going to have to find a way to survive without her because I still had not found the woman of my dreams. I still had not found a beautiful woman to break through the walls of my social anxiety. Therefore, my search for the one had to continue without her after she left the library forever.

I knew none of these beautiful angels were going to be able to replace her. I knew there could never be an angel as inspirational as my beautiful blonde library angel. I knew that she was irreplaceable. So I knew she was always going to be my most powerful source of inspiration even after she left. Yet I also knew that she was not the woman of my dreams since I never said one word to her other than the time I thanked her for being so beautiful. I will never forget that bubbly giggle after I thanked her for being so beautiful. How could I ever forget this bubbly giggle when it was the only time I ever approached her at the library. I never could find the courage to have a conversation with her, or even say hello to her. I literally spent two and a half years at the library obsessed with this angel without ever saying anything else to her. Thus I never once believed that she was the woman of my dreams while at the library. How could she be the woman of my dreams when she did not even know that I existed? This is why I believe my real search for the woman of my dreams started when she finally left the library for good. I believe it started with this fiery redhead who started to work there. I truly did believe with all my heart that this fiery redhead was going to be the one to carry the torch for her. I truly did believe my beautiful blonde library angel and her friends were leading me to this fiery redhead.

This fiery redhead had a physique that I will never forget. She had this wonderful physique because she was a soccer player. Don't ask me how I learned that she was a soccer player because I never asked her or overheard her say anything about being a soccer player. However, I somehow knew she was a soccer player because of her incredible figure. I even remember thinking of her athletic figure one night as motivation to complete one of my runs. I remember being so out of breath that night that I did not know how I was going to keep running. Then I remembered the incredible figure of this fiery redhead, and she inspired me to keep running. There was even a point during the last part of my run when I visualized this fiery redhead from the library as my inspiration to keep running. After this inspirational run, I was starting to believe this fiery redhead might be my new angel after my blonde angel finally left.

Another reason why I started to believe that she might be the one to carry the torch for her after she left was because of how I was introduced to this fiery redhead. I will never forget how I was introduced to her because of who she was walking with that day. I remember her walking toward me and talking with my beautiful blonde library angel. It literally felt as if the torch was being passed to her that day because they were both so beautiful. I could not hear what they were saying as they were walking toward me that day. Yet it really did not matter because this moment felt so perfect that I did not really want to hear what they were saying. Then there was another time when I overheard her talking to someone about this guy that she liked, and I thought she might be interested. This only intensified my feelings toward her because I felt over time something might happen with her. I knew that this fiery redhead was way out of my league. I knew there was too much of an age difference for me to have a real chance with her. I knew she probably had thousands of guys pining over her at school. However, I could not help how I felt about this fiery redhead when I went to the library to write.

My passion for writing allowed me to see a path to her when there was no real path to her. My passion for writing inspired me to believe that maybe someday I might have a chance with her if I stayed true to my spiritual journey. Then one day, I discovered her name as I overheard some of the librarians talking. This only helped to intensify my beliefs that she might be the woman of my dreams because I was then able to find pictures of her. This fiery redhead was the only library angel that I found pictures of besides my beautiful blonde library angel. So after I found these pictures of her, I could not stop thinking she might be my new library angel. Thus I was prepared to stay at the library until she left once my beautiful blonde library angel left the library forever. This time I had with my fiery redhead and my beautiful blonde library angel was so inspirational that I never wanted them to leave. Sadly, these beautiful angels eventually left the library, and I then had to continue my search for the one outside the library.

I had two weeks to prepare for the loss of my beautiful blonde library angel. I first learned that she was leaving when I heard her say she finally gave her two weeks' notice. After I heard this, I took some time off from work because I did not want to miss my chance to see her. Sadly, I was going to get only two more chances to see her at the library during these two weeks. However, one of these two days was going to be that magical Tuesday when I never expected to see her there. So I was glad that I took time off from work to see her because had I not taken this time off from work, I might have missed my last chance to see her at the library. Unfortunately, I was not going to have the same time to prepare for the loss of my fiery redhead.

The library lost its magic once I realized that the fiery redhead was never going to reappear at the library. It took me about two weeks to realize that she had also stopped working at the library once my beautiful blonde library angel left. I was probably more devastated by losing my fiery redhead from the library than the loss of my beautiful blonde library angel. Of course, I missed my beautiful blonde library angel once she left. Of course, I wanted to keep seeing her angelic beauty at the library if she still worked there. However, I had more than two years with her at the library before she left, and then two weeks to say goodbye to her. Sadly, the same could not be said about my fiery redhead because I had no time to prepare for her exit. So I could not continue going to the library after the loss of both of my library angels because it was too painful to be there without them being there to inspire my writing. I was ready to keep going to the library after the loss of my beautiful blonde library angel. I was ready to keep going there because I still had a connection to her with this fiery redhead. Then, when this fiery redhead left the library, I knew that it was also time for me to leave the library since it had lost its magic.

There were still two beautiful angels working at the library when I left. There was a beautiful ebony angel that was still working there. Plus, there was this new blonde library angel that started working there the same day when I said goodbye to my beautiful blonde library angel. Thus I could have continued to go to the library to continue my spiritual journey with them. Unfortunately, it was too painful for me to even try. So I knew it was time to leave the library.

I never planned to return to the library after it lost its magic. I never imagined there being a time when I might want to return after it lost its magic. Then I fell into another pit of darkness, and I felt myself being drawn back to it. There were no beautiful angels working there other than this beautiful black-haired library angel. This library angel was attractive. Yet she was nowhere near as inspirational as my two library angels. Plus, I was dealing with the discomfort I felt from all the other librarians who knew me from when I was there before. However, I kept being pulled back to the library because of my memories of my library angels. So eventually, I did find my way back to the library after a two-year absence. Before I write about my return to the library, though, I must first write about my spiritual journey away from it.

I believe my beautiful blonde library angel was one of the loves of my life. I do not know if she was the love of my life. However, I do believe that she was one of the loves of my life. I believe there were four beautiful angels that were the loves of my life. The first was Annabelle, who was my French soulmate. The second was this beautiful blonde angel from high school who wrote me a letter to tell me she was interested. The third was this beautiful blonde sales angel working at Bon Gout, who I will introduce later. Finally, we get to my beautiful blonde library angel, who I could only thank for being so beautiful. Thus, I am well aware of this being an unreciprocated love. However, this does not change how I feel about her since I still believe this is love because I believe my connection to her goes beyond words. I believe that my love for her is more of a spiritual love. I never felt this kind of love with my other three angels. All my other loves were based upon my dreams of building a life with them as my wife. Yet I knew that this was something that was never going to happen with her. I knew I never had a chance with her while I was obsessed over her at the library. Actually, it was not until she finally left the library that I started to imagine that there might one day be some path to her.

I had to find a new place to write after my beautiful blonde library angel left the library. My original French Bistro was going to be my new place to write because there were all these beautiful angels that were still working there. Plus, there were all these beautiful angels that went there to eat as well. So I knew this was going to be my main source of inspiration after my beautiful blonde library angel left even if my fiery redhead had remained at the library. I knew I was going to continue to go back and forth between the library and my original French Bistro. I was going to go to the library when this fiery redhead was working. Then I was going to spend the rest of my time at my original French Bistro since there were so many angels there. These were my plans for getting over the loss of my beautiful blonde library angel. Then my fiery redhead also left the library, and I knew my plans had to change. I knew I was going to start spending all of my time at my original French Bistro since it was too painful to go to the library.

I never saw the fiery redhead at the library again after she left the library around noon that Saturday. She did reappear to me two more times at my French Bistros. The first time I saw her at one of my French Bistros was when she went to get some food with her mother. So she was only at my original French Bistro for a few moments when I saw her. I doubt she even saw me at my original French Bistro when she was there. However, I definitely saw her there getting her food, and it felt great to see her again. Then the second time I saw her at one of my French Bistros was when I saw her arrive at my new French Bistro with her friend. This time she was at my new French Bistro for about half an hour. I could not believe my eyes when I first saw her arrive. It had been about a year since I last saw her at the library. So I never expected to see her again. Then there she was, eating with one of her friends, and I was so grateful to her for reappearing in my life. After this, I think she reappeared two more times at my new French Bistro. However, I had trouble recognizing her because she looked older and more sophisticated than she did at the library. I was always so intimidated by this fiery redhead.

I never really stood a real chance with this fiery redhead because I was always too intimidated by her. I was also intimidated by the beauty of my beautiful blonde library angel. However, there was always something about my beautiful blonde library angel that had me feeling more comfortable with her than I did with this fiery redhead. I think it might have been her personality because she never felt uncomfortable with my obsession with her. Again, she may have been uncomfortable. She may have been so uncomfortable that this was why she finally decided to leave the library. However, I never got the impression that she was uncomfortable, which is why she still remains my perfect angel two years after she finally left. I will never forget my beautiful blonde library angel. This will be a theme throughout all my books. I believe the only woman who will ever get me to forget her is the woman of my dreams.

I thought that my spiritual journey was leading me to the fiery redhead as the woman of my dreams. I knew she was out of my league. I was too intimidated by her athletic figure to even think of approaching her when she was working at the library. I was also too intimidated by her personality to even think of approaching her. This fiery redhead was so quiet and reserved that I knew I could not approach her. I knew the woman of my dreams had to be more socially outgoing than this if I was going to have a chance with her. I knew that I was never going to make the first move because of my social anxiety. I knew I could not approach them because I had no clue what to say to these angels if I approached them. After all, how could I ever dream of approaching them to talk to them when I could not even say hello to them?

This is the life of someone with social anxiety. This is something no one will ever understand unless they truly do have social anxiety. I could go years obsessed over one of my angels and never even say hello to them. I know that this might make my beautiful angels uncomfortable. I know that this makes them think of me as this rude person who is too scary to approach because he never talks and always seems angry and depressed. Unfortunately, this is who I am, take it or leave it. I wish I could change who I am. I wish I could be someone else. However, I doubt I will ever change. I will always have social anxiety. I will always love to see beautiful women. I will always feel inadequate around beautiful women and most of humanity because of my lack of confidence. I will always have a fear of humanity because I see all people as bullies. So I have to learn to accept who I am because I will never change. I do not care how much I may like an angel, I will never make the first move. After all, I could not approach my beautiful blonde library angel. So how could I ever approach any other angel I am obsessed with? Thus, I believe there is only one path to the woman of my dreams, and this is with my passion for writing. I still believe that one day one of my angels will read one of my books and make the first move. I know that this may never happen. However, I do not see another path to the woman of my dreams because the older I get, the more I must accept myself.

I must stay true to my spiritual journey. It may never lead me to the woman of my dreams. I may grow old and alone never knowing what is like to find true love. This is a very dark future that I hope will never happen. This dark future has me going home most nights crying at times since I can't believe how cruel this world is to have me live this lonely existence.

I do not know if there is a god. I am not a religious person. I doubt I will ever believe because how do you want me to believe in something that could be so cruel? I never wished for this life. I never asked to live this life without love because I am a man without a voice. I never asked to love something I will probably never have—beautiful women. However, I do love beautiful women, and I do have social anxiety. Sadly, this is something that I will probably never be able to change about myself either. So I have to learn to accept my love for my angels.

My love for beautiful women is also why I will never kill myself. I do not care if it is taboo to write about suicide. I do not care how it sounds to tell people that my love for seeing beautiful women was the only thing that kept me alive at times. I could be banned from my locations of inspiration because I make my angels uncomfortable by looking at them. I might be alone for the rest of my life because women do not like me thinking of them as beautiful angels. Yet my obsession with beautiful women is the one thing that never dies. I could find myself within the darkest depression and be so afraid of humanity I want to cower away and die, yet once I see a beautiful woman, all of this disappears for that brief moment when I see them. Currently, I have been banned from all my locations of inspiration because of my obsession with beautiful women. I was so devastated by being banned from my locations of inspiration that I fell into another pit of darkness. I fell into another pit of darkness because they had me thinking that it was wrong to love beautiful women so much. They had me feeling so ashamed for my love for beautiful women that I was considering suicide. Then I started to find salvation in the unlikeliest of places. One of these places was work because I was still working at Bon Gout, which was still my perfect place to work. I knew it did not pay great, and I knew I could make more money if I went somewhere else to work. However, none of these places were as inspirational a place to work as was this work because there were so many beautiful angels there.

Another place where I was starting to find salvation after my fall into another pit of darkness was television. I did not feel safe writing at any location of inspiration after my fall into another pit of darkness because I was so afraid of being banned again. I tried to find another location of inspiration. However, I was not comfortable at any of these places because it was either too warm or I felt as though people knew I was there to look at angels. Thus the only place I felt safe writing was at home, where I turned to celebrities or beautiful angels from television as my angels of inspiration once again. Currently, my angels of inspiration are these beautiful angels from this reality show called *Love Island*. I'd never heard of the show before I fell into another pit of darkness. So by the time I get my book published, no one may have ever even heard of this show. However, this is the perfect show for me to watch right now since these angels are wearing these skimpy bikinis showing off their great bodies. Thus, Kyra, Bailey, Olivia, and Shannon are my angels of inspiration as I am writing about my search for a new angel of inspiration. These are the perfect angels of inspiration for me right now because I never have to feel uncomfortable looking at them since they are not real. Of course, these angels are real. However, they are not real because I doubt I will ever meet them.

Television is a wonderful thing when you need an escape from reality. I believe that television is something that people sometimes take for granted at times. However, when you are feeling suicidal because you love beautiful women, then there is nothing better than television. Where else could I go to watch beautiful women without worrying about the ramifications of others because I was looking at beautiful women. So television was a great place to turn to when I wanted to see some angels without the fear of being vilified for it. Yet I also knew that I was never going to meet these angels, and even if I did, I cannot talk to any of them. So as great as television is, it is not going to lead me to the woman of my dreams. Thus this brings me back to what made my work at Bon Gout so important. I believe that my work at Bon Gout might someday lead me to the woman of my dreams. This is something that I believe because one of the most unbelievable things was happening at work. I was finding the courage and confidence to say hi to some of my angels at work. I even had conversations with a few of them.

This is where my spiritual journey has led me to as I am currently writing the second book of my spiritual journey to finding the woman of my dreams. I am writing my second book about two years after my beautiful blonde library angel left the library. I am currently writing my story from home and at the library while I occasionally try out a new location of inspiration. Sadly, this search for a new location of inspiration has not gone very well because I have not been able to find a location of inspiration as inspirational as my two French Bistros. I was able to get over the loss of my original French Bistro rather quickly. I got over its loss so quickly because I still had my new French Bistro to go to for inspiration. Unfortunately, the loss of my new French Bistro was a much more difficult loss to get over due to what I lost. I doubt I will ever be able to get over the loss of my new French Bistro. However, before I write about my new French Bistro, I must first write all about my spiritual journey at my original French Bistro.

# My Spiritual Journey At My Original French Bistro

My spiritual journey at my original French Bistro started with the discovery of this beautiful black-haired angel who worked there. This beautiful black-haired angel was one of the most beautiful angels I had ever seen since the discovery of my two library angels. She had this great figure and this bright white smile that I will never forget. However, as beautiful as she was, it was not her beauty that really drew me to her. What really drew me to her was her flamboyant personality. This angel had one of the most cheerful personalities that I ever felt. I could not get over how nice and welcoming she was every time I went there to write. I will never forget how she always said hi to me and asked about my day when I went there to write. So after I was introduced to this beautiful black-haired angel, I could not stay away. I had to see if this beautiful black-haired angel might be the one. I knew she was out of my league. I knew she was too beautiful for me to have a real chance with her. After all, there was no way that I was the only person she was this nice to everyday. Plus, I could not ignore the glaring engagement ring she was wearing. So started my spiritual journey at my original French Bistro.

This beautiful black-haired angel was at my original French Bistro for only about two months. I kept hoping I might be wrong about her being gone from my original French Bistro. I kept hoping that one day I might see her again. Sadly, I never did see her again. I did see this angel that looked like her about a year later. She had black hair and a great figure.

She was wearing glasses and had that same flamboyant personality. Plus, I saw her visiting with some of the employees there. Yet I still had no way of knowing for certain if this was her. Also, she was there with her boyfriend and these other guys. So I chose to believe that this was not her since I did not want this memory of her to ruin my great memories of her. I know my beautiful black-haired angel was at my original French Bistro for only a short time. I know she was there for only two months. However, this angel was so inspirational for that short time because she was the first angel of inspiration I was going to discover outside of the library.

My beautiful blonde library angel was still working at the library when I first saw my beautiful black-haired angel at my original French Bistro. I knew I was going to keep going to the library to see my beautiful blonde library angel if she was still working there. Yet I also knew that my days of seeing her at the library were numbered. So I had to prepare myself for the worst. I had to prepare myself for the day when she was going to leave the library forever. I still did not know when she was going to leave the library. However, I knew that it was fast approaching because I knew she was only there as a student aid. So I had to start thinking about where I might find my inspiration after she left. Then I saw this beautiful black-haired angel working at my original French Bistro, and I knew that this was going to be a great place to write.

My original French Bistro was this great new place to write because it had all these beautiful angels working there. There was this beautiful black-haired angel who introduced me to my original French Bistro. Again, I know she was only there for the summer. Yet this summer was so inspirational that she had me thinking she might be my new angel of inspiration.

My beautiful blonde library angel was my first angel of inspiration. I doubt there will ever be an angel more inspirational than my beautiful blonde library angel. Even two years after she left, I still feel her presence at the library. So I doubt that I will ever find an angel as inspirational as she was because she was such a special angel. Yet as inspirational as she was, she was not the only angel of inspiration I had during my spiritual journey to finding the one. There were also these beautiful angels working at the library who were inspiring me when she was not at the library. There was a beautiful Irish angel who was the first angel that I saw myself with at my snowy log cabin. There was a beautiful brunette angel whom I thought of as Annabelle 2 because she reminded me so much of my French soulmate,

Annabelle. I also remember there being a beautiful black-haired angel who was there at the start of my journey. Finally, there was this beautiful creative brunette angel who I believe had to be really good friends with my beautiful blonde library angel since they were spending so much time together.

All these library angels were very beautiful angels. Their beauty was helping me to see that I could be inspired by other angels when she was not at the library. Yet none of these beautiful angels were as beautiful or as inspirational as my beautiful blonde library angel. I knew none of these angels could replace the way I felt about her. I knew she was too powerful an angel to be replaced. Yet what these angels did show me when she was gone was that they could carry the torch for her when she was not there. So these library angels introduced me to the power of transference. Yet it was not until I was introduced to this beautiful black-haired angel working at my original French Bistro that I was going to find my new angel of inspiration.

My beautiful black-haired angel was the second angel of inspiration in my spiritual journey to the woman of my dreams. Her beauty was the first thing I noticed when I first saw her at my original French Bistro. I cannot say enough about her figure because she had an incredible body. Yet those bright white teeth were the most memorable things about her beauty.

I loved seeing her smile because you could literally see that twinkle within her teeth when she smiled because they were so bright. This brings me to what I really loved about this beautiful black-haired angel from my original French Bistro. What I really loved about my beautiful black-haired angel was her flamboyant personality. It was her flamboyant personality that had me going back to my original French Bistro over and over again. I loved that she noticed me every time I was there. I loved not being invisible to a beautiful woman. Unfortunately, what I did not love was that I could not say anything to her after she greeted me because of my social anxiety. I wanted nothing more than to have a conversation with her. Sadly, this never happened because my mind always went blank after she asked about my day.

My spiritual journey to the woman of my dreams officially started with me discovering this beautiful black-haired angel. My beautiful blonde library angel will always remain the most inspirational angel in my spiritual journey. I do not think that I will ever be able to say enough about the importance of this angel in my spiritual journey. Without her, I would have never found my passion for writing and the confidence to follow my path to the woman of my dreams.

However, after my beautiful blonde library angel, I believe that this beautiful black-haired angel was the second most important angel in my spiritual journey. There have been more than twelve angels of inspiration since I discovered my beautiful blonde library angel at the library. All these beautiful angels are inspirational angels that I will never forget. However, none of these angels were as significant as her since she was the one who introduced me to my path to the one. So my beautiful blonde library angel gave birth to my spiritual journey to the one. Then my beautiful black-haired angel was the one who showed me that there was a path to finding the one.

This beautiful black-haired angel was the first beautiful angel of inspiration that I discovered outside the library. The first two years of my spiritual journey to finding the one were spent at the library. I never needed another place to write during these first two years because my beautiful blonde library angel and her friends were all that I needed for inspiration. Then one by one, these library angels started to disappear, and I knew that eventually, my beautiful blonde library angel was also going to leave. I dreaded this day. I did not want to lose the most important angel of my life. Unfortunately, I knew there was nothing I could do to stop this from happening because of my social anxiety. I knew I could never say anything to her. Thus I knew that one day she was going to leave, and I might never see her again. So I started to prepare myself for this dreaded day by finding another place to write. I had to find another place to write because I knew the library was going to lose its magic once this blonde angel left.

My search for a new location of inspiration led me to my original French Bistro. It led me to my beautiful black-haired angel. I now had two angels of inspiration that I believed were guiding me to the woman of my dreams. My beautiful blonde library angel was the first. My beautiful black-haired angel was the second. After I was introduced to my beautiful black-haired angel, I was traveling back and forth between the library and my original French Bistro to write. I could not stop going to the library because of my beautiful blonde library angel. I knew nothing was ever going to happen with her realistically, yet spiritually, she was still the most important angel in my spiritual journey, and thus the most important person in my life. So I was never going to stop going to the library if she was there. Then I found this beautiful black-haired angel, and I started to split my time between the library and my original French Bistro.

I knew my days with my beautiful blonde library angel were numbered. I knew my beautiful blonde library angel was going to leave the library, never to return. I was so dreading this day. Yet I knew there was nothing I could do to stop it from happening because I could never say anything to her to get her to stay. So I had to find a way to prepare myself for the loss of this angel who was the most important person in my life. I also had to find a new place to write because I knew the library was going to lose its magic once she finally left. I thought I found a place once I was introduced to the beautiful black-haired angel. So I was ready to say goodbye to the library after she left. I was ready to spend all my time at my original French Bistro. Then my beautiful blonde library angel introduced me to my third angel of inspiration.

My third angel of inspiration was this fiery redhead that my beautiful blonde library angel introduced me to as I saw them walking toward me at the library. This moment is another one of those moments that I will never forget. I will never forget this moment because after I saw them walking toward me, I literally felt the torch being passed to her. I literally felt my spiritual journey was telling me that she was going to be my new angel of inspiration. So I started to believe that my spiritual journey at the library was going to continue with her. Unfortunately, I was mistaken, because she left right after I lost my beautiful blonde library angel.

My beautiful black-haired angel stopped working at my original French Bistro before I lost my two library angels. I knew that I could not stop going to my original French Bistro after she left because there were too many other beautiful angels working there. Also, there were these random angels who went there to eat and study who were my inspirations as well. So I was not ready to stop going to my original French Bistro after my second angel of inspiration left. Yet I was also not ready to stop going to the library because I now had two angels of inspiration there. I still had my beautiful blonde library angel who was at the library. Plus, I now had this fiery redhead. So the library was still my main source of inspiration. Yet I was not ready to lose my original French Bistro as a place to write. So after I lost my beautiful black-haired angel, I started my search for a new angel of inspiration to keep me at my original French Bistro.

My search for a new angel of inspiration was going to eventually lead me to my fourth angel of inspiration. My fourth angel of inspiration was this beautiful blonde angel who was later promoted to supervisor at my original French Bistro. I knew I never had a chance with this beautiful blonde supervisor because she was too young and beautiful for me to be with her. Also, I knew she had a boyfriend because I saw them having lunch together during her breaks. This made me very uncomfortable because it reminded me that I could never be with her. I probably should have stopped going there to see her once I started to feel uncomfortable. However, I could not stop going there to see her because she was still inspiring me to do my best writing. She continued to be my angel of inspiration until I thought she quit before the Coronavirus hit. So this angel was my inspirational angel because she outlasted so many angels.

My original French Bistro turned into my favorite place to write after the loss of my beautiful blonde library angel. I was hoping the library might still be a source of inspiration after my beautiful blonde library angel left. I was hoping my fiery redhead was still going to be my angel of inspiration after she left. Then my fiery redhead left the day after I said goodbye to my beautiful blonde library angel, and I knew my time at the library was over. I kept going to the library for another two weeks, hoping to find out that I might be wrong about her being gone. Sadly, as these two weeks passed, I soon found out I was not wrong, as the library lost its magic.

My original French Bistro was going to be my only source of inspiration after my beautiful blonde library angel left the library. I did make a few more attempts at returning to the library to write. I had to see if I could try to recapture some of the magic of the library now that I had lost my last connection to my beautiful blonde library angel. Sadly, this was something that I could not recapture, and I realized it was too painful for me to go there to write.

I knew I needed a new location of inspiration after my beautiful blonde library angel finally left the library. I knew that my original French Bistro was going to be my new location of inspiration because of all the beautiful angels who worked and ate there. I was overwhelmed by all the beautiful angels who worked and ate there. Rarely was there a time when I did not see an angel of inspiration at my original French Bistro. So I knew this was the place to write after the library lost its magic because I knew I still had the beautiful blonde supervisor working there. Actually, this beautiful blonde supervisor was not a supervisor yet. It was not until after I said goodbye to my beautiful blonde library angel that she was promoted. So her promotion was partially what made her such an inspirational angel because she was the only angel that I had left.

My beautiful black-haired angel was the first angel of inspiration to leave after she stopped working at my original French Bistro. I still kept going there after she left because there were so many beautiful angels working and eating there. However, none of these angels were my angels of inspiration at the time. It was not until my beautiful blonde library angel left that I found my new angel of inspiration there. Yet I think I always knew that this beautiful blonde supervisor working at my original French Bistro was going to be one of my angels of inspiration. I knew it was either going to be this beautiful blonde supervisor or this beautiful angel working at a nearby gas station. This angel at a nearby gas station was also vying to be my new angel of inspiration because I was actually talking to this angel. Granted, these were only brief conversations. Yet we were able to talk, and she was the only angel I was talking to after my beautiful black-haired angel left my original French Bistro. So I was not sure which of these angels was going to be my new angel of inspiration after I lost my library angels. Yet I knew it was going to be one of them. Actually, it turned out to be both of them. The beautiful blonde supervisor was going to be my fourth angel of inspiration, and the one at the gas station my fifth.

My beautiful blonde library angel will always be the most inspirational angel of my spiritual journey. She will always be the angel I turn to for inspiration during my darkest hour because I doubt I will ever find an angel who was more inspirational than her. I may find an angel more beautiful than her; however, I will never find an angel more inspirational than her since she arrived into my life when I needed her the most. Then I also had this inspirational day to say goodbye to her, which made her even more inspiring. My beautiful blonde library angel finally left the library on Tuesday, May 28th, 2019. This Tuesday was so great because I got one final chance to admire her angelic beauty before I thought she was going to be gone forever. Then I had that following Friday to say hello to her spiritual presence, which I still continue to feel to this very day. So I doubt I will ever find an angel of inspiration more beautiful or inspirational than my beautiful blonde library angel. Sadly, this angel has now left the library.

My beautiful blonde library angel has never been back to the library since that inspirational Tuesday. I doubt I will ever feel her magic at the library again. I hoped the fiery redhead was going to carry the torch for her after she left. However, I was wrong about this because she left right after her. Thus started my spiritual journey at my original French Bistro.

I left the library at one on Saturday because my fiery redhead left for the day at one. I thought about staying at the library after she left because of these two new angels that got there. However, I was so hungry that I had to leave. So I left the library, and I went to continue my writing at my original French Bistro because I wanted something to eat. I did not realize this was going to be the last time I was going to feel the magic of the library once I left. I did not realize that my time at the library was over after this until I fell into another pit of darkness. Unfortunately, this was going to be the last time that I was going to feel its magic for two years.

I arrived at my original French Bistro at about two that Saturday. I was not sure where my spiritual journey was going to lead me now that my beautiful blonde library angel was gone. I only knew that my spiritual journey to the woman of my dreams was not over. I still had not found an angel with the social confidence to make the first move. So I knew I had to keep searching for the woman of my dreams until I found the one. I still believed that my path to the woman of my dreams was by writing and getting my books published. I still knew I was never going to find success the normal way because of my social anxiety. So I knew I had to keep writing even though my beautiful blonde library angel was gone. However, I was not sure if I was going to be able to keep going to the library once she was gone. I was not sure about how painful it might be to go there once she was gone. Yet I planned to keep going since I thought that this fiery redhead was still going to be there. Although I also knew that it was time to phase out the library as my main source of inspiration. I had to search elsewhere for inspiration.

I knew someday the library was going to lose its magic. I did not realize that the day when it was going to lose its magic had already arrived. I only knew that it was going to lose its magic once I lost my last connection to my beautiful blonde library angel. So as I walked into my original French Bistro, I had questions about how my spiritual journey might continue. However, the one thing I never questioned was my source of strength and inspiration. I never doubted that my strength derived from my passion for writing. I also knew the inspiration for my writing derived from my beautiful angels, or so I thought at the time. Later, I was able to start to find that I did not need my angels to be present for my inspiration. However, I will get into this more toward the closing of my book. For now, though, I believed that my angels of inspiration had to be present for me to be inspired. So after the library, I went to my original French Bistro to find what angels of inspiration I had left. As I walked into my original French Bistro, I sat by the window because this was where I first realized the story of my first book. Then I started writing about my spiritual journey when I saw there were these two beautiful blondes working.

One of these beautiful blonde angels was this tall beautiful blonde angel with glasses. The other beautiful blonde angel was the beautiful blonde supervisor who sat right where I could see her as she was eating lunch. Of course, her boyfriend was there with her to remind me that I could never be with her. Yet I could not see him. I saw only her. So this was a great way for me to continue my spiritual journey after I thought I'd lost my beautiful blonde library angel. After seeing these two beautiful blonde angels, I knew my spiritual journey had to continue at my original French Bistro. I never imagined losing this French Bistro as my location of inspiration. Then I lost it as my location of inspiration because of the weirdness of my anxiety.

# THE WEIRDNESS OF
# MY ANXIETY

The weirdness of my anxiety is something nobody will ever understand. Nobody will ever understand how I am unable to say anything to my angels no matter how much I like them. This is the story of my life. This is my life's handicap. I am a man who will obsess over a beautiful woman without ever saying a word to her. I could go days, weeks, months, or even years without ever saying a word to her unless it is something I have to say to her for work. However, I will never say anything that might lead to us having a conversation for fear that this might lead her to find out about all my inadequacies. So I go into my obsession with these beautiful angels knowing that I will never say anything to them. I am a man who has never even been able to find the courage to say a simple hello to them. I know this makes me look angry and rude, and as if I am not interested, which is so frustrating. Sadly, this is who I am, and I do not see this changing anytime soon. I know I will never be a socially confident man. I will never be a man who is able to say hello to a beautiful woman first since I fear what follows "Hello."

The weirdness of my anxiety is something that eventually got me banned from my original French Bistro. I was banned from my original French Bistro because I moved to sit near this beautiful angel who worked there. She was apparently a minor. I had no idea that this beautiful blonde was a minor when I moved to sit near her. I did not even know that she was this beautiful blonde employee that worked there. All I knew about her when she first arrived was that she might be a beautiful woman, and I had to get a better look at her. So I started to move closer to her to get a better look to see if she was beautiful. I had to get a better look because all I could see when she first arrived was that she was blonde and wearing a red jacket. So I started to move closer and closer to her to see if she was worth my time. Unfortunately, this was a costly move since this move was what got me banned from my original French Bistro.

I started to fall into another pit of darkness after I was banned from my original French Bistro because its loss meant the loss of my last connection to my beautiful blonde library angel. I knew my beautiful blonde library angel was always going to be a part of my spiritual journey because I was always going to feel her spiritual presence with my passion for writing. I knew that I was always going to feel her spiritual energy when I wrote about my spiritual journey. Sadly, I also knew that my beautiful blonde library angel was gone from the library, and I had only one angel left from my time when she was still working at the library. I knew that this beautiful blonde angel at my original French Bistro was my last connection to her.

This beautiful blonde supervisor working at my original French Bistro was my main source of inspiration after my beautiful blonde library angel left the library. I was thinking this fiery redhead from the library was going to be my main source of inspiration after she left. Then she quit a few days after my beautiful blonde library angel left, and I knew I was going to have to find a new angel of inspiration. My search for a new angel of inspiration eventually led me to this beautiful blonde supervisor. This beautiful blonde supervisor carried the torch for my beautiful blonde library angel after she left. This angel was the only angel of inspiration I was going to have to carry the torch for her until I found my way to my new French Bistro. There was still the angel at the nearby gas station after my beautiful blonde library angel left. Then she also left when she was promoted and started to work at another gas station. I thought about going to see her at this other gas station after she was promoted. However, I decided against it because I knew she was engaged. Also, I knew that I was still not going to be able to have more than a brief conversation with her. So my time with this angel of inspiration was over, and the only angel of inspiration who was left was this beautiful blonde supervisor. So this beautiful blonde supervisor turned into my angel of inspiration because she outlasted all the other angels.

I still remember all the events that eventually got me banned from my original French Bistro clear as day. I still remember how I had to get a better look at this beautiful blonde angel at my original French Bistro because I had to see her beauty. I had to get a better look at this blonde angel who walked into the French Bistro. I remember feeling the need to move closer to her to get a better look. So, I remember it was the mystery and beauty of this beautiful blonde angel that had me moving closer to her, not the actual person. I also felt the need to move closer to her because there were no other angels there that day. So after I saw her arrive, I started walking around to see if there was a place to sit close to her. I tried to get a look at this beautiful blonde angel when I passed her as I was walking around. However, my anxiety was stopping me from looking at her. My anxiety had me too scared to make eye contact with her. I must have passed by her two times without making eye contact before finally finding a booth near her to sit. Then as I got ready to sit down, she grabbed her lunch and left. Once I saw her move, I finally realized she was this blonde employee who never liked me looking at her. I was once again getting rejected by one of my angels that I was obsessed over without ever saying a word to her.

I wish I had gotten a better look at this beautiful blonde angel when she first arrived. I wish I knew she was this employee that was constantly moving away when I sat near her. Sadly, I did not know it was her when she first arrived. I only knew that she was a beautiful woman I had to get a better look at after she first arrived. So I had to move closer to see this beautiful, mysterious blonde angel. Sadly, once I finally saw who this angel was, I knew that this was going to be a costly move. However, it was a costly move that I was going to have to live with because I did make the choice to move closer to her to get a better look. I knew I was not going to say anything to her once I got close to her. I knew I was only moving close to her to uncover the mystery of this beautiful blonde angel at my original French Bistro. Sadly, she knew none of these things once I was finally able to sit near her. All she knew about me was the weirdness of my anxiety. She saw me only as a creepy old man who was basically stalking her.

There were two other times when she got her food and moved to let me know that she was obviously not interested. I knew this beautiful blonde employee was not interested because every time I sat where I could see her, she stopped whatever she was doing and moved. Each time that she did this, I felt the pain of being rejected by her all over again. I hated this feeling, and I never wanted to feel it again. So I tried not to sit where I could see her. I tried to avoid her. Unfortunately, I was having a string of bad luck with her because I kept moving to where she happened to be sitting. This was happening time and time again until finally I was banned from my original French Bistro. Again, I was not trying to make her uncomfortable by sitting near her; it was simply my bad luck that she was sitting where I sat for inspiration. It was also my bad luck that she was some beautiful angel that was a minor. Obviously, if I had known all these things, I might have made more of an effort at not making her so uncomfortable. Unfortunately, I did not know all these things, and this string of bad luck was why I was banned.

I moved to a table hidden from all the employees at my original French Bistro after this beautiful blonde angel moved away from me and made it clear that she was not interested. I was still able to see some beautiful angels who were studying there when I made this move. So I was ready to go into my world of isolation to escape the pain of being rejected by this angel. Sadly, I was not able to find this escape because once I moved to this table to write, I was banned.

The dreadful moment finally arrived. It all started with me seeing the manager and a shift supervisor walk toward me at my original French Bistro. I had no clue what was happening when I saw them walking toward me that day. However, I knew that it was not a good thing because I was feeling so uncomfortable as I watched them get closer. Then once the manager finally approached me, she told me this employee was so scared of me that she was shaking and crying. Then she told me she had to call corporate to get them involved. Finally, she said that I was never allowed back at my original French Bistro. I could not believe I was banned from my original French Bistro. I could not believe I scared this angel so much that I was being banned.

I was shell-shocked once I learned that I had been banned from my original French Bistro. I had no words for what was happening after they told me that I had been banned. All I could say after I was banned was, "OK." Then I switched to automatic pilot. I packed all my stuff and got ready to leave my original French Bistro for the last time. It was raining as I left my original French Bistro for the last time, and I did not care. I did not care because I was walking in a daze after I was banned. I could not believe what had happened. I could not believe I was never allowed back at my original French Bistro again. I was angry. I was devastated. I was depressed. I was embarrassed. I had not felt this bad since the loss of my dad.

I called my mom to get a ride home as I felt the rain fall down upon me after being banned from my original French Bistro. I did not mind the rain falling down upon me because the rain felt like the perfect weather for how I was feeling. I started to fall into another pit of darkness after I was banned from my original French Bistro. I never felt anything like what I felt after I was banned from my original French Bistro. It was not so much the loss of the French Bistro that had me so devastated as it was how I felt once I was banned. They had me feeling like a criminal after I was banned. They had me feeling that it was wrong for me to love to see beautiful women. I was so confused and devastated once I was banned that I could not think clearly. Hence, I felt the dark clouds and the rain were the perfect weather for how I was feeling.

I was walking to Bon Gout because it was only about ten minutes away. I was going to walk to Bon Gout to wait for my mom there. Also, I was hoping to go there because I wanted to talk with whoever was at the entrance about what happened. Then before crossing the intersection to go to Bon Gout, I decided I had to see if I was banned from all my French Bistros.

I had to find out if the loss of my original French Bistro also meant the loss of my new French Bistro. I had to find this out because I knew I was able to survive the loss of my original French Bistro if I could still go to my new French Bistro. My new French Bistro was my favorite place to write because of all the beautiful angels who went there to work and eat. So I could not lose this as my place to write. So I went back to ask if it was also lost. Sadly, I was unable to get the response I was hoping for when I asked the manager. Instead, she said she had no control over what I did outside of the establishment. She also said that she knew corporate knew of me from my book. Finally, she reminded me I was not allowed back, and I left my original French Bistro for the last time. I left my original French Bistro with all these mixed emotions.

I was feeling a sense of loss because I was losing my last connection to my beautiful blonde library angel. The beautiful blonde supervisor working at my original French Bistro was my last connection to my beautiful blonde library angel. She was the last angel of inspiration I had left from when my beautiful blonde library angel was working at the library. I was also feeling this sense of loss because I was losing one of my locations of inspiration. I knew if I still had my new French Bistro to go to for my writing, then I could get over this loss. However, I was still not sure if I could go to my new French Bistro. So I was definitely feeling a sense of loss after I left this French Bistro. I was also feeling hurt because I felt as if I was being bullied all over again. It had been thirty years since the last time I was bullied during middle school. I was still tormented by my years of being bullied from childhood. However, I thought that my years of being bullied were over. I never once imagined I might be bullied again as an adult. Then I realized my years of being bullied were not over after I got banned from my original French Bistro. This was a painful thing to realize, and I was afraid of what might happen. I feared I might lose my passion for writing since I was afraid of telling the world what happened.

These feelings of being bullied were why it was so important for me to go to my new French Bistro after getting banned from my original French Bistro. I felt I had to go to my new French Bistro to see if I could see all the beautiful angels who worked there. More importantly, I had to go to my new French Bistro to see if I still had a place to go for my writing.

Luckily, I was soon going to find out that my new French Bistro knew nothing about what had happened at my original French Bistro. Once I learned that I still had my new French Bistro to go to for my angels of inspiration, I was able to find my way out of my pit of darkness. However, getting over the loss of the beautiful blonde supervisor was more difficult to get over.

It felt as though all the employees at my original French Bistro made a consensus choice to make me feel uncomfortable at my original French Bistro after the Coronavirus hit. It all started when I went to order something one Sunday, and the person taking my order was very rude. I could not believe how rude he was, and I thought about saying something. Then they took about five to ten minutes to get my food ready, and I was the only person there. So I was really uncomfortable with this experience. However, I tried my best to shrug it off. Then I went back during the week, and this blonde that eventually had me banned was also rude. She started to argue with me about the size of the drink I ordered. However, I said nothing because of my debilitating social anxiety. I was afraid that if I said something, then it might lead to a confrontation.

Things were not always this way. Things were better before the virus because the employees there were much more welcoming. Plus, there was my beautiful blonde supervisor there for inspiration. I never really felt as welcome as I did at my new French Bistro. However, I was not feeling uncomfortable at my original French Bistro. Then this all started to change after the virus. I kept returning hoping things might improve. Sadly, they never did improve even after I made two attempts at trying to explain the weirdness of my anxiety to them.

My first attempt at trying to explain the weirdness of my anxiety was after I said something to one of the employees there. I said something to this employee because I saw him shaking his head and mumbling something after he saw me walk by him. I felt I had to say something to him after this because I could not take how he was making me feel anymore. He was making me feel uncomfortable because of how he was looking at me all the time. Also, there were all the times I thought he was gossiping about the weirdness of my anxiety. I felt I had to finally say something to this guy. Finally, after I said something, I felt so much rage toward this guy when he was working that I decided I had to try to tell one of the supervisors.

I felt the need to say something because I could not continue to keep my mouth shut anymore. I was tired of being a man without a voice. So I approached this supervisor to tell her my side of the story. I started to explain why I confronted this guy. I told her that I confronted him because a few weeks ago, one of the girls there called me a weirdo as she was leaving. The supervisor then asked me for the name of the employee. However, I was unwilling to tell her because I feared some type of confrontation if she found out I had placed a complaint about her. Then the supervisor told me that she needed to have the employee's name to address the situation. However, I was still hesitant. Finally, she asked me what I was hoping might happen.

I was really uncomfortable with this question because I did not think it was my place to give a solution. I thought they were management and I was a customer, and quite a loyal one. I had spent quite a bit of money there over the years. Sadly, I guess this did not matter much to them.

My first attempt at explaining the weirdness of my anxiety went unheard. I returned to my seat, still shaking and enraged after I tried to get them to hear my side of the story. A few days passed and nothing happened. I was starting to feel ignored and unheard. I tried to let it go. Then one day during lunch, I tried to approach the manager about what happened because I felt she might be more sympathetic and understanding. However, after I told her what happened, she did not present me with a solution. Instead, she told me things I did not want to hear because they turned my worst fear into reality. She told me that when I published my first book, some of the angels there were uncomfortable. I could not believe what I was hearing. I could not believe I was making them uncomfortable when all I ever did was praise their beauty. Then she told me the legal department got involved to see if action could be taken. She finally said no action could be taken, and the issue went unresolved. I did not know how to react to all of this. I so wanted to revert to my invisible man complex after hearing this. Unfortunately, I could not since I was surrounded by so many people. So I apologized and left.

I doubted I was ever going to feel comfortable at my original French Bistro again. I knew I was not going to feel comfortable there when certain employees were there. So I tried going there whenever they were not working, and if they were working, I tried to avoid them. However, this was getting difficult to do because there were so many employees there to avoid.

There was the guy I said something to that I was trying to avoid. There was the supervisor that I tried to explain the weirdness of my anxiety to who I was trying to avoid. There were these two beautiful angels that I was trying to avoid. I was hurt every time they moved to sit somewhere else because I felt that they were nonverbally rejecting me every time. One of the two employees was this blonde that eventually got me banned from my original French Bistro. Then the other beautiful angel was a beautiful black-haired angel with glasses who looked like the angel who introduced me to Panera Bread. There were other times when I did not feel uncomfortable with her since she looked at me and even said hi. So she was also inspirational.

There was one more beautiful angel that I felt uncomfortable around at my original French Bistro. I was also uncomfortable around the angel who called me a weirdo. This angel was someone I still found attractive, yet I was not inspired by her anymore. Thus I was now starting to think of her as my angel of darkness. I was trying to avoid my angel of darkness. Unfortunately, I was not always able to avoid her because she was at my French Bistro so much.

My routine of obsessing over my beautiful angels because I am unable to find the courage or confidence to socialize with them is probably what made these angels uncomfortable. I fear all my beautiful angels will ever see when I'm writing at my locations of inspiration is the weirdness of my anxiety. Unfortunately, I find that it is impossible for me to escape the weirdness of my anxiety most of the time, so I have had to learn to accept it as my way of being.

I started to develop the weirdness of my anxiety while obsessing over my beautiful blonde library angel at the library. It all started with me spending all my time at the library writing about how my beautiful blonde library angel was making me feel when I was there. During my time at the library, I was playing musical chairs with her trying to find the best place to sit to see her best because she was not always at the same spot during her four-hour shift. She spent the first hour of her shift putting away non-children's books at one side of the library. Then she spent the second hour putting children's books away. After this, she went to the back for about an hour, where I could not see her at all. Finally, she spent the last hour of her shift socializing with the other librarians at the counter before they closed for the night. So this was how the weirdness of my anxiety started. It all started with me moving around the library to get the best view of my angel because she was my reason for being there. I knew I was risking making my beautiful blonde library angel uncomfortable with the weirdness of my anxiety. However, this was a risk I was willing to take since she was also inspiring me to think, *What if?*

# What If?

What if my beautiful blonde library angel was my soulmate? What if I found my one true love when I walked into the library that one hot Saturday? What if I missed my chance to be with her because of my social anxiety? What if my beautiful blonde library angel is the closest thing that I will ever get to finding true love? What if these two and a half years I spent with her at the library were the best years of my life? What if I spend the rest of my life searching for a beautiful woman as special as her and I never find her? What if my only chance of ever finding true love left with her that fateful Tuesday as I watched her leaving the library for the last time? What if I spend the rest of my life searching for someone as special as her, and I never find her?

I am starting to fear that this might be a real, strong possibility because there is no denying the strong connection that I felt for my beautiful blonde library angel. It has been over two years since I last saw my beautiful blonde library angel at the library. Yet I still feel her spiritual energy each and every time I walk into the library. I still feel her spiritual energy every time I write about my spiritual journey toward finding the woman of my dreams. I still find myself finding my way back to her every time I start to fall into another pit of darkness. I do not need to see my beautiful blonde library angel to feel inspired by her. Sure, it helps to have pictures of her to remind me of her angelic beauty. Sure, it is great to know that she is still working at a bakery nearby so I am able to see her angelic beauty when I go there for some tea. Yet even if I could not see her, I could still feel her spiritual presence in my passion for writing. I could still feel her spiritual presence in my passion for writing because I still have my memories of her. These memories that I have of her are why I keep finding myself writing about her when I am writing about my spiritual journey to finding the woman of my dreams. Sadly, I doubt the world will ever understand how I feel about my beautiful blonde library angel.

I doubt the world will ever understand the inspirational power of my beautiful blonde library angel unless they read my books. I doubt the world could ever understand how I could feel such love for a woman when I was only able to thank her for being so beautiful. Sadly, I knew my love for her could never be reciprocated because I could never say anything to her. However, this did not change how I felt about her because she led me down a path that I will be following for the rest of my life when I saw her as this symbol of hope for finding the one. I do not know if the woman of my dreams exists. I do not know if I will ever find an angel who is able to defy the odds of normal society to actually make the first move. I doubt I will ever find an angel with the compassion and understanding to see past the weirdness of my anxiety. However, every time I write about my spiritual journey to finding the one, I feel this hope return.

I feel this hope return because of my beautiful blonde library angel. I doubt I will ever find another angel to equal the inspirational power of my beautiful blonde library angel. I do not doubt I will ever find an angel to equal, or maybe even surpass, her beauty. However, I doubt I will ever find an angel to equal her timing. Again, my beautiful blonde library angel entered my life when I had lost all hope because I had lost my hope of being a truck driver. After this, she remained a part of my life until I was able to write and publish my first book. Then I had two weeks to prepare for her loss after I overheard her telling a coworker that she was leaving. This led me to having my inspirational Tuesday with her, where I got to say goodbye to her physical presence. Then I was able to say hello to her spiritual presence at the library that following Friday. Thus as beautiful as she was, her timing was what really made her so inspirational. Then there was the fact that I never approached her to be hurt by her. I now see my never approaching her as a good thing because this turned her into my perfect angel. Finally, what makes her even more inspirational is finding out that she never left town when I found out she was at a nearby bakery.

My beautiful blonde library angel is this perfect angel that I will never be able to stop writing about unless I find the woman of my dreams. I believe the woman of my dreams is the only angel that might ever equal the inspirational power of my beautiful blonde library angel. Sadly, the further away I get from my time at the library with my beautiful blonde library angel, the darker the path gets to finding the woman of my dreams. I thought my search for the woman of my dreams was going to take place at my French Bistros. Then my angels of inspiration at my French Bistros turned into my angels of darkness as they got me banned from there. Every time I got banned from a location of inspiration, I fell further and further into my pit of darkness. I never felt more lost than I did after the loss of my three locations of inspiration. I knew I could not continue obsessing over my angels the same way. Yet I also knew how important my angels were to my life since I also could not deny how I felt when I saw an angel.

I felt so inspired by my beautiful angels that I was able to imagine this world where anything was possible when I saw them. This imaginary world was so inspiring that it had me asking myself, *What if?*

What if there was a path to my angels of inspiration? What if these beautiful angels that I was obsessed with were actually interested? What if one day my patience and persistence paid off and it led me to be with one of these angels I was obsessed with? What if someday one of these angels I was obsessed with actually approached me to ask me why I was spending so much time at my locations of inspiration?

What if?

These two words were why I kept returning to my world of isolation. These two words were where I was finding my hope. I was not finding my hope from reality because my reality was so dark because of my social anxiety. I knew I could not talk to my beautiful angels no matter how much I liked them. It was so frustrating and depressing to not be able to talk to my angels. I hated to be a man without a voice. I hated not being able to let them know how I felt. I hated that I could never say hello to them because I was so afraid of them. I feared there was no escaping my dark reality. So I started to spend all my time within my world of isolation asking myself, *What if?*

One day I was sitting at my original French Bistro writing when the beautiful blonde supervisor sat near me during her lunch break. This beautiful blonde supervisor almost never sat near me at my original French Bistro. She rarely sat anywhere where people could see her because she usually liked to be hidden when she took her lunch break. However, this time was different. This time she sat where everyone could see her at this booth right near where I was sitting. I could not get over the fact that she felt comfortable enough to sit near me that day. I felt so inspired by her after she sat there that I started to imagine a path to her that day. I started to imagine this path to her when I saw that she was not wearing an engagement ring. I saw she was not wearing a ring when she returned to work. I was so inspired by her that day that I was even thinking that she was purposely showing me her hands to let me know she was single. Sadly, this feeling did not last more than a day because I eventually saw her having lunch with her boyfriend again during her breaks. However, I will never forget how inspired I felt by her because she decided to sit near me at my original French Bistro. I will never forget the hope I felt because she sat there. I will never forget how this hope I felt had me asking myself the question, *What if?* What if this beautiful supervisor might one day be the woman of my dreams?

There is no denying the inspiration I feel from seeing my angels of inspiration. The world could try to stop me from seeing them as my angels of inspiration. They could ban me over and over again from going to my locations of inspiration to see them. They might even vilify me because of this love that I have for seeing beautiful women. Yet my love for seeing my angels is undeniable because they inspire me every time I see them. Sadly, after I was banned from my new French Bistro and another coffee shop, I was really hurt and confused. I was feeling so hurt and confused because I knew how good I felt whenever I saw my angels. Yet I felt the world was telling me I was wrong for wanting to look at beautiful women. I felt the world was telling me that I was not allowed to look at beautiful women. Yet I still continued to search them out since my love for my angels was such an important part of my life.

I love seeing my beautiful angels. I am unable to say anything to my beautiful angels when I see them. This is probably what makes my angels so uncomfortable. This is why all my beautiful angels see of me is the weirdness of my anxiety. I wish things could be different. I wish I could be someone like Sam Malone. Lately, Sam Malone has been someone I have really been admiring since he was such a ladies' man. I even started watching the entire series of *Cheers* because I admired him so much.

Cheers has always been one of my favorite comedies. So I always loved watching it for laughs. Although, this time I was watching it as more of a character study. Sadly, I knew I could never be a Sam Malone because of my debilitating social anxiety. I knew I could never talk to beautiful women like he did because I lacked the confidence to socialize with beautiful women. Yet this never stopped me from imagining what it might be like to be him, or to have a friend like him. I so admired Sam Malone! I so wished that I could have had the charisma and social confidence of Sam Malone!

I was never going to be a Sam Malone. I was never going to be someone who had the social confidence to make the first move with a beautiful woman because of my social anxiety.

I did learn one more thing from watching Sam Malone when I watched the very last episode of *Cheers*. The last episode of *Cheers* had him walking off into a dark pool room like a cowboy walking off into the sunset. This was something I really admired about Sam Malone because I saw this as him choosing his bar as his true love over a beautiful woman. I felt a special connection to him after this because I felt the same way about my passion for writing. I believe my passion for writing is one of the true loves of my life. I believe that if I am never able to find the woman of my dreams, then at least I've found my passion for writing. Of course, I still hope to one day find the woman of my dreams. However, if I never find her, at least I still have my passion for writing to turn to for comfort and solace. I know my passion for writing will always be one of my true loves. I know I will always have my passion for writing to go to no matter how dark my existence gets. Sadly, as great as my passion for writing is, I also know I will never have a chance with the woman of my dreams unless I learn a few social skills.

I know I have to learn how to socialize with beautiful women to make them more comfortable. I wish that there was another way to be with the woman of my dreams besides socializing. I wish I could find my way to the woman of my dreams with my passion for writing. I wish I could write my books to introduce myself to them, and then they might make the first move. Sadly, I am slowly starting to realize that this will never happen because they will never feel comfortable with me unless I start to talk to them first. I tried to write my way to some of my beautiful angels. I tried to write them letters to let them know how I felt about them. I tried to write them these letters to avoid having to go through the anxiety of having to talk to them. Sadly, this never worked because after I wrote them these letters, I still had to socialize with them to continue to build a connection with them, or worse, they had me banned. So, sadly, I now know the truth. I know I must learn to socialize with them if I ever hope to have a chance with them. Yet I am still unable to socialize with them because I still have to deal with my fear of humanity and my social anxiety. As a matter of fact, now it is even more difficult to socialize with them since I now feel I know they are uncomfortable with the weirdness of my anxiety.

However, I also know that not all my angels were uncomfortable with the weirdness of my anxiety. I know my beautiful blonde library angel was not uncomfortable with the weirdness of my anxiety. Again, I know she might have been uncomfortable with me always being at the library. However, if she was uncomfortable with me being there so much, she never let it show.

The weirdness of my anxiety started with my beautiful blonde library angel. It started with me going to the library to see this beautiful blonde librarian that I was obsessed with. After I got my first look at this angel from the library, I could not stop thinking about her. I could not stop thinking about her, and I did not try to stop thinking about her. She was my sole reason for living after I lost my future as a truck driver. Her angelic beauty was all I thought about and all I cared about because everything else I thought about was pure darkness. The idea of going to work and having to deal with humanity again was pure darkness. The idea of having to work at some factory where I had to deal with the excruciating heat of a factory was pure darkness. The idea of dealing with the disapproval and disappointment of my parents was pure darkness. This pure darkness that I was consumed with was what led me into my pit of darkness. My only escape from my pit of darkness was the thought of seeing this angelic beauty at the library again.

This reality of pure darkness was not a reality that I wanted to be a part of anymore. I could not see myself spending the rest of my life doing extroverted work. I knew that I was most likely never going to have a family since I could not socialize with beautiful women. Yet I knew I had to make money, and I knew I still loved beautiful women. So I felt trapped because I knew what I had to do and what I loved, yet I also knew the severity of my social anxiety. Then I remembered seeing this beautiful blonde librarian at the library, and my life was changed forever because seeing her angelic beauty was all that mattered. Thus started my obsession with her. I could not get enough of seeing her angelic beauty. I did not care about my world of pure darkness anymore. I did not care that I did not have money or that I did not have a girlfriend. All I cared about was getting to see her angelic face. I knew she was out of my league. I knew my social anxiety was still keeping me from talking to her. Yet none of these things really mattered to me anymore. I only cared about seeing the angelic beauty of my angel at the library.

I do not want to live in a world where I am not able to be honest with people. I loathe having to be fake with people. This is why when you see me, then I am usually that angry man walking around who never smiles. I smile only when I laugh. The rest of the time, I look angry because I am angry. I look depressed because I am depressed. I look scared because I am scared. I do not like being fake, which is one of the reasons why it is so difficult for me to keep any type of work. It is so difficult for me to work because to work, you need to be fake when at work. Do I need money? Yes, I need money. Yet do I want to do what I need to do to make money? No, I do not want to do what it takes to make money because this usually means having to spend hours at work being fake, all because management expects you to care about only work. Yet there is so much more to life than spending hours at work trying to make money. I feel people value money too much since the more money they make, the more money they then want.

I spent all my life trying to do the work thing without much success. It was not until I found work at Bon Gout that I found a semblance of success because I finally found work there that I could somewhat tolerate. It is not great-paying work. I often need to work somewhere else for extra money. However, it is work that I am able to tolerate because of the employees there and because there are so many angels of inspiration who work and shop there. I will often find myself making a list of at least twenty-five angels who work and shop there during the day. This is all the inspiration that I need at work. Money is not my inspiration for going to work. I do need money to survive. I do need money to make it as a writer. Yet earning money is not my motivation for working. My motivation for working is my angels at work and my need for money to promote my first book and to get my second book published once it is finally written.

I hate work because I hate having to be fake around people at work. I hate that I must pretend to care about things I do not really care about when I am at work. I want to be part of a world where I am able to tell people the truth. I want to live within a world where I am able to tell people I love beautiful women. I want to live in a world where I am able to tell people that seeing a beautiful woman is the only reason I am alive most of the time. There is nothing, and I mean nothing, like seeing the beauty of one of my angels. I mean, there are truly times when I think I want to die. Then I see one of my angels, and I remember why I am alive. So the world may try to take away my ways of seeing my angels. They may ban me from my locations of inspiration time and time again. Yet my love for seeing my angels will not die because I never want to live in a world where I am not able to see my angels of inspiration.

This was something I learned during the Coronavirus. This was something I learned while working at a call center where only five people were working. Before the virus hit, there was at least one angel there, and I literally found any excuse possible to see her. I knew this angel was married and was the boss's daughter. Yet this did not mean I could not look at her beauty. Then I lost her as my angel when the Coronavirus hit. I tried to work at this call center without her as my inspiration. I tried to bring pictures of other angels to work for inspiration. However, these pictures were not working. I needed to see and feel inspired by actual women and not mere pictures of them. So I started to go to Control and my new French Bistro before work to see some actual women. Then I slowly started to self-sabotage myself at this call center because I felt I had to feel the presence of these women at Control and the French Bistro. I felt trapped at this call center. So I knew I was going to eventually quit or get fired since I had no angels of inspiration there. The money meant nothing if I could not see one of my angels of inspiration while I was working there. I tried to stay there for a few months, then I had to leave.

The inspirational energy of beautiful angels is one of the many things my beautiful blonde library angel introduced me to during my obsession with her. I always knew I loved the beauty of beautiful women. I was always obsessed with their beauty. I remember spending all of my Floridian childhood at the Fort Lauderdale beach and the mall to see their beauty. Then I saw their beauty at this bookstore and at the University of Akron when I moved to Ohio. I saw one of the most beautiful angels I ever saw when I moved to Alaska. She was this beautiful brunette angel from Texas with the greatest tan I ever saw. There were also all these beautiful angels from Russia and Hawaii when I was there. Yes, that's right, Hawaii! After leaving Alaska, I found my way to truck driving. Finally, its loss then led me to my beautiful blonde library angel.

I spent two years at the library with my beautiful blonde library angel. I was obsessed with this angel after I saw her that one hot Saturday. I knew I had no chance with this beautiful blonde librarian because she was way out of my league. So I never dreamed of approaching her. Then one day, I was sitting at the library writing my book and I started to think to myself, *What if?*

What if my beautiful blonde library angel was putting library books away near me because she was trying to look over my shoulder to see what I was writing? What if she was trying to see what I was writing because she liked me as much as I liked her? What if after looking over my shoulder to see what I was writing she made a comment? What if this one comment then led to us talking to each other when I went to the library? What if these conversations then led us to build a relationship with each other? What if this relationship then led us to dating each other? What if after a few dates with her she turned into my girlfriend? What if after spending a few months or years with her I finally proposed and she said yes? What if once we got married, I found out she was pregnant and we actually had a family? Finally, what if this one comment she made led her to be the woman of my dreams?

# The Woman Of My Dreams

The woman of my dreams may not exist. I could spend the rest of my life searching for the woman of my dreams without ever finding her. I could not hold back my tears as I was leaving the library one night because I was thinking I may have already found the woman of my dreams. I always knew my beautiful blonde library angel was the most inspirational angel of my life. I always knew she was the angel that gave birth to my spiritual journey to finding the one. Yet what I never allowed myself to think was that she might have been the love of my life. Then as I was leaving the library that night, I started to think about her not being at the library. I started to think about what was missing from the library, and I started thinking about her. I started to think about how special she was because I felt so comfortable around her. I spent two and a half years at the library obsessing over her, and she never left. She was also comfortable enough with me being there that she rarely ever hid from me when I was there. Sure, there were moments when she was out of sight. However, I never got the feeling that it was because I was making her uncomfortable. This was another reason why my beautiful blonde library angel was so special. Her social confidence was what made her special. Then I started thinking that maybe she was also interested. I started thinking she might have been the woman of my dreams.

I literally could not hold back the tears as I was walking to the car that night. I did not know why I was feeling the way I was feeling when I was walking to the car. All I knew was I was feeling something dark when I left the library that night. I spent most of the previous day writing at this new coffee shop because of this beautiful blonde coffee shop angel. This blonde coffee shop angel is probably turning into my new current obsession. Yet I spent most of this day at the coffee shop writing about my beautiful blonde library angel. It has been two years since my beautiful blonde library angel left the library. It has been over two years since I last felt her magic at the library. Yet she is still all I think about whenever I write about my spiritual journey to finding the one. I do not care how many months or years pass, she still continues to be the most inspirational angel of my life. There have been other angels to carry the torch for her after she left. There was the beautiful black-haired angel with a super-friendly personality who introduced me to my original French Bistro. Then there was the beautiful blonde supervisor who took her place. There was a beautiful angel at the gas station. There was this beautiful blonde sales angel who I really thought was the woman of my dreams. Yet every time I started to write about my spiritual journey to finding the one, I returned to her. Then one night, I felt this darkness take over as I was walking to my car. I was not sure why I was feeling such darkness until finally I realized it was because I was missing my beautiful blonde library angel.

I knew my beautiful blonde library angel was still working at this nearby bakery. I realized that there was still hope for her. Yet I also knew that I could not talk to her if I saw her because of my debilitating social anxiety. I also knew that I could not see her at the bakery because it was closed for maintenance. So my beautiful blonde library angel was once again gone from my life. I had no way of seeing her. Yet this did not stop me from thinking about her and writing about her because as I said, I do not need to see her to feel her presence. I feel her spiritual presence whenever I write my books about her. So I have always known my beautiful blonde library angel was the most inspirational angel of my life because of my writing.

I was feeling such pride before I left the library because I completed another chapter of my book. I was feeling great about writing my second book because everyday I was off, I wrote another chapter of my book. So I was feeling really good before I left the library. I was even able to find the courage to say goodbye to one of the librarians that was working there. This librarian has been there since I started my spiritual journey to find the woman of my dreams. I always knew this angel was there, yet I never thought much of her because of my beautiful blonde library angel and her friends. Then last night, I started to think she was also attractive. I knew she was older. However, I was thinking that this might be a good thing because it meant she was more my age. So I was feeling very proud of myself for saying goodbye to her as I left.

I was feeling great when I left the library. I walked out of the library feeling such confidence because I said hello to this beautiful older brunette angel. Then as soon as I walked out of the library, I felt a darkness flow through me from out of nowhere. I was not sure why I felt this darkness as I was walking to my car. All I knew was that I was not able to find my way out of the darkness once I felt it. Luckily, it was dark outside and there were no people around when I started to feel this darkness arise from out of nowhere. So I did not have to hide what I was feeling, and I was able to try to figure out why I was feeling this darkness. My heart was aching from the darkness that I was feeling as I left the library that night. It did not matter how much I tried. I could not stop myself from feeling the tears flow out of me because of this darkness. I never did cry. However, I definitely felt everything that you felt when one cries. So this was how I was feeling as I walked through the darkness to get to my car. Yet I was still not sure why I felt this pain and darkness. Then I thought about my beautiful blonde library angel. I started to think about how I was missing her. I was thinking about how special she was, and about how comfortable I was when she was at the library. So finally, I knew why I felt this darkness. I knew I felt this darkness because I was missing my beautiful blonde library angel.

I will never find anyone as inspirational as my beautiful blonde library angel. I will never find anyone as special as my beautiful blonde library angel. I always knew this about my beautiful blonde library angel. So thinking about my beautiful blonde library angel was not anything new. However, what was new was thinking that she was more than simply an angel of inspiration. Last night, I realized she was more than my angel of inspiration. Last night I realized she may have been the love of my life. She may have been the woman of my dreams.

I always knew that she was special. I always knew she was my angel of inspiration. I always knew that she was one of the four loves of my life. I always knew I never felt what I felt for her with any other angel. Sure, there were angels that I thought I loved before. There was Annabelle from France, who was one of the loves of my life. There was my beautiful blonde angel from high school who wrote me a letter to tell me she was interested. There is still a part of me that believes this angel could be the one. However, I also know that there is too much distance and time between us for her to ever be the one. Then there is the beautiful blonde sales angel who I promise I will get to later in this book. Lastly, there is the mystery angel who I have not met yet who might be the woman of my dreams. All these beautiful angels are special. Yet as special and beautiful as they are, they are not my beautiful blonde library angel.

My beautiful blonde library angel might be gone from my life. I hope she is not gone from my life. I hope I will see her again. Yet I also know that if I saw her again right now, the chances of me saying something to her are very unlikely. I know that as much as I think she might be the woman of my dreams, I still cannot say anything to her. I still believe she is too young for me to have a chance with her. I still believe she is too beautiful for me to have a chance with her. I still believe she might be unavailable if I saw her again because there is no way that I am the only one who knows of the greatness of my beautiful blonde library angel. Finally, I believe she is still too socially confident to notice someone who is so quiet and shy. Yet as time passes and she keeps reappearing in my life, I start to feel hope again. So maybe my spiritual journey with her is not over. Maybe, she will reappear to me one day, and when she reappears to me, I will have actually grown and found the social confidence to socialize with her.

I love my beautiful blonde library angel. I know my love for her might never be reciprocated. I know I might never see her again. I know even if I see her again, I most likely will not be able to say anything to her. I know that people will tell me that I am wrong for feeling how I feel about my beautiful blonde library angel since they feel it is wrong to love her.

I know there are people that feel this way because these same people were the same people who got me banned from my new French Bistro. They were also the same people who told me that I was not allowed back at the coffee shop across the street from her. Sadly, this world is overrun by these people, and I am not really able to defend myself against these people. These people are the bullies of the world. These people are the extroverts of the world with a voice, and I am a man without a voice. So when they ban me from a location of inspiration, there is only one thing I am able to do, which is to accept it, and then write about it in my books.

I know the weirdness of my anxiety is weird. This is why I call it the weirdness of my anxiety. I know the normal way of doing things with beautiful women is to socialize with them before you approach them with a letter. I know you have to socialize with beautiful women before they are comfortable with you being around them so much. Sadly, socializing is something I might never be able to do to make them comfortable. This is why I write my books.

I write my books since I doubt I will ever be comfortable enough to say anything to a beautiful woman. I doubt I will ever find the courage to tell a beautiful woman how I feel about her the right way. I fear my angels will always be uncomfortable because of the weirdness of my anxiety. Sadly, even if one of my angels is interested she will eventually lose interest because of my social anxiety. I was trying to change this about myself. I was trying to find the courage and the confidence to say something to one of my angels. I was even starting to find success at socializing with one of my angels at my new French Bistro. Then I was banned when I gave her a letter to let her know how I felt about her. I was so devastated after being banned that I was starting to fall into another pit of darkness. Yet as devastated as I was after being banned, I still found a way to move forward since I still had my beautiful blonde library angel. I knew my beautiful blonde library angel was still someone I could turn to since she was still at this bakery.

I was slowly finding my way out of my fall into another pit of darkness because I found this coffee shop to go to that was right across the street from my beautiful blonde library angel. I was starting a new routine of going to get a tea from her at this bakery. Then I went to this coffee shop to do some writing because there were all these beautiful angels who worked and ate there.

I was still missing my new French Bistro. I was still devastated after I lost it as my favorite place to write. However, I was starting to find my way out of my fall into another pit of darkness. Then it happened again. I was banned from another location of inspiration, and I believe this one was the most painful of them all because of how quickly it happened. I never got a chance to really feel inspired at this new coffee shop before I was banned. After I was banned from this coffee shop, I literally lost all my will to move forward. I could not believe how I had been banned from all my locations of inspiration. I was not sure how to move forward. I was literally thinking about killing myself after this. I could not live in a world where it was wrong to look at my angels. I could not imagine living life where I could not see my angels. After I was banned from this coffee shop, I started to think about never leaving my house again. I thought about going back to a time when all I had was television. I knew I could still watch my beautiful angels with my TV since this was what I did before my spiritual journey.

So I started writing from home for about a day, and it did work. Yet I could not stay home to write.

I felt safe writing at home. I knew I could always turn to TV for some angels of inspiration. I knew I could always turn to movies, reality TV, soap operas, and teen shows to see my beautiful angels, if nothing else. Yet I also knew that I had no shot of ever being with the beautiful angels from television because they were not really real. I mean, they were real people. However, they were not real people I was ever going to get because they were so far away. Thus I knew I had to leave the house to be around real women if I ever hoped to find the one. I knew it was getting painful to leave the house since humanity was hurting me so much. However, I also knew I could not hide at home because I was never going to meet the woman of my dreams hiding away at home. I knew I could find safety, and even some inspiration, at home. However, what I was never going to find hiding at home was the real thing. I was not going to find the woman of my dreams at home. So I had to venture back out into the real world no matter how painful it was to venture back out. I had to get back out there because I felt there was still some hope of finding the one. I knew many of the doors were now closed. However, I knew I had my work at Bon Gout. I also knew I still had my passion for writing and my books.

I was scared of what might happen if I kept writing about my spiritual journey. Everywhere I looked, all I saw were bullies when I left my world of isolation. I never saw this changing since I felt as if everyone was judging me because of the weirdness of my anxiety. Every time I saw a beautiful angel, I found my inspiration for a moment. Then right after I felt this moment of inspiration, I felt as if everyone was judging me for looking at one of my angels. So, I never felt safe because I was constantly wanting to see my beautiful angels. Yet I always felt wrong for looking at them. I was afraid of going to new places for inspiration because I was afraid of being banned from these places, or worse. So I was living my life afraid of people saying something because I loved beautiful women. I could not live this life anymore. So I started to really think about killing myself. I was starting to think about how death might be my only escape from my fear of humanity. After all, I knew that no matter how scary it was, I could not stop looking at beautiful women. I knew I was always going to be searching for ways to see beautiful women, right or wrong since life is not worth living without seeing beautiful women.

This was what I learned from my beautiful blonde library angel. My beautiful blonde library angel taught me I will always love beautiful women. I will always look forward to seeing my angels. I will always want to go places where I am able to see my angels. Sadly, these places are also places where I must deal with humanity since my beautiful angels are also people.

I know I must learn to deal with humanity if I ever hope to be with the woman of my dreams. I know I need to learn how to leave my world of isolation to be with the woman of my dreams. I know my world of isolation is not a real world. I know my dark existence is the real world. Unfortunately, I am terrified of this real world because I believe that all people are bullies within this real world, and I am finding that there is a great deal of truth to this statement.

I doubt I will ever feel safe around humanity after what happened at my locations of inspiration. I was so traumatized by what happened at my locations of inspiration that I do not know how to feel comfortable with anyone anymore. I am even finding it difficult to look at beautiful women. I still look at beautiful women. However, I feel that threats lie around every corner whenever I try to look at them. I believe that all beautiful women have a boyfriend waiting to confront me because I wanted to look at them. I fear all parents are waiting to say something to me because I looked at their beautiful daughters. I am especially afraid of mothers because I feel they know what it is like to be a beautiful woman. I feel as if these beautiful mothers were hurt by men before, and they see me as one of these men. Thus they see me as one of these bad men, and I am unable to show them that I am not them due to my social anxiety. So what chance do I have of being with the woman of my dreams if this is what they see? Unfortunately, I have no chance since I have to deal with my fear and the rest of humanity's fear.

This fear of humanity is something that will never go away. My love for beautiful women is something that will never go away. So how am I ever supposed to find my way to the woman of my dreams when I feel everyone feels I am wrong for loving beautiful women? Unfortunately, I am not sure how I will find my way to the woman of my dreams, which is why I am starting to believe that I will never find the woman of my dreams because she does not exist. Yet I also know I have to try to find my way to her because without my search for the woman of my dreams, my life is meaningless and hopeless. I do not want to live life without meaning or hope. So I know I must continue my search for the woman of my dreams because it is my only reason for living. Thus this means my passion for writing is my reason for living because I believe that this is my path to finding the woman of my dreams. Thus I must write for survival!

I believe my path to the woman of my dreams is through my books. I believe my spiritual journey toward finding the woman of my dreams is my reason for living. So I have to write until the day I die, or until I find my way to the woman of my dreams. Sadly, the more time that I spend without my beautiful blonde library angel, the darker my existence gets. I may never see my beautiful blonde library angel again. I hope that this is not true. Yet I fear this may be true because I am not sure if she will still be at the bakery when maintenance is over. I am not sure why the bakery is closed right now. I only know what it says, which is that they are closed for maintenance. So once again, I have to live without my beautiful blonde library angel not knowing if she will be back. I believe she will be back because I believe her to be a very responsible person. So I doubt she is gone forever this time, which means all hope is not gone. Thus there is still hope that one day my beautiful blonde library angel might be the woman of my dreams. I know how unlikely it is that this might happen since it never happened at the library. Yet I know that there is still some hope that she could be the one if I am able to see her.

My beautiful blonde library angel is the love of my life. I may never be with my beautiful blonde library angel. I may never see my beautiful blonde library angel again. She may be gone from my life forever. Although if I listen to my heart, then she will be back. However, her return does not mean that she will be the woman of my dreams because I know I must say something to her to have any chance with her. I know I will most likely have to socialize with the woman of my dreams for her to be the woman of my dreams. The woman of my dreams could still be the one who makes the first move. I still believe that she could be the one to initiate a conversation with me since I now know that angels like this exist. However, I also know that even if these angels do exist, then I still need to socialize with them. I must socialize with them to build a connection with them. I must socialize with them to learn what lies beyond their beauty. I must socialize to feel comfortable with them. However, more importantly, I must socialize to get them to feel more comfortable with me when I look at them.

I wish I could find my way to the woman of my dreams with my passion for writing. I wish I could write my books to find the woman of my dreams. I still believe that this is possible. I still want to believe that one day the woman of my dreams will read my books and search me out because she was attracted to me through my passion for writing. However, I know how unlikely it is that this will ever happen because this is simply not the way of the world. I know we live in a world where socializing is the only way to feel comfortable around people. Sadly, I am still unable to socialize because of my social anxiety. However, I thought that I was learning how to socialize with people at my new French Bistro. Then the loss of my new French Bistro led me to my fall into another pit of darkness. Alas, I had to regain my confidence to deal with humanity all over again. However, before I write about my fall into another pit of darkness, I must write about how my spiritual journey led me to my introduction to my new French Bistro.

# My Introduction To My
# New French Bistro

My introduction to my new French Bistro started when I was hired to work at this political call center. I knew I had to leave my work at Bon Gout when I was working only one day a week. I knew I had to leave my work at Bon Gout because I was not making enough money to make it as a writer. I knew I needed more money to market my book better. I could not do anything with five hours of work a week. I was only able to pay for gas and maybe one meal a week with this money. Thus I knew it was time to leave Bon Gout. I still hated the idea of leaving my work at Bon Gout. I still remember how it was at the other grocery store. Sadly, my work at this grocery store was not the same as my work at that grocery store. Sure, there were these two wise old grandmothers whom I liked at this grocery store. Sure, there was a beautiful blonde angel there for inspiration. However, this was nothing compared to the beautiful angels who worked and shopped at the other grocery store. It also had more wise old grandmothers for me to socialize with when I was there. Thus as much as I tried to turn my work at this Bon Gout into my work at my old Bon Gout, I was never that successful at doing so. I often found myself bored there, which often had me thinking about leaving because I knew I could be making a great deal more money than this at a call center. Then when they cut my hours to one day a week, I knew it was time for me to look for some new work. I knew that leaving my work at Bon Gout was now inevitable. So I had to get ready to say my goodbyes.

I knew I was not making enough money at Bon Gout. I knew I could earn more money working at a call center. I knew call centers were offering full-time hours for the same pay that I was making at Bon Gout. I also knew it was not that difficult to find work at a call center since they were always hiring. Unfortunately, I also knew why they were hiring. I knew I could always find work at a call center or a factory because it was such horrible work. I knew I never wanted to work at a factory again because of the heat. Thus I knew I had only one option for finding work after I finally decided to leave Bon Gout. I knew call centers were my only option.

I always believed I could find work at a call center. I always knew call centers needed people to work for them because of their high turnover rate. Yet I also always knew how much I hated the idea of working for them due to my social anxiety. I hated the idea of spending my days at work having to socialize with people. I kept telling myself that they could not see me because we were talking to each other over the phone. I kept telling myself these callers could not do anything to me because I could always disconnect the calls. I knew the worst thing that could happen if I disconnected the calls too much was that I could get fired. Then I knew I could find work at another call center because call centers were always hiring. Telling myself these things was what got me to work at these places everyday. Then the problem with me working at these places was that once I was there taking calls, I felt I needed to find some escape.

I knew how miserable I was working at these call centers. I knew how trapped I felt there once I had to start taking some calls. I felt there was no escape from these call centers once I started my shift there. I knew I could always walk out of my work at these call centers. Yet I also knew how much I needed the money to help my mom with the finances and for my book. I knew I needed the money to survive. I knew I needed the money to make it as a writer. I knew I was always going to need to make money. So I knew I could not leave my work at the call center once I was hired there, which was also why I never wanted to start working there. This was why I had so much trouble leaving Bon Gout. Yet I also knew I was not making enough money working at Bon Gout, and I was going to make good money working at a call center. So I knew I had to return to a call center once I decided to leave Bon Gout. I knew that factory work was never something I wanted to return to unless I was truly desperate. So I felt I had only one option if I left Bon Gout, and it was to work at a call center. This was one of the main reasons why I never wanted to leave Bon Gout. I did not want to leave Bon Gout because I did not want to feel trapped at a call center again. Then they cut my hours down to five hours a week at Bon Gout, and I knew it was time to leave. I knew it was time for me to find new work.

I started the process of applying for new work at a call center by applying to about a hundred call centers. My plans were to keep applying to call centers until the count reached one hundred. I was not sure if I was going to be able to reach a hundred call centers if I kept applying to these call centers. However, I did not believe that it was going to be that difficult to apply to one hundred call centers since there were so many call centers needing employees. Luckily, I found work at a call center before I ever reached my goal of one hundred call centers.

I found I could apply to at least twenty call centers a day without any difficulty once I started to apply for work at these call centers because of technology. All you had to do to apply for work nowadays was answer a few questions to let them know you were interested. Other times, you did not even have to answer these questions. Oftentimes, all you had to do was click a button to apply for work. So at first, I was feeling great about my search for work. Then my fear was that it was too simple to apply for work. My fear was that I was never going to hear from these employers after I applied for work with them because it was too good to be true. Then my fears were alleviated when I started to get call after call for an interview. I could not believe how many interviews I was getting once I started to look for work. I literally had ten interviews to work at a call center after only two hours of looking for work. I started my search for work upon a Monday. Then I had ten interviews scheduled to start my new work at a call center. Now not all these interviews were for call centers. Some of them were for me to work at rehab centers and for customer service. So I was not only looking for work at a call center. Yet I knew call centers were what I was looking for since I was looking to make as much money as possible, as soon as possible. I knew I was not planning to stay at this call center forever. I was hoping to be at this call center only until I made it as a writer. So I felt a call center was the best place for me to work after I left my work at Bon Gout.

It did not even take me a full week to find my new work at this political call center. I started applying for work at call centers on a Monday. I believe I applied to about fifty places that Monday after I finally decided it was time to leave Bon Gout. Again, it was not difficult to apply for work at fifty places once I decided to find new work because of technology. It took me only about two hours to apply to these fifty places. Then I had all these interviews to go to during the week. I had my first interview that following Tuesday at this political call center. I did not expect much from this interview, though, because I had worked for them before. I worked for them before, and I was fired from them before. So I never expected to get hired by them again after being fired. Then I went to the interview, and it went really well. I obviously never told them that I got fired from this company before, and they never asked. Thus I left the interview feeling really good about my chances to work for them again. I knew they wanted to hire me right then and there because they said so. All they had to do was wait for my background check, and I was hired if it went well. I was never worried about my background check because I had never done drugs before. I was also never arrested. So I knew I was getting hired; it was only a matter of time before I found out what I already knew was going to happen.

I spent this Tuesday at my original French Bistro because my beautiful blonde library angel did not work at the library Tuesdays. This meant that I was spending my Tuesdays at my original French Bistro to be inspired by the beautiful blonde supervisor who worked there. Therefore, once the interview was over, I returned to my original French Bistro to apply for more work as a precaution and to be inspired by this beautiful blonde supervisor. I knew that my interview went well. I knew all I was waiting for was my background check. So I knew I was not really going to look for work once I got to my original French Bistro. I knew that I was really going there to see the beautiful blonde supervisor who was working at this French Bistro.

I left my interview at this political call center believing that it was only a matter of time until I was hired to work for them. I knew the interview went well. I knew I was only waiting to see if I passed the background check. So I knew it was only a matter of time before I found out that I was hired to work for them. Then I got back to my original French Bistro, and I got an email from them saying that I was hired, and they wanted me to start training with them. I thanked them for the opportunity, and I told them I had to give my notice to Bon Gout. I usually never really cared about giving my two weeks' notice where I was working. Honestly, I usually never had anyone to give two weeks' notice to before since I was usually not working when hired. However, this was one of those rare occasions when I wanted to give my two weeks' notice because I hoped to one day return to Bon Gout. Thus I wanted to leave with a chance to return.

I gave my two weeks' notice when I returned to work at Bon Gout. I explained to the manager that I did not want to leave Bon Gout because I really did love working for them. Yet I was not getting enough hours there, and I knew this was probably never going to change. He might be able to give me two or three days a week rather than only one day a week. However, I knew this was the best he could do because there were others there who also wanted the hours. He understood why I was leaving and knew that this was a great opportunity because he knew of the call center. So I worked at Bon Gout for two more weeks before starting my tenure at this new call center. I knew I was taking a risk by leaving Bon Gout because I knew I might never have another chance to return to my perfect work for writing. Yet I also knew that this was a risk that I had to take because I was not making enough money there. So I got through my two weeks there, and then I started my new work at this political call center. I was not nearly as excited to start my work at this call center as I was when I returned to Bon Gout. However, I was very excited about the financial opportunities that I was presented with when I started working there.

I was guaranteed full-time hours at this political call center. There were even weeks when I could get more than forty hours while working at this call center. So I was going to be making good money at this call center, which was a welcome change from being broke so much. Another great thing about working at this call center was that I was able to create my own work schedule while working there. I was able to create my work schedule around the times when my angels of inspiration were not at work. Thus I worked when I was the least inspired. Unfortunately, this work at this call center was not perfect work because I hated the calls there.

I hated the calls I had to make and take there because I was mostly dealing with conservatives while working there. I hated having to deal with conservatives so much because I found it difficult to show them any respect. I found it really difficult to show them respect because when I think of conservatives, I think of bullies. So I found it was really difficult to be respectful to conservatives because I had no respect for bullies. How could I have any respect for people who had no respect for other people? How could I have any respect for people who I knew wanted to kill or meme someone simply because they disagreed with them? So I had no respect for the people I was working for, and I could not fake my respect for them either. Every time I took a call from these people or I called them, I was rude to them. I was either rude to them or I disconnected my calls when I could not deal with them anymore. Obviously, this did not sit well with the management there because they knew I was rude to their clientele. However, somehow I was able to stay at this call center for a year before I was finally fired. I do not know how I was able to last a year at this political call center. However, somehow I managed to stay there for a year before finally getting fired. I always knew I was inevitably going to get fired from this call center. I always knew it was only a matter of time until management got tired of my rudeness to customers and I was fired. Sadly, I simply did not care.

It was sad that I did not care because I had such respect for the manager there. This manager was a very nice lady who always said hello when we passed each other. Plus, she did try to help me to deal with the clientele there. I really do believe she wanted me to keep my employment at this call center. Sadly, no matter how much respect I had for her, I could not fake my respect for the clientele there. I could not act like I cared about their money or their beliefs when I felt what they believed was evil. This was what I believed, and I could not ignore what I believed. The money I was making there did not matter. The respect I had for the manager could not make me stop believing what I believed. Maybe, it might have been better if I had simply quit. Yet I also knew I was making good money when I was there. Thus I tried to remain at this political call center until I was fired since I also wanted to get my money's worth.

I found it very difficult to do well at work because I could not fake my respect for the clientele there. This disrespect for the clientele was eventually what got me fired from this call center. I will never forget that moment when it finally happened. I was following my normal routine of talking to my best friend at work and disconnecting my calls. I was at a point where all I was doing was disconnecting my calls with customers one after another. I stopped caring about what happened to me at work. I was only there to talk to my best friend and the other coworkers. Then I got called to the office, and it finally happened. I remember I walked into the office with the manager I had great respect for, and she told me I was fired. So the inevitable moment finally arrived. After it finally happened, I left work without saying a word.

I could not say anything to defend myself to the manager. I had too much respect to argue with her about what she was saying because I knew everything she said was true. I knew I was being rude to the customers. I even knew I deserved to be fired. I felt the best course of action was to simply say nothing and leave because it was time. There was no reason for me to try to explain myself or to try to defend myself to her. There was no point in me saying anything to her other than sorry. So I did say sorry. Then I left without saying a word. I could not say anything for two reasons. I could not say anything because I knew everything they said was true. I also could not say anything because I felt so much shame and regret. I did not feel this shame and regret because of how I treated the customers or the employers there. Although, I was feeling it for the manager who I had great respect for there. Yet not for anyone else at this call center. So why was I feeling this shame and respect? I was feeling this shame and respect because I knew I was fired for something I could not change about myself. I was fired because of my social anxiety and my fear of humanity, and this was something I could not change. However, I knew I had to find a way to change this about myself if I ever hoped to make money.

The world did not care about my debilitating social anxiety. The world did not care about my fear of humanity. The world only cared that I was able to make money. The world only cared that I tried to find a way to act as close to normal as I was capable of acting. Unfortunately, I was not able to be fake. I could not pretend to care about what I did not care about for any reason including money. The only things I cared about was seeing my angels, listening to my music, drinking my soda, the cold, and writing about my spiritual journey. Sadly, I was the only person who cared about what I cared about because the rest of this world cared only about me making them money. So I had to work to survive. Yet I also knew the importance of my passion for writing. I knew my passion for writing was all that I cared about in this world. Yet I knew there was more to my passion for writing than writing. I knew getting published was also important, as was marketing my books to make any money as a writer.

The library was still my main source of inspiration when I started to work at this call center because my beautiful blonde library angel was still working there. My original French Bistro was my secondary source of inspiration because of this beautiful blonde supervisor. I felt as if this was enough inspiration for me before I started to work at this call center. Then I started to work at this call center that was across town from both locations of inspiration. So, I was thinking about going to this new French Bistro near this call center for inspiration. I somehow always knew about this French Bistro since I passed by it when I went to the movies. However, I never really thought about going there until I started to work at this call center because I felt I had enough inspiration from the library and my original French Bistro. Then I thought about going to this French Bistro because it was so close to the call center. I was not expecting much from my new French Bistro. I was simply going there to save time because I had to drive across town to write at my other locations of inspiration. Then I saw all the beautiful angels who were at my new French Bistro and I knew I made a good choice to go there.

There were at least ten beautiful angels working at my new French Bistro. There were these two beautiful supervisors that were working there. One was this beautiful redhead who sat across from me when I was eating. I could not believe that this beautiful redheaded supervisor was comfortable enough to sit where I could get such a good look at her beauty as she ate lunch. This beautiful redheaded supervisor was my introduction to my new French Bistro. Then there was this other supervisor who was also my introduction to my new French Bistro. This second supervisor was this beautiful brunette who was very socially confident. I knew this beautiful brunette supervisor was way out of my league. I knew she was way too beautiful and was way too socially confident for me to ever have a chance with her. So I never dreamed of trying to approach her when I first started to go to my new French Bistro. Then her social confidence was so contagious that I started to think I might have a chance with her. I knew I might be wrong about ever having a chance with her. Yet I felt I needed to try since she was so special.

These two beautiful supervisors at my new French Bistro were my introduction to my new French Bistro. I was equally attracted to both these supervisors when I started my spiritual journey at this new French Bistro because they were both so attractive. Yet they were also so different because of their personalities. The beautiful redheaded supervisor was more quiet and reserved, which made her the more realistic angel when I started my spiritual journey there. Then as I spent more time at my new French Bistro and felt more confident around the beautiful brunette supervisor, I started to think that she might be the one. Sadly, I was very mistaken about her. Yet I have no regrets about approaching her because I could not help how I felt about her. So maybe the redheaded supervisor was the one. After all, she was the first angel of inspiration that I was drawn to when I first walked into my new French Bistro. However, I felt my spiritual journey was leading me to my beautiful brunette supervisor. I felt my spiritual journey was showing me all these signs that she might be the one. Sadly, I was wrong about her.

These two beautiful supervisors were not the only beautiful angels working at my new French Bistro. There was also this beautiful redheaded cashier working there who looked very much like the fiery redhead from the library. She looked so much like her that I started to believe it might be her. Then I realized she was more beautiful than the fiery redhead from the library. So I instead found myself thinking she might be my new angel of inspiration, until she left right after I thought this about her. There was also a beautiful black-haired angel and a beautiful Asian angel, and each helped me to start my spiritual journey to my new French Bistro.

# MY SPIRITUAL JOURNEY TO MY NEW FRENCH BISTRO

My spiritual journey to my new French Bistro started while my beautiful blonde library angel was still working at the library. It started right before she left with me needing a new place to work because I was not getting enough hours working at Bon Gout. I did not want to find a new place to work because I still considered Bon Gout the perfect place to work for my writing. Yet I also knew that I was going to need to find another place to work because I was only working two or three days a week at Bon Gout. I was averaging about only twenty hours a week at Bon Gout. So I was not able to help my mom out with the finances while working there. More importantly, I was not able to pay to market *The Beautiful Blonde Library Angel* more while working at Bon Gout. I had sold only about nine copies of my first book while working there, and I knew I had to sell much more than this to make it as a writer. So I had to find another place to work to help out my mom with the finances and to get my name out there more.

I had to find a new place to work. I had to make more money than what I was making while working at Bon Gout. I did not want to leave my work at Bon Gout, though, since I knew it took so much for me to finally find my way back to Bon Gout. I first left this work at Bon Gout when this grocery store near my house hired me to work for them. I was offered less money to work for them and about the same number of hours as I was getting at Bon Gout. So I was never sure about my decision to leave Bon Gout. However, I thought this was a good decision at the time because I felt I was going to have more room to grow there since it was part of a union. So after a great deal of soul searching, I decided to give my notice to Bon Gout because I was hoping to build a future for myself at this grocery store. Then as soon as I started my work at this grocery store, I knew I made the wrong decision. So I instantly started trying to find my way back to Bon Gout. Thus started my gut-wrenching process of trying to return to Bon Gout.

I never wanted to leave Bon Gout when I went to work at this grocery store. I never wanted to leave my work at Bon Gout because it was the perfect work for my writing. I loved how some weeks I was getting five to seven days a week, then other weeks I got two or three. This fluctuating schedule was great for my passion for writing. It worked out great for my writing because there were weeks I got good money, then there were weeks I could write more.

Another reason why I loved my work at Bon Gout so much was because of my coworkers. I was working with mostly old ladies at Bon Gout. I referred to these old ladies as my wise old grandmothers because they reminded me so much of my grandmothers. My grandmothers were the two people I felt the most comfortable with socially. There was my French grandmother during my wonderful French childhood. Then there was my American grandmother from Florida after I left my wonderful French childhood. I loved both my grandmothers equally. I loved them so much since they each had a way of making me feel socially comfortable around them. My French grandmother reminded me of this Becassine doll from the area, and my American grandmother looked like Lucille Ball. Sadly, both my grandmothers passed away after I was done with high school. So I lost both my grandmothers as my beings of comfort. I still had my dad and my best friend as my being of comfort after they passed away. However, once I moved to Ohio, I lost my best friend. So then the only person I had left who I was socially comfortable around was my dad until he, sadly, passed away.

I was not sure how I was going to survive the loss of my father. My father was my last physical connection to my wonderful French childhood. I knew my memories of my wonderful French childhood were not going anywhere because of my love for French music. Sadly, as wonderful as I felt when I heard French music, nothing could bring back what I lost. I lost everyone from my wonderful French childhood, and there was no bringing them back. I learned my best friend from France and my favorite cousin committed suicide. I learned both my grandparents from France passed away. I learned that most of my other cousins moved away after I returned from my return trip to France. Finally, I learned that Annabelle got married soon after my return trip from France. So I could never go back to my wonderful French childhood. My father was the only person I had left of my wonderful French childhood. Then, when my father passed away, all that I had left of my wonderful French childhood was my French music.

I was not only losing my last connection to my wonderful French childhood with the passing of my father, but I was also losing the only person I was able to socialize with outside of therapy with his passing. My father was my best friend and my worst enemy. I felt I could always be myself with my father. I never had to hide who I was with my father. I could talk to him about anything, and I mean anything. My father was the first person I told about my beautiful blonde library angel. He was the only person I could tell about my obsession with my beautiful library angels. He never judged me for not talking to any of my angels. Sure, he did occasionally joke with me about not being able to talk to them. Yet, I knew he was joking and I never got mad when he joked because I never took it seriously. I am not sure if my father ever really understood my social anxiety because he was always such a socially confident person. I will always be grateful to my father for his social confidence because this is why I am alive. I believe that my mother has the same social anxiety that I have, which is why we never talk. Yet my father never had social anxiety. So he was able to make my mother feel socially comfortable when they were younger. Then this eventually led to them getting married and my existence. Thus I will always be grateful to my father for his social confidence. However, the real reason I am grateful for his social confidence is that he was all I had when I moved to Ohio. Sadly, once I moved to Ohio, all I had were my parents. Thus my father was truly all that I had.

My father was my best friend. He was my social confidant after I moved to Ohio. However, I did not have a perfect relationship with my father. There were times when we got into such heated arguments that we did not talk to each other for days. There was even one argument that led to us not talking to each other for months. These months of not talking to my father were some of the darkest months of my life. I hated not having my father as my best friend. Even when I had my therapists to talk to, I still treasured my father more than anything because he was the one relationship I had that was real. He was the only person I knew all my life, and I knew he was not going anywhere until that sad day when he was gone. I did not want to think of that dark day when he might be gone forever. I did not want to imagine a world without my father. Then that day finally arrived, and I had to learn how to live life without my only being of comfort. I had to learn to live my life without my best friend and my worst enemy.

I could not imagine a life without my father. I never had a perfect relationship with my father. There were moments when I hated my father because he said such hurtful things. I could not believe how hurtful he could be at times. Then there was the fact that he never washed his hands or took a shower, which was so disgusting. However, as much as I hated all these things about my father, he was still my best friend since he was so much like my French grandmother. I could not believe how I could always feel socially comfortable with him when I could go the rest of the day without ever saying a word to anyone else. My father had such a special gift of being able to socialize with anyone no matter what they thought of him. There were often times when I was ashamed of him, or embarrassed, because of the things he said to people. Although, when I think back on these moments now, I think I was actually jealous of him. After all, these were things that I could never dream of doing with people. I never could tell people what I thought free of judgment. My fear of humanity and my social anxiety always stopped me from socializing with people comfortably. So I always admired how my father and my French grandmother had the social confidence to say things to people no matter what they might think.

This was the same gift my French grandmother had when she was alive. She was such an interesting person because she always had something to say. I never dreamed I would meet someone else like her until I left France and moved to America. My American grandmother was the only other person I ever met who was like my French grandmother. I was able to talk to Grandma June about anything. I am not sure if I could have talked to her about my love for beautiful women since this was not something I often thought about at the time. So mostly, I spent my time telling her about my love for television. I mostly talked to her about television since this was what I thought about at the time. I do not remember what I talked to Grandma June or my French grandmother Augustine about when we talked. All I really remember about them is how socially comfortable I was with them, which was why I loved them.

They both had the gift of gab. They both were great storytellers. I have so many wonderful memories of my time with both my grandmothers. I remember walking the cows with my French grandmother at the farm. I remember never feeling like I was working with my French grandmother because it was more about spending time with her and hearing her stories. Most of my memories of my wonderful French childhood consisted of the time that I spent with her. This and my life at the farm. Then there was Grandma June. Most of my memories of Grandma June were of her babysitting me and of all my time spent with her in the Florida Keys.

I have so many great memories of Grandma June. One memory I have of her is playing Pac-Man with her one night. I also have these memories of her rubbing my back when I was a child. Grandma June was so nurturing. Grandma Augustine was also nurturing because she often hugged me and pinched my cheeks. I think all grandmothers love to pinch cheeks. I am not sure why. Yet I do remember watching these old shows where the grandchildren hated grandmothers pinching their cheeks. These are not the only memories I have of Grandma June. I also have my memories of us getting into a Jacuzzi after dinner. I also remember my mother being there, which brings me to another great thing about Grandma June. I loved how Grandma June was able to help me feel closer to my mother. Finally, I have one more great memory of Grandma June. This memory is of us sitting at the dining room table late one night. I remember I was eating some type of a dessert while she was telling me some of her great stories.

Grandma June was my American grandmother. Grandma Augustine was my French grandmother. I will always treasure my memories of both my grandmothers. I love my parents. I love my family. However, no one was more special than my two grandmothers. Sadly, they both passed away soon after I returned from France after college. I first lost Grandma Augustine to old age. Then I lost Grandma June to cancer a few years later. Once I lost my two grandmothers, my father was my last connection to my wonderful French childhood. So my father was the only person left who had the gift of gab. So my time with my father was something I truly treasured for two reasons. The first being that he was my last connection to my wonderful French childhood. The second being that he was the only person left who I was socially comfortable around after I moved to Ohio. My father always had something to say to me even if it was only a simple hello as I was leaving the house. I am not saying we always had these great conversations. Although we did often have some great conversations. Then other times we simply said hello to each other, and this was all that I needed sometimes. Unfortunately, once my father passed away, I was afraid of being a man without a voice forever.

I wrote about seventy pages about the loss of my father after he passed away. I spent about two months writing after the loss of my father. My passion for writing was the only voice I had left after the loss of my father. I could not find my voice when I was around people after the loss of my father. I had no therapist to talk to after he passed away because my therapist was let go at the same time as I lost my father. Thus all I had after my father passed away was my passion for writing and my beautiful blonde library angel. So once again, my beautiful blonde library angel was leading me out of my fall into a pit of darkness. Eventually, I was able to find some way of socializing with people again. At least I could socialize enough to return to work. After the loss of my father, I was spending most of my time at the library writing because I lost my voice after he passed away. Then I started to find my way back to my dark reality when I was finally assigned a therapist. Finally, I was ready to return to the world of work when I received an email to work at Bon Gout again, and I jumped at the chance to return to Bon Gout.

I was afraid I was never going to find my way back to Bon Gout. I knew I was never going to return if the manager had any say. The manager at Bon Gout never liked me because I was always breaking the rules there. I hated to follow the rules there because there were so many rules to follow. I could not have a cell phone in the cart. I could not have my Pepsi in my cart. I could not walk away from the cart. I could not eat any of the food samples. I never followed any of these rules. So the manager was always bitter toward me because of how I always broke the rules. Thus I knew I was never going to be able to go back to working for Bon Gout at the grocery store where she was the manager. Hence I thought I'd lost my chance of ever returning to my perfect work for writing. Then I got an email to work at Bon Gout again. However, this was at another grocery store, which was too far away. So I had to turn down my first opportunity to return to Bon Gout because I did not have a car. I was afraid this was it. I was afraid this was my last chance to return to Bon Gout. Then soon after my father passed away, I got an email to return to work for them at another grocery store. This grocery store was right around the corner from where I was originally working. So I was ecstatic about this opportunity, and I did not want to do anything to miss out on a chance at returning to Bon Gout.

I went to see the manager at this grocery store right after I got the email. I was hired right after I had the interview. So finally, I found a way back to Bon Gout. I knew it was at a different grocery store. However, I was still excited to be back at Bon Gout because I thought this might lead me back to Bon Gout if the manager ever left. So I was still ecstatic to be back.

I tried to make the most of my time at this grocery store. I went to visit my wise old grandmothers during my breaks from work. Then I also went to visit them after work. I also started to find some coworkers that I liked to socialize with at this new grocery store. Unfortunately, I never felt this job at this grocery store was as great as the first grocery store.

There were two coworkers that I liked to socialize with at this grocery store. One coworker I liked to socialize with was this mother who was very outgoing. I felt I could tell her anything because she was very outgoing and nonjudgmental. I told her all about my book and my social anxiety. I also told her about all the angels I was obsessed with. There was one more reason why I liked to talk to this mother, and this was because of her attractive daughter. I was hoping that maybe by socializing with her I might be able to socialize with her daughter. Sadly, this never really happened. There were moments when we socialized with each other. However, these moments never turned into anything because I never really felt comfortable around her. There was even one time when I drove her home. I was hoping that this might help because we had these great conversations during the drive. Then she went home, and I was never able to really socialize with her again. This is the story of my life. I will have moments where I might be able to socialize with beautiful women. Then, I am unable to continue to socialize with them because my social anxiety returns to remind me that I am unable to socialize with women.

There was one other coworker I loved to socialize with at this grocery store. This coworker was my favorite person to socialize with because I felt so comfortable around her. I could spend hours talking to her. I could talk to her about my beautiful angels without her judging me for not doing anything to be with them. I often told her about my spiritual journey with my beautiful blonde library angel. Plus, I talked to her about my attraction to this beautiful blonde working at this grocery store. This beautiful blonde was the only angel working at this grocery store. So there was not much inspiration there. However, this blonde was very beautiful. So I found myself spending a great deal of time trying to see her. Sadly, most of the time, I could not get a good look at her because she was so far away. I also talked to her about my attraction to the other coworker's daughter. Sadly, this was also when I found out that the daughter liked this other guy that was working there. So I think this was why it got really difficult for me to socialize with the daughter since I was not about to deal with the competition.

I loved talking to this old lady at this grocery store. I felt as though I was talking to my grandmother when I was talking to her. Unfortunately, this old lady was only working at this grocery store one or two days a week because she was recovering from cancer. Sadly, her recovery from cancer was only temporary because I learned she passed away a few months ago. I was very sad to learn that she had passed away because I loved talking to her so much. My time at this grocery store lasted only about a year, maybe less. I tried to make the most out of working at this grocery store because I knew how much I loved working for Bon Gout. Sadly, I never found my work at this grocery store as enjoyable as my work at the other grocery store. This one old lady with cancer was probably my fondest memory of my time there. So a part of me often wonders if my only reason for being there was simply to meet her. Sure, I enjoyed socializing with the other coworker. I also remember her daughter, whom I thought might be the one for a brief moment of time since she had autism. I thought this might be some way of connecting with her since I had social anxiety. However, nothing happened with her because my social anxiety was so much more debilitating than her autism. There was also this beautiful blonde angel who worked there who I occasionally said something to as she got samples from me. However, my fondest memories at this grocery store were of all of my conversations with Linda.

I left this job at this grocery store because I was getting about only ten hours a week. I could not continue to work there when I was still pursuing my dream of being a writer. I had to make more money than this to market my book. Plus, I had to get more money than this because I had to pay for car insurance and I had to try to help my mom out with the finances. So I knew I had to find other work. Yet I did not want to leave Bon Gout because I still felt that this was the perfect work for my writing. Then I went from working two days a week to working only one day a week, and I knew it was finally time for me to find another place to work.

It did not take me much time at all to find another place to work. I applied to a few call centers because I knew this was the best way to get more hours. Then I got an interview to work for this political call center, and I was hired soon after the interview. I was not thrilled about leaving Bon Gout to work for this call center. Yet I knew I had to leave since I needed money. I never liked dealing with the calls at this call center since I was mostly dealing with conservatives, and when I think of conservatives I think of bullies. Yet I tried to keep this work because I got good money there, and I was able to create my own schedule while working there. I was still able to see my beautiful blonde library angel when I started to work at this call center. My original French Bistro was still part of my spiritual journey because of the beautiful blonde supervisor. Yet I knew she was not single and my beautiful blonde library angel might be leaving soon. So I was thinking about continuing my spiritual journey at my new French Bistro.

# My New French Bistro

My new French Bistro was my new location of inspiration. I could not believe how many beautiful angels there were at my new French Bistro. There was this beautiful redheaded cashier who looked like the fiery redhead from the library. Again, I first thought she was the fiery redhead from the library until I realized she was even more beautiful than her. There were these two beautiful angels cleaning the dining room who were also very beautiful. One was this beautiful Asian angel who was only there for a few weeks. I do not remember much about this Asian angel other than the fact that she was very shy and beautiful. This beautiful Asian angel liked to mostly keep to herself when she was there. This gave me the impression that she was very uncomfortable working there because everyone else was so engaging. There was also this beautiful black-haired angel who was much more outgoing. This beautiful black-haired angel was often smiling and laughing with customers. Lastly, there were the two beautiful supervisors.

These were the five beautiful angels who first introduced me to my new French Bistro. The beautiful Asian angel at my new French Bistro was the first angel to leave once I started my spiritual journey at my new French Bistro. I was not that surprised that she was the first to go because I always felt she was very uncomfortable being there. The beautiful redheaded cashier was the second angel to leave. I was more surprised when she left. Yet I was still not too surprised that she left either because I felt she was also uncomfortable being there. I was more depressed than anything when she left. I was so depressed when she left because I thought she might be my new angel of inspiration there. I was starting to spend a great deal of time at my new French Bistro because of all the beautiful angels working there. Thus I was thinking it might be time for me to single out an angel of inspiration at my new French Bistro. The beautiful redheaded supervisor was the first angel I thought of when I started to single one out.

I singled out this fiery redhead as my new angel of inspiration because she looked so much like the fiery redhead from the library. She was actually more beautiful than the fiery redhead, which meant that I was even more inspired by her. So I thought that maybe this was who my spiritual journey was leading me to after I was introduced to my new French Bistro. Then I saw that she left my new French Bistro right after I started to think this about her. So I realized I was wrong about her and that I now had to find a new angel of inspiration there. I was still not ready to think of the two beautiful supervisors as my new angels of inspiration. I still could not bring myself to imagine either one of them as being the woman of my dreams. I still felt they were both too beautiful and confident for me to have a chance with them. So I instead turned my attention to the beautiful black-haired angel who was cleaning the dining room. I could not ignore the beauty of this black-haired angel anymore. She had such a shapely figure. Yet her personality was what I really noticed about her. Again, she was always smiling and laughing with the customers, which made her even more beautiful. So after the beautiful redheaded cashier left my new French Bistro, this black-haired angel turned into my angel of inspiration.

This beautiful black-haired angel cleaning the dining room remained my new angel of inspiration for a few months. I never imagined her leaving my new French Bistro because I felt she was so happy there. Then a few weeks passed without me seeing her there. Yet I still thought she was working there. I simply thought she was working when I was not able to be there. So I probably had to rearrange my schedule to see her again. Then I went to get something at Control, and I saw that she was now working there. At first, I was upset to learn that she had left my new French Bistro. I was upset to learn that I had lost another one of my angels of inspiration at my new French Bistro. Then Control turned into one of my locations of inspiration during COVID, and she was my beautiful black-haired angel of inspiration once again.

The beautiful Asian angel cleaning the dining room was the first angel of inspiration I lost once I was introduced to my new French Bistro. The beautiful redheaded cashier was the second angel of inspiration I lost once I was introduced to my new French Bistro. Then the beautiful black-haired angel was the third angel of inspiration to leave my new French Bistro. I was still not ready to think of these two beautiful supervisors as my angels of inspiration. I still felt they were too beautiful and confident for me to ever have a chance with them. However, this was starting to change as more of my angels left and they were the only ones still there. So each time one of my angels of inspiration left, their inspirational energy grew. Then over time, the story of my spiritual journey at my new French Bistro was all about them. Sure, there were other angels of inspiration at my new French Bistro who were my inspiration. However, these two beautiful supervisors were always the angels of inspiration that I returned to while I was there. These two beautiful angels were always the angels I was most attracted to at my new French Bistro. Yet I could never decide which one I liked the best until the redheaded supervisor finally quit.

The two beautiful supervisors were always my go-to angels of inspiration at my new French Bistro. I could not write about my spiritual journey at my new French Bistro without writing about these two beautiful supervisors. I never dreamed of having a chance with the beautiful brunette supervisor when I started my spiritual journey at my new French Bistro. She was too socially confident and beautiful for me to ever dream of being with her. So the beautiful redheaded supervisor was the angel of inspiration I dreamed of being with at the start. She was the one I thought I had a chance with at the start of my spiritual journey. Although, I never really thought I had a real chance with her, which was why I could not say anything to her. So nothing ever did happen with the beautiful redheaded supervisor. She was too quiet and reserved for me to ever think she could actually be the one because I could never be the initiator.

The beautiful brunette supervisor working at my new French Bistro was always the woman of my dreams. I always found her to be the most inspirational angel at my new French Bistro. However, I never imagined that one day I might find the courage to actually approach her. At the start of my spiritual journey at my new French Bistro, I could not even imagine her as being my angel of inspiration. This beautiful brunette supervisor was simply too beautiful and confident for me to imagine her as being the one. Then over time, I started to believe that maybe she might be the one because of her social confidence. The more time I spent at my new French Bistro, the more I started to think she might be the one. Sadly, I was wrong about her being the one. Yet as great as the loss of my new French Bistro was, I have no regrets about approaching her because at least now I know she was never really the one.

I have no regrets about the time spent at my new French Bistro. I have no regrets about approaching this beautiful brunette supervisor. I know what it cost me to approach her. I know I may never get over what happened after I approached her. However, I have no regrets about approaching her to let her know how I felt because I really did believe she was the one. Sadly, I now know I was wrong about her being the one. I now know that she was not the one. However, I might never have known this if I had not approached her. So I might have continued to go to my new French Bistro for the rest of my life, thinking she was the one without knowing the truth.

So no, I have no regrets about approaching her. My only regret is that I grew impatient with my spiritual journey when I started to rush things with this beautiful brunette supervisor. So I guess I do actually have two regrets after approaching her. The first being that the world was unable to understand the weirdness of my anxiety after I approached her with the letter. Then the second being that I did not listen to my spiritual journey better. I still believe this beautiful brunette supervisor might have been the one if I was able to be more patient with her.

I believe my spiritual journey was telling me to be patient. I believe I might have actually had a chance with this beautiful brunette supervisor if I listened to my spiritual journey. Sadly, I grew impatient with the universe because I also felt she might lose interest if I never intervened. So I decided to write her a letter to let her know how I felt about her. I was afraid I might never be able to tell her how I felt because of my social anxiety. So I felt the letter was my only way of ever letting her know how I felt. So I spent about a week writing her the letter. Then I set a deadline for when to give her the letter. I knew there was no turning back once I decided to write her this letter and give it to her. I knew I had to give it to her no matter how anxious I was about doing so, and boy, was I nervous. My new French Bistro was actually packed the last ten minutes before they closed. So I was not sure if I could give her the letter. I was sitting there at my new French Bistro ready to give her the letter if I could find the courage. I had the letter written and ready to give to her. I had this little Tigger toy to go with it and a card as well. OK, so now, when I think back to it all, I realize that this was way too much too soon. However, I did not care then because I felt it was all or nothing. I believed I had to approach her because if I did not, I might never find the courage to ever let her know how I felt.

I believed I had to approach her if I ever hoped to have a chance with her. I believed writing her a letter to tell her how I felt about her was my only chance with her. However, this was not what the universe believed. This was not how my spiritual journey was telling me to approach her. My spiritual journey was telling me to take my time with her. It was telling me to simply keep going there and try to say hello to her and see what happened. I had been going to my new French Bistro for about two years, and I was actually starting to say hello to her. Then right before I approached her with the letter, I was even able to compliment her. This compliment even led to a smile and a thank you from her. So this was something I was really feeling good about because it took so much courage to compliment her. Then this compliment led her to saying more than the usual as I was leaving.

Things were going great with this beautiful brunette supervisor before I decided to approach her with this letter to tell her how I felt. The universe was actually showing me a path to being with her if I was patient with her. Then I grew impatient with the universe. So I decided to write her a letter to pour my soul out to her. I knew this was too much too soon. I knew I was going too far. I knew this was not the way things worked. I knew I was taking a risk by going this route. Yet my social anxiety was telling me that I had to do this because she might lose interest if I did not take a risk. I believed from my past experiences with beautiful women that if I did not take a risk, then she might never know the truth, and she might lose interest. So I decided to go with what my instincts were telling me to do rather than listen to the universe.

I decided to write her a letter about how I felt about her. I decided I had to give her this letter that Friday night no matter what since it was my only path to her. I now know that this was not my only path to her. I now know that there was another path to her. I now know, or at least believe, that there was another path to her if I had been more patient and listened to the universe. Sadly, I did not listen to the universe. I was not patient with her because I was tired of being alone. I was tired of spending my nights alone. I was tired of wondering if she was interested. So I decided I had to give her this letter because I had to know the truth about how she felt. I did not care how many people were there. I did not care about what the universe was saying anymore. I had the letter written. I had the card. I had the Tigger toy. I knew what the plan was for giving it to her. So now all I had to do was find the courage to actually give it to her. I did not care how many people were at my new French Bistro. I did not care how anxious and uncomfortable I was about giving it to her. I knew I had to take this risk and give it to her. So I finally found the courage to give it to her when she walked away. I knew I had only one opportunity of giving it to her, and it was when she was not there, because of my social anxiety.

I first thought about giving her the letter when she was mopping because she was all alone. I actually took a few steps toward her with the letter. Then I sat right back down since I knew she was working and this was not a good time to give it to her. So I sat there with the anxiety of not knowing if I was ever going to be able to find the courage to give it to her. Then I saw her at the counter with her notebook, and I thought this might be the right time. However, there were so many people around her that I got scared again. Finally, she walked away from her notebook, and there was no one around other than this cashier who I also liked. Yet she was not the beautiful brunette supervisor. So this was when I took the risk. I grabbed the letter, the card, and the Tigger toy, and I dropped them all off by her notebook. After dropping them all off, I went back to the table, got everything into my backpack, and I left through the back door. I could not see her because I was afraid of her saying something to me after I gave her the letter. I knew I still could not say anything to her because of my social anxiety. I knew I still could not say anything to her because she was one of my beautiful angels. So I was still scared to socialize with her. However, I was able to tell her how I felt by writing her a letter. Thus I truly did believe that this letter was my only way to the beautiful brunette supervisor. I knew I took a major risk by giving her the letter. I knew this was not the normal way of doing things. However, I also knew I was not normal. So I took the risk because I felt she might understand.

I believed she was the woman of my dreams. I believed that this beautiful brunette supervisor was the one who might understand the weirdness of my anxiety. So I decided she was worth the risk. I really did believe all these things before I approached her. Thus, I decided there was no turning back. I had to give her the letter, and I was so proud I gave it to her.

This moment changed my life forever. This moment led me into another pit of darkness because it led to the loss of my new French Bistro. My new French Bistro was probably my best place to write because it was cold and it had so many beautiful angels working and eating there. There were so many beautiful angels working and eating there that I often spent entire days there writing. After the beautiful black-haired angel left my new French Bistro to work at Control, there were so many revolving angels of inspiration who took her place. There were actually too many for me to remember. However, I do remember some of these beautiful angels because I thought they might have been interested. I remember there was this beautiful blonde porcelain-like angel who was a cashier there at first. Then she cleaned the dining room before she left. There was this beautiful brunette angel who cleaned the dining room who I really thought was interested because she passed by me so much when I was writing. Plus, she stood at this spot where I could get a good look at her beauty. So it felt as if she was actually modeling for me when she was standing there. Sadly, I will never know if she was interested because I could never say anything to her. Then there was this beautiful black-haired supervisor with glasses who was at my new French Bistro for the same amount of time as the two beautiful supervisors. Finally, there was this beautiful black-haired Latin-like angel, who got there before I was never allowed back at my new French Bistro. This beautiful angel was so beautiful that she was dangerous. I knew she was young, yet she was so beautiful, and I really thought she was interested.

These were only some of the beautiful angels working at my new French Bistro. I believe I could spend an entire book writing about the beautiful angels working there. Sadly, I was never able to say anything to any of these beautiful angels unless it was to order food. I could never get past the pedestals I put these angels upon to talk to them. I kept hoping eventually they would be the ones to initiate a conversation with me if I kept going there. Sadly, this never happened. So I always felt anxious and depressed when I first went to my new French Bistro because I knew I was not going to say anything. I knew I was always going to be invisible to these beautiful women. I knew they were never going to say anything to me, and I was never going to say anything to them. Thus, I always arrived and left anxious and depressed.

This was how I spent my two years at my new French Bistro. This was how I left my new French Bistro. I will never know if I had a chance with any of these beautiful angels at my new French Bistro because I could never say anything to them. My new French Bistro was such an inspirational place to write because of all the angels working there. However, it was also inspirational because of the beautiful angels who ate and studied there. There were times when I was literally surrounded by beautiful angels when I went there to write. These were the moments when I knew why I was a writer. These were the moments when I loved being alive. I did not care about anything else when I was a part of these moments. I did not care what anyone thought about me during these moments because of all these angels. I did not care that I could not say anything to them because I only cared about seeing these angels. These moments were rare at my new French Bistro. Yet they were moments I will never forget.

I looked to the left, and there was a beautiful angel sitting there. I looked to the right, and there was a beautiful angel. Sometimes there were tables full of beautiful angels. So I had to simply pick the one that was the most beautiful to be my angel of inspiration. I looked at the cash registers, and there were all these beautiful angels working there. I looked at the counter where they prepared the food, and there were all these beautiful angels. Finally, as I looked across the room, I saw there were more beautiful angels. I was literally surrounded by beautiful angels at my new French Bistro during these moments. This is what I lost after approaching this beautiful brunette supervisor. I lost these magical moments that felt like moments from heaven.

How could I ever get over the loss of my new French Bistro? How will I ever get over losing a place that was so inspiring? I doubt that I will ever get over the loss of my new French Bistro because this was my favorite place to write. Actually, this is not true because I still believe that the library was my favorite place to write until the beautiful blonde library angel left.

The library was my main source of inspiration when I was first introduced to my new French Bistro because my beautiful blonde library angel was still working there. I knew the day was fast approaching when she was going to leave the library. However, that dreaded day was not here yet. So I was still going to the library to see her and the fiery redhead since I was still thinking she was going to be the one to carry the torch for her when she left. My original French Bistro was still my secondary source of inspiration because of the beautiful blonde supervisor. However, I knew nothing was ever going to happen with her because she had a boyfriend. As a matter of fact, their relationship was a part of the reason why she was my angel of inspiration. I always saw their relationship as a perfect relationship like Ken and Barbie's or Glen and Maggie's. Thus I never dreamed of ruining this perfect relationship because I might have lost her as my angel of inspiration if she was not with him anymore. So I knew it was time for me to start thinking about finding another location of inspiration to, hopefully, find the woman of my dreams.

My new French Bistro was going to be this new location of inspiration because of all these beautiful angels that worked there. I was thinking if I kept going to my new French Bistro, then something might happen with them. So I was still going to the library because of my beautiful blonde library angel. I was going to my original French Bistro for the beautiful blonde supervisor. I was also still going to the gas station for my brief conversations with the beautiful angel working there. Then I was going to my new French Bistro for my new angels of inspiration, and also to see my new angel of inspiration who gave me my glimpse into happiness.

# MY GLIMPSE INTO HAPPINESS

My glimpse into happiness was my introduction to what my life could be like if I actually found the woman of my dreams. I never allowed myself to go down this path of true happiness before because of my social anxiety. I knew I could not talk to beautiful women because my social anxiety made it impossible for me to have a conversation with these women. So I never allowed myself to go down this path of true happiness. I never allowed myself to imagine what it might be like to actually meet the woman of my dreams. I never allowed myself to imagine what it might be like to actually talk to a beautiful woman. I never allowed myself to imagine what it might be like to actually have a family and children with this woman. I never allowed myself to imagine what it might be like to actually be with the woman of my dreams. I had been writing about it since I started to write about my spiritual journey to finding the one. Yet I never dreamed I might actually find a beautiful woman who might actually be the initiator.

I always believed I was writing a fictional fairy tale about my spiritual journey to the woman of my dreams. I never dreamed there might actually be a beautiful woman out there with the social confidence to initiate a conversation with me at any of my locations of inspiration. Then when it actually started to happen, I could not believe it. I could not believe one of these beautiful angels was actually talking to me, and it felt as if she was comfortable doing so as well. Then what was even more shocking was that I was actually able to talk to her as well. I could have been defensive when she asked me why I was always at my new French Bistro. I could have been defensive because before she approached me, I saw her talking to another cashier. I saw her looking at me and laughing when she was with this other cashier. So after seeing her with this other cashier, I was feeling uncomfortable because of the weirdness of my anxiety. Therefore, her approach could have gone much worse because I could have been very defensive.

This beautiful brunette freckled angel at my new French Bistro was unlike any other angel I had ever met before. My spiritual journey to the woman of my dreams started five years ago with my beautiful blonde library angel. My beautiful blonde library angel is the most inspirational and most important angel to my spiritual journey. There will never be an angel like my beautiful blonde library angel because she gave birth to my spiritual journey. However, I was never able to socialize with her, and I never imagined myself having a real chance with her. Then there was the beautiful blonde supervisor who always had a boyfriend. Now there was the beautiful angel from the gas station who I was able to have these brief conversations with when I went to see her. Yet I always knew she had a boyfriend because she always mentioned him during our brief conversations. Then there were all the angels of inspiration at my new French Bistro who were very beautiful, yet I never said anything to them.

This beautiful brunette freckled angel was the only angel of inspiration who ever approached me at my locations of inspiration. I knew she was young. So maybe, I was wrong for thinking of her as being the woman of my dreams. However, I was unable to help myself since I had never met a beautiful angel like her before. I had never met a beautiful angel with the social confidence to initiate a conversation with me before. So I could not help how I felt about her. I could not stop myself from thinking about the possibilities of what might happen with her. She may not have been the most beautiful of all my angels of inspiration; however, I believe she was the closest I ever got to the actual woman of my dreams. Sadly, I was not sure how to socialize with her once she entered my life. I never knew how to react if I was lucky enough to have one of my angels say something. I obsessed over these angels for years, yet if they ever showed interest, I never knew how to respond. I either acted rude and aloof, causing them to believe I was uninterested, or I scared them by doing too much. Sadly, this is the story of my life.

My social anxiety is what keeps me single. My social anxiety is what keeps me from ever finding the woman of my dreams. My social anxiety is the reason why I am still writing my books about my spiritual journey to the woman of my dreams. My social anxiety is something that I have to live with for the rest of my life. It will never go away. I will never feel socially comfortable around people because I do not know how to be socially comfortable. I will also never feel comfortable around people because of my fear of humanity. My fear of humanity will always cause me discomfort when I am around people. I am feeling this social discomfort right now because this guy is standing by me at this coffee shop surrounded by so many people. I am really feeling uncomfortable right now because he is standing here talking to people. I am not quite sure why I am feeling so uncomfortable right now. It could be because of my history of being banned from my locations of inspiration, or it could be jealousy. I think I am feeling jealous of him because he is able to do something I will never be able to do, which is to socialize.

I will never be the center of the party. I will never be that guy who is able to initiate a conversation with someone. I do not care how bored I am when I am at work. I do not care how much I know that socializing is the only way to make a beautiful woman comfortable. I will never be that person to socialize with someone because I have never mastered small talk. I might be able to somehow find the courage to say hello to a beautiful woman, yet that is very rare. I might even be able to tell someone about my social anxiety and my love for beautiful women. I may even be able to have serious conversations with someone. However, small talk is a skill I never learned, and I may never learn because I am not able to be fake. I am not able to, or as my therapist says, I choose not to talk about things that I do not care about with people. I do not care about football or cars. I do not want to talk about the weather since I hate the heat and everyone hates the cold. I do not want to talk about politics since I fear getting into an argument.

This is the story of my life. I am a man without a voice because I do not know how to socialize with people. I do not know how to act like I care about something when I do not care. I am too true to myself at times. I do not know how to lie about what I think. I love beautiful women, and I will always love beautiful women. Sadly, nobody wants to hear about my love for beautiful women. Beautiful women do not want to hear me talk about other women. Men have been trained to hide their love for beautiful women, or at least this is what I believe. So I have to keep my love for beautiful women a secret since I have no one to tell about my love for them. Sadly, I never see this changing, which is why I am a writer. I am a writer because I feel this is the only place where I am able to express my love for beautiful women. This brings me to another reason why I was really jealous of this guy at the coffee shop who was talking to people.

I was jealous of him because I thought he was dating this beautiful blonde coffee shop angel. I knew I was most likely never going to say anything to this beautiful blonde coffee shop angel. I knew she probably had a boyfriend because she was so beautiful. Yet I did not want to see her boyfriend because if I did, I knew my fear of humanity was going to skyrocket. I knew that it was going to skyrocket because I was afraid he might be there for her protection. I was afraid he might be there because once again I was making one of my angels uncomfortable. I had only been going to this coffee shop for a few weeks. I never thought I was going to find another location of inspiration after my fall into another pit of darkness. Then this coffee shop near my work was slowly starting to turn into my new location of inspiration. It was turning into my location of inspiration since it was so cold and close to work. Also, I was starting to buy tea and food there, so they knew me as a paying customer there. Then there was the fact that they did not know me there. So I could go there without all the history of my other locations of inspiration. However, none of these reasons were the real reason why I always liked being there.

The beautiful blonde coffee shop angel was the real reason why I liked going there so much. This beautiful blonde coffee shop angel is slowly starting to turn into one of my angels of inspiration. However, she is not my only angel of inspiration. I also have been going to the library because of this beautiful brunette library angel that works there certain days of the week. Then there is this beautiful blonde coffee shop angel that works across town. Finally, there is still my beautiful blonde library angel. Although, I do not really get to see her right now since the bakery where she works is closed while I am writing. Yet she is still a vibrant source of inspiration because I still find myself writing about her more than any other angel of inspiration.

My beautiful blonde library angel will always be the most inspirational angel to my spiritual journey. The beautiful blonde supervisor will always be an angel of inspiration that I will never forget because she was so inspirational at my original French Bistro. The two beautiful supervisors at my new French Bistro will also be my angels of inspiration. All my angels of inspiration are unforgettable because they each inspired me so much at one time. However, the beautiful brunette freckled angel to approach me at my new French Bistro was very different from all these other angels of inspiration. She will always be one of my most memorable angels of inspiration since she was the one who gave me my glimpse into happiness.

Several weeks had passed since the beautiful black-haired angel left my new French Bistro to work at Control. I was still not ready to decide which of the two beautiful supervisors I found more inspiring. So I knew it was time for me to look for a new angel of inspiration because I was not ready to leave my new French Bistro. I was not sure who this new angel of inspiration was going to be because there were so many angels that worked there. Then I was paying closer attention to this beautiful brunette freckled angel that was working there. This beautiful brunette freckled angel was working at the cash registers and cleaning the dining room. She was everywhere, and I could not ignore her anymore. So I knew this beautiful brunette freckled angel was turning into my new angel of inspiration. Again, she may not have been the most beautiful angel; however, she had such a vibrant personality that this never really mattered. I even found myself forgetting about the two beautiful supervisors when she was around.

My search for a new angel at my new French Bistro led me to this beautiful brunette freckled angel. I started to think of her as my new angel of inspiration when I saw how down-to-earth she was when she was talking to customers there. I was starting to believe that I might actually be able to say something to her one day because I saw how she was with the customers.

I had only been observing her a few weeks before the unbelievable happened. I was feeling very uncomfortable sitting at my new French Bistro after I saw her at the registers. I was thinking they were saying something about the weirdness of my anxiety. So I was trying to absorb myself into my writing to get over the discomfort that I was feeling. I was trying to tell myself that I did not know what they were talking about when I saw them talking. They could have been talking about anything. I was not even sure if they even knew that I was there. Then as I was starting to get over the discomfort, the most unbelievable thing happened. She was there asking me why I was always at my new French Bistro. So again, I could have gotten all defensive when she asked me why I was always there. However, shockingly, I did not get defensive. Instead, I told her I was an aspiring writer and that I was always going to be there when I was not at work. Then we started to talk some more, and she told me that she wanted to be a teacher. So this led us to have our first conversation, and it went surprisingly well. Finally, she looked at her watch and told me that she had to get back to work. Then before getting back to work, she told me when she was working again. She told me that she was working Saturday morning again. Thus not only did we have our first conversation with each other, she felt comfortable enough with me after this to tell me when she was working again. This conversation was the first of many I was to have with this beautiful brunette freckled angel.

I saw her again at my new French Bistro that following Saturday. We said hi to each other twice that day. She even smiled at me when we said hi to each other those first two times. However, I could not bring myself to say anything to her those first two times because I felt awkward trying to say anything to her then. It was not until she was cleaning near where I was writing that I was finally able to say something to her. I was sitting at a booth hidden from everyone when she was there cleaning. At first, I was not sure if I was going to be able to say anything to her because I was so scared and anxious. Then I removed my headphones and said something about work. I am not sure what I said to her about work. I probably simply asked her sarcastically if she was having fun at work. Then after I asked her about work, she started telling me about her brothers and her sisters. She then said how much she hated ignorant people.

This statement right there drew me to her even more because I felt the exact same way about people. I have always hated closed-minded and ignorant people because they feel it has to be their way or the highway. We talked some more after this before she returned to work. Actually, I think she did most of the talking, and I was simply trying my best to focus on what she was saying. I was so nervous when she was talking that I was having a really difficult time listening to what she was saying. So I was simply trying to calm myself down enough to not make her uncomfortable. I actually found myself hoping she might return to work because I was so uncomfortable. It was not so much that I did not want to listen to her anymore because I loved listening to her. Yet my social anxiety was making me so uncomfortable that I wanted to find an out. This was all new territory to me, and I was scared. So finally, she went back to work, and I ordered some food to have my lunch. After our second interaction with each other, I was feeling really good about how things were going with her. Then when I was leaving, I passed by her and I asked her if she liked to read because I was going to give her my book. Then she said no, not really, which I chose to ignore since I wanted to give her my book. So

I then asked if she wanted a copy of my book. She said to go for it. Then I left, feeling this great pride.

She was not working Sunday, which I saw as a good thing. I saw this as a good thing because I saw this as a good time for me to spend the day at my original French Bistro. I could have gone to my new French Bistro for the two beautiful supervisors and the other angels. However, I felt more inspired to see the beautiful blonde supervisor at my original French Bistro.

The beautiful brunette freckled angel returned to work Monday. She was literally the first person I saw when I returned to my new French Bistro since she was at the cash registers. I remember her waving and smiling at me when I first arrived, and it felt wonderful to see her. Then I started my normal routine of looking for the best place to sit to see this beautiful brunette freckled angel. I found a place to sit where I could see her at the registers, and I started to write. Then after a few hours passed, she started to clean the dining room. She probably must have passed by me a few times before we had our third social interaction with each other. I am not too sure what we talked about when we had our third conversation with each other. I only know it must have gone well because it was not that awkward of a conversation. Then I remember she asked me if I had my book. It was a relief to hear her ask me about my book because after I asked if she wanted my book, I was afraid it was a mistake to offer her my book. Then I decided to tell her that I forgot it because I did not want to give it to her that day. I decided to lie to her about having my book because I wanted to wait to give it to her. I wanted to wait because I felt it was better to give it to her on Christmas Eve. Finally, she got back to cleaning, and I started to write for a few more hours. I spent the rest of my day at my new French Bistro because I did not want to leave. Then I eventually saw her leave, and I found that I was feeling much more relaxed since I had nothing to be anxious about when she was not there. Finally, I went home.

It was Christmas Eve. I walked into my new French Bistro where I saw the beautiful brunette freckled angel taking orders at the cash registers. I am not sure if she saw me when I arrived because she was busy talking to customers when I arrived. So I was not able to say anything to her when I first got to my new French Bistro. This was very discouraging because I knew this was the day when I had to give her my book. I knew this meant that I was going to have to say something to her once I tried to give her my book. Yet I was feeling really anxious about approaching her because she did not notice me when I arrived. Every other time we socialized with each other, I felt more comfortable because she initiated the conversation. At times, I was the one to initiate the actual conversation. However, I was comfortable with initiating these conversations with her since she initiated them when she said hi when I first arrived.

I had to find the courage to approach her since I felt I had to give her my book. I approached her two times before I finally gave her my book. The first time I approached her, it was simply to ask her when a good time might be to give her my book. She said she was through with work at two and I could give it to her then, which may have been best. However, I had to leave early because I had a therapy appointment that Christmas Eve. So I told her I was leaving before two. Then she said I could give it to her now since she could put it under the counter. So I went back to my seat to try to find the courage to make my second approach and actually give her my book. I did not spend too much time at my seat trying to find the courage, though, because I was afraid I might talk myself out of giving it to her. So I finally returned to the counter to give her my book. Then I went back to my seat, where I spent about another hour writing at my new French Bistro before I left. After leaving, I was ready to tell my therapist all about everything that happened with this beautiful brunette freckled angel. However, after leaving, I felt I had to return to greet her a Merry Christmas which I eventually did.

This was the last time I saw this beautiful brunette freckled angel before getting my glimpse into happiness. I went to therapy after I left my new French Bistro for the last time that Christmas Eve. I wanted to go to the library before I went to therapy because I wanted to print out everything I wote down about what happened with this beautiful brunette freckled angel. I wanted to tell him about everything that happened. I did not want to leave anything out because nothing like this ever happened to me before. I thought I had finally met the woman of my dreams, and I was so excited. However, I was not able to get to the library because I did not have the time to go there without being late for therapy. I felt it was much more important to not miss a minute of therapy than it was for me to go to therapy with all that I had written. So I finally got to therapy, and I told him about everything that had happened with this beautiful brunette freckled angel. Then after telling him about her, there was this uncomfortable, awkward silence. This silence was so horrible because I knew I had to keep talking to her if I hoped to build a relationship with her.

This is where the real fear arises for me when I have to talk to a beautiful woman. I might be able to somehow find the courage to say hello to a beautiful woman occasionally. I might even be able to have a conversation with her if I am really brave. However, the real anxiety derives from trying to have a conversation with her over and over again. I never dreamed I might be able to do this with one of my angels. I also never believed an angel might help me with this fear and initiate a conversation. Then I was approached by this beautiful brunette freckled angel. Sadly, nothing was to happen with her after my glimpse into happiness with her that Christmas Eve. Thus my spiritual journey with this beautiful brunette freckled angel all fell apart after I got my glimpse into happiness during this one magical Christmas Eve.

# One Magical
# Christmas Eve

One magical Christmas Eve was when I got my glimpse into happiness. I wished the beautiful brunette freckled angel a Merry Christmas. I told my therapist all about this beautiful brunette freckled angel who I started to think might be the woman of my dreams. I left my therapist looking forward to having the house to myself for Christmas Eve. It was so rare when I had the house to myself because my mom was almost always home when I was home. However, this Christmas Eve was one of those rare occasions when I was going to have the house to myself. She was going to my family's house for dinner, and I was not because I was able to find some excuse for not going there. I never liked going to my family's house for dinner because of my social anxiety. I did not care that you got free food for going there, or that we only went there one time every year. I never liked going there. I found it boring because I had no one there I was comfortable socializing with when I was there. There was my aunt who I occasionally enjoyed talking to when she was able to socialize. Sadly, she got old and could not think right anymore. So anytime I went to these family gatherings, I sat off to the side, where I reverted to my invisible man complex. This was how I spent most Christmas Eve, when I went to my family's house for dinner. So I dreaded going to my family gatherings because I found this worse than work because with work, at least I was getting paid to be uncomfortable. Luckily, I could find my way out of being at my family's house this one magical Christmas Eve.

I was looking forward to having the house to myself this one magical Christmas Eve. I knew my mother had already left for dinner. So I knew I was going to have the house to myself as soon as I got home. I was not sure what I was going to do when I got home because I rarely had the house to myself. Yet I knew I had to cook some quiche, and I wanted to take care of some laundry. Yet other than that, I was not sure how I was going to spend my time at home alone.

I was still thinking about this beautiful brunette freckled angel when I got home on Christmas Eve. I was still excited about giving her my book. I was also excited because when I tapped her on the shoulders to wish her a Merry Christmas, I found out her name. I always knew what her first name was because of her name tag. However, I never knew what her last name was until I saw her sweater before I left my new French Bistro to go to therapy. At first, I did not think too much about seeing the name on the back of her sweater. Then as the night progressed and I left therapy to go home, I realized that I now knew her first and last name. So I was thinking that this might be another angel who I might be able to find pictures of to remind me of her angelic beauty when I was not at my locations of inspiration. So I knew what my plans were for when I got home to have the house to myself now. I knew I wanted to spend time home alone cooking, doing laundry, looking for her pictures, and listening to music.

Christmas music was my favorite thing about Christmas Eve. There was so much Christmas music that I liked to listen to on Christmas Eve. So I rarely was able to find the time to listen to it all. However, there were two artists that I always found the time to listen to every Christmas Eve. The first was Trans-Siberian Orchestra because Christmas Eve never feels much like Christmas Eve until I start to listen to their music. Then the second artist that I always made time for every Christmas Eve was Pavarotti. I loved listening to Pavarotti because no one had a more beautiful voice than Pavarotti. There was the great Satchmo, Louis Armstrong. There was the smoky-voiced Rod Stewart. Then there were the artists who I always loved listening to yet never realized they also had these beautiful voices as well. Billy Joel and Elvis Presley were these two artists. However, none of these artists had a voice more beautiful than Pavarotti. Although, this was not the only reason I loved listening to Pavarotti every Christmas Eve.

Another reason I loved listening to Pavarotti was because of this French concert. This was one of my Christmas Eve traditions. Listening to this concert turned into a Christmas Eve tradition years ago after I bought my father a videotape of this concert. I bought it for him as a present for Christmas because I thought Pavarotti was his favorite artist.

Unfortunately, he never watched the video because he was never technically savvy enough with VCRs. Then I started to watch this videotape every Christmas Eve at midnight, and this slowly turned into the one Christmas Eve tradition that never disappeared. I had many Christmas Eve traditions I tried to continue. Then as I got older, I could not keep them going. However, watching this old video of Pavarotti singing at an old French cathedral was one tradition that was never lost because it reminded me of my father. This is the power of music.

Music is the most inspirational thing this universe has to offer. I love beautiful women. I love how I feel every time I see one of my beautiful angels because as much as I hate humanity, I also love their angelic beauty. I also love the cold because I feel so much energy when it is nice and cold. Rare is a time when I will complain about the cold; even if I am shivering and shaking from the cold, I still will not complain. Although, it might get difficult to write when I am shivering too much. However, the cold energizes me so much when I write that I am able to write about two or three pages within an hour sometimes when it is really cold. Then, when it is too warm, I will spend two or three hours trying to write one page. Finally, there are other times when I will try to look over a chapter and ruin it because it is too warm. So I literally need it to be cool or cold when I am writing. The sweet taste of Pepsi or unsweetened tea is another thing I love when I am writing. Yet as much as I love a good drink, seeing my beautiful angels, the cold, and my passion for writing, nothing is more inspiring than my music.

My passion for music is the one thing more powerful than my love for beautiful women. I could live without seeing a beautiful woman. I might not be that inspired if I am not able to see one of my angels. I might struggle to write well without one of my angels. However, the one thing I have learned from my spiritual journey is that eventually, I will be able to get over them not being there because of my passion for music. So my passion for music might be the one thing more powerful than my love for beautiful women. Actually, I am not sure how true that statement is even because my writing and the cold might also be more powerful. Thus I am not sure how to rank the five elements that create my world of isolation because every one of these elements helps me do some of my best writing. Sadly, my love for seeing beautiful women is the only one that might cause me pain because of my fear of humanity. Therefore, it is during these times of fear that I turn to my love for music for inspiration.

My passion for music is something that will never go away unless I lose my hearing. I will always love music because there is so much music out there to enjoy. My favorite music to listen to will always be French music because of the language and the music. New Age music might be my second favorite type of music to listen to because it is so enlightening and spiritual. Then Latin music is my third favorite type because it is so lively and romantic. Plus, much of what I listen to with Latin music reminds me of my wonderful French childhood. Then there is American music, which I love to listen to for certain artists such as Bon Jovi and Avril Lavigne. Unfortunately, I often find it difficult to enjoy American music because of my years of being bullied. Finally, there is Christmas music which is another type of music that I love. Sadly, I allow myself only two months a year to listen to it. Yet this does not mean that it is not one of my favorite types of music. I simply chose to keep it to these two months to never get tired of it. My favorite Christmas songs are "Christmas Cannon Rock" from Trans-Siberian Orchestra and "Christmas" from Blues Traveler. Although, these are not the only Christmas songs I enjoy listening to at Christmastime. I also love Vince Guaraldi, Elvis Presley, Luther Vandross, and Pavarotti. Yet there is no artist I love listening to more at Christmas than Trans-Siberian Orchestra. After all, Christmas is simply not Christmas to me without Trans-Siberian Orchestra.

I drove into the garage thinking about my beautiful brunette freckled angel. I thought about how this beautiful angel at my new French Bistro was unlike any angel I'd ever met before. I had never met an angel like this before. I'd never met an angel with the social confidence to approach me and start asking me about my life before. Then after a few more conversations with her, I could not stop thinking about her. I could not stop wondering if she might be the one.

I knew what I was looking for from the woman of my dreams. I knew she had to be beautiful. I knew she had to be compassionate enough to be able to understand the weirdness of my anxiety. I knew she had to be available because I never wanted to be the man to take someone away from another man. I knew how difficult it was to find the woman of my dreams. So I never wanted to be the cause of another man's misery. Finally, I knew the woman of my dreams had to be socially confident. Social confidence was the most important thing the woman of my dreams had to possess. I believe I could look past some of these other qualities in the woman of my dreams. However, social confidence is the one thing the woman of my dreams must possess because I will never be the initiator of a conversation with a beautiful woman. I do not care how much I like a beautiful woman. I will never be the one to approach her and this is something I have to accept about myself. After all, if I never could approach the beautiful blonde library angel, and she was the love of my life, how could I ever approach another angel? So I knew if the woman of my dreams existed, then she had to be the initiator. She simply needed social confidence to start a conversation with me because I could not be the initiator.

I knew I could never be the initiator with a beautiful woman because of my social anxiety. I knew how difficult it was to say a simple hello to one of my angels. So I knew that I was never going to be the initiator no matter how much I liked one of my beautiful angels. Unfortunately, I also knew how difficult it was to find a beautiful woman who could initiate a conversation with a man. I knew this was not the way of the world. I knew it was a man's responsibility to start a conversation with a beautiful woman to let her know you were interested.

I knew beautiful women did not have to socialize with men because of their angelic beauty. I knew all a beautiful woman had to do was simply exist to get a man's attention. I also knew there were men out there with the social confidence to socialize with beautiful women. I knew I could not compete with these men because my social anxiety was such a handicap. Therefore, I felt I had to simply accept the sad fact that the woman of my dreams might not exist.

I had to accept that I might never find love. I had to accept that there might not exist a beautiful angel with the social confidence to approach me to initiate a conversation. I knew that I was never going to change because the more beautiful the woman, the more I could not talk to my angels. This was my life's handicap, and I knew if I was not going to change for my beautiful blonde library angel, then I was never going to change. So I knew whoever the woman of my dreams may be, she had to be the initiator. However, I was really starting to doubt a beautiful woman like this existed. I had been going to my locations of inspiration for about three years now, and none of my angels ever said anything to me unless I went to order some food. So I was really starting to doubt the existence of a beautiful woman with the social confidence to be the initiator. Then one day, I was writing at my new French Bistro and it happened. One of my beautiful angels was standing right there asking me about my life. I could not believe it. One of my angels of inspiration was actually talking to me, and it was more than a simple hello. Sadly, I was so unprepared for the chain of events that followed with her that I was not sure how to react. Although, I did feel great about the chain of events before my glimpse into happiness and before going to therapy that Christmas Eve. Then I had that awkward silence during therapy, which was so uncomfortable because I knew it was a sign that my social anxiety was still my handicap.

I knew there was no escaping my social anxiety. I knew I could never be the most socially confident man when I was with a beautiful woman. I knew this was one of the main things keeping me from being with a beautiful woman. I knew there was no way for me to escape my social anxiety. After all, I literally spent two and a half years at the library obsessed over my beautiful blonde library angel. I sat there playing musical chairs because I wanted to see her angelic beauty. Yet never once, did I ever think about saying anything to her because to me, she might as well have been an A-List celebrity who was not real. I never dreamed of saying hello to her or asking her about her day. I never once imagined a path to her because she was unapproachable. It was not until she left the library that I started to imagine that maybe one day there might be a path to her. Although, I still never really believed I could be with her because I still could not socialize with beautiful women. I still knew that the beautiful woman had to be the initiator. Sadly, I knew how rare it was to find these beautiful angels because I had not met one since high school. My best friend was the only one I ever met since the beautiful blonde from high school who wrote me a letter. Yet neither of these angels were where I went to write.

The beautiful brunette freckled angel was the only angel at one of my locations of inspiration who ever approached me to initiate a conversation. I knew she was probably too young for me to be thinking of her as the woman of my dreams. However, I could not help myself from thinking about her that Christmas Eve when I got my glimpse into happiness. I remember driving into the garage that night after therapy and thinking, *What if?*

What if this beautiful brunette freckled angel was actually the woman of my dreams? What if all these conversations with her were the start of a great romance? What if these conversations led to us getting married one day and to us actually having children? What if I had actually found a beautiful angel who was actually interested? I could not believe how happy I was feeling that Christmas Eve. I never felt anything like this before. I never felt such hope before, and all I wanted to do when I got home was keep this hope alive as I started this one magical Christmas Eve.

This one magical Christmas Eve at home started with me driving into the garage and thinking I might actually have a future with this beautiful angel at my new French Bistro. I knew this was dangerous territory for me because of my social anxiety. I knew my social anxiety always stopped me from experiencing true happiness. However, I could not stop myself from imagining all these what-ifs that one magical Christmas Eve. I had never met an angel as socially confident as her before. So I did not care about the dangers of thinking about her that night because I was thinking maybe this was the start of something wonderful. Finally, I got home after therapy, and I got my glimpse into happiness during this one magical Christmas Eve.

I started to do some laundry before going upstairs to cook some quiche. I went to my computer to start listening to the Trans-Siberian Orchestra. I was not sure when my mom was going to get home that night because she was not at work. However, my best guess was that I was going to have the house to myself for a good four hours that night. So I was going to try to listen to as much Trans-Siberian Orchestra as possible while I had the house to myself. I was going to try to listen to their entire Christmas trilogy as I was home alone. I usually listened to only their songs at Christmas. Then Christmas Eve I tried to listen to the story that Ossie Davis narrates since it was too difficult to write and listen to the narrator. I found I was going back and forth between listening to their music, cooking, doing laundry, and writing. I was not sure if I really enjoyed having the house to myself that much because I was so busy. However, I was trying to make the most of this time since it was so rare when I was home alone.

I could not stop thinking about my glimpse into happiness during this one magical Christmas Eve. I could not stop thinking about this beautiful brunette freckled angel who started socializing with me at my new French Bistro. Then I remembered that I knew her first and last name. So I started to look to see if I could find some pictures of her to see her angelic beauty while I was thinking about her. She was not difficult for me to find at all once I typed her name into the computer. She was one of the first angels to appear once I entered her name into my computer. Then I was thinking about looking at her some more to see if it said anything about her relationship status. However, this was when I thought about stopping because I was thinking I might regret finding this out. Eventually, though,

I did look to see what it said, and happily, it said nothing. So I was able to imagine she was single. This led me more and more into thinking about my glimpse into happiness with her. Sadly, though, the more I started to think of my glimpse into happiness, the more reality was creeping its ugly claws into the happiness that I felt.

I had one magical Christmas Eve where I was able to think about my glimpse into happiness. I will probably never forget how happy I was when I was thinking about this possible future I might have with her. I was not thinking about my social anxiety that Christmas Eve because I did not want my dark reality to start creeping its claws into my happiness. So once my mother finally returned home, I went downstairs to write my father a letter. I started writing my father a letter every Christmas since his passing to feel connected to him again. I felt that this was a way for me to feel spiritually connected to him even if he was not alive anymore. I wrote all about what happened with this beautiful brunette freckled angel. Then after I wrote about her, I started to look at her pictures again. Sadly, this was when I started to feel the dark claws of reality creep its claws into my happiness again. I felt my dark reality creep back in as I remembered that awkward silence during therapy since I knew I now had to keep talking to her.

This glimpse into happiness was all I was going to have with this beautiful brunette freckled angel because nothing more happened with her after this one magical Christmas Eve. I continued to go to my new French Bistro to see her after this one magical Christmas Eve. Unfortunately, I was feeling really uncomfortable around her when she was working. We had a few more brief conversations when she was there. However, these brief conversations were quite rare. So I started to realize that she was never really interested; she was merely being friendly when she was talking to me at my new French Bistro. This was difficult to accept after my glimpse into happiness. Then what was even more difficult to accept was that I felt she might be uncomfortable with me being there, and was even trying to avoid me when I was there. I tried to keep telling myself that I was overdramatizing things. Although, I sadly do not think I was after everything that transpired there. Eventually, I had to stop going to my new French Bistro because I lost my car. Then I saw her a few more times before COVID hit. Then she disappeared during the Coronavirus, and I never saw my beautiful brunette freckled angel again.

All I have left of this beautiful brunette freckled angel are my memories of this glimpse into happiness that one magical Christmas Eve. Two years have passed since I had this glimpse into happiness. I thought I forgot all about my beautiful brunette freckled angel after so much time passed since last seeing her. However, I guess I will never forget my beautiful brunette freckled angel because she was the first angel to give me a glimpse into happiness. I still seriously doubt I will ever find another angel like her. Although, now I do believe that angels like her do exist. Sadly, she was now gone from my new French Bistro, and I needed to find a new angel to inspire me there after COVID. So I started to look to the two beautiful supervisors who were still working there. I was still not sure which one I preferred. However, I felt my angel of inspiration at my new French Bistro now had to be one of the two beautiful supervisors.

# The Two Beautiful Supervisors

The two beautiful supervisors at my new French Bistro were always the most inspirational angels at my new French Bistro. The beautiful redheaded supervisor was the first of these two supervisors to inspire me at my new French Bistro. I will never forget my introduction to my new French Bistro for two reasons. The first being all the beautiful angels I saw working and eating there. The loss of all these beautiful angels will always be the greatest loss after losing my new French Bistro. Never did a day go by when I was at my new French Bistro when there was not at least one beautiful angel working or studying there. Then the other reason why I will never forget my time at my new French Bistro is these two supervisors. I never could decide which of these two beautiful supervisors I liked better. I felt inspired by each one of them for different reasons. I was inspired by the beautiful redheaded supervisor because she was so quiet and reserved. This had me believing that she might be the one at the start of my spiritual journey there. Then as I started to spend more time at my new French Bistro, the beautiful brunette supervisor turned into my angel of inspiration. Thus, it is impossible to write about my new French Bistro without writing about these two beautiful supervisors.

The beautiful redheaded supervisor was my introduction to my new French Bistro. I walked into my new French Bistro for the first time, overwhelmed with all these beautiful angels. Everywhere I looked, there was a beautiful angel. They were either working at the counters, taking orders from customers, eating there, or they were studying. I could not believe all the beautiful angels at my new French Bistro, and it got really difficult for me to think clearly. Also, I had not yet developed a routine at my new French Bistro on my first day there. So I had no clue where the best place to sit was once I was first introduced to my new French Bistro. So I decided to sit at a booth with my back to everyone since I needed to recuperate from what I saw.

This beautiful redheaded supervisor sat right across from where I was sitting as I was trying to recuperate from seeing all these beautiful angels at my new French Bistro. I could not believe that this angel was sitting right across from me where I could see her angelic beauty. After she voluntarily decided to sit there, she instantly turned into my angel of inspiration at my new French Bistro. However, I was still too overwhelmed by all the other beautiful angels working and studying there to really think of her as my angel of inspiration. Plus, I could not ignore the beautiful brunette supervisor who was also working at my new French Bistro. However, I lacked the confidence to even think of her as being one of my angels of inspiration.

This beautiful brunette supervisor at my new French Bistro was so beautiful that I could not imagine myself ever having a real chance with her. I could not even look at her when I was first introduced to my new French Bistro because she was so beautiful. She had this beautiful black hair and these beautiful brown eyes. This all meshed well with her dark eyelashes. However, the most beautiful thing about her was her golden dark glowing tan. This beautiful brunette supervisor working at my new French Bistro may not have been the most beautiful angel I had ever seen. I still believe that mantle is held by the beautiful blonde library angel or the beautiful tanned Texas angel from Alaska. However, she was definitely one of the most beautiful angels I ever saw. Then there was what really made her so special. Her personality was what made her so special since she was so friendly and cheerful with everyone.

These two beautiful supervisors were my introduction to my new French Bistro. The beautiful redheaded supervisor started out as being my angel of inspiration. I could not believe she voluntarily sat right across from me at my new French Bistro. This was something else I loved about my angels at my new French Bistro. I loved that they sat where I could see them voluntarily. I loved how welcoming this made me feel because I knew it was their choice to sit there. Now she did not sit right across from me that first day. She was sitting at this booth across the aisle from me that day. However, she was sitting there facing me, which allowed me to get a good look at her angelic beauty. Then she stayed there for her entire break. I was so mesmerized by her beauty when she was sitting there. She looked so beautiful sitting there with her strawberry red hair and those beautiful blue eyes. She looked as beautiful as the brunette supervisor, yet her beauty was a more approachable beauty. Her beauty was more pale-skinned and freckled, which made her look more down to earth. So my chances with this beautiful redheaded supervisor felt more realistic. However, I still could never find the courage to say anything to her since she was too quiet and reserved for me to ever approach her.

My spiritual journey at my new French Bistro started with the beautiful redheaded supervisor being my angel of inspiration. I could not stop thinking she might be interested when she sat across from me during her break on my first day there. I knew I was lying to myself by telling myself this because she probably did not even notice me sitting there. However, I could not help myself. I was so attracted to her that I started to imagine the impossible with her after she sat there. Then as more time passed, I started to sit where I could see her as my angel of inspiration. Yet I spent more time sitting where I could see the beautiful brunette supervisor because I did not want to make the beautiful redheaded supervisor uncomfortable. I still felt the beautiful brunette supervisor was way out of my league. So it did not bother me too much if I made her uncomfortable. Then as I spent more time at my new French Bistro, I was drawn more and more to this beautiful brunette supervisor because of her social confidence. So eventually, I was finding it difficult to decide which beautiful supervisor was more inspirational.

My path toward seeing the beautiful brunette supervisor as my angel of inspiration was much slower than my path to seeing the redheaded supervisor as my angel of inspiration. I had a much more difficult time believing she was the one because of her social confidence. Then the more I spent time there, the more this was changing as I was drawn to her social confidence. I could not believe how cheerful and friendly she was all the time. There were literally times when she went around talking to the customers. I was never one of these customers she said something to when she went around talking to the customers. However, I could not stop myself from thinking that one day she might start talking to me if I continued to go there. Then I started to believe I saw a path to her being the woman of my dreams as I spent more time there.

My path toward seeing her as the woman of my dreams started with the loss of my beautiful brunette freckled angel. I was always attracted to the beautiful brunette supervisor. How could I not be attracted to this beautiful tall skinny tanned angel that looked like a cheerleader? Later, I also learned that she was a gymnast because she was wearing a sweater that said she loved gymnastics. So maybe she was not a cheerleader. However, to me, a cheerleader and a gymnast are close to the same thing. I also learned that she was a vegetarian from my time of observing her and being obsessed with her, which told me she really cared about her health. Finally, I knew what car she drove. I was learning all these things about her from my time at my new French Bistro. I knew the weirdness of my anxiety was always bordering upon stalkerish behavior. I knew it was not normal to learn so much about a beautiful woman without ever saying anything to them. However, this was who I was, and I never saw it changing because my social anxiety was my life's handicap. So I was learning all these things about her, which made me feel closer to her. Yet I knew I could never do anything with any of this information because of my fear of humanity and my social anxiety. I believed that I was never going to approach her because I could not talk to her. Then one day I decided to write her a letter to tell her how I felt about her. Sadly, this was a costly mistake because it was what led me to lose my new French Bistro. Thus my spiritual journey at my new French Bistro started with the beautiful redheaded supervisor. Then my spiritual journey at my new French Bistro was over when I finally found the courage to approach my beautiful brunette supervisor. My spiritual journey at my new French Bistro was over the moment I lost the woman of my dreams at my new French Bistro.

It was not right away that I thought the beautiful brunette supervisor was the woman of my dreams. It was not until I started to see all these signs leading me to her as being the one that I started to believe that she might be the woman of my dreams. At first, I was trying to ignore these signs because I knew she was out of my league. Then the more I saw these signs leading me to her as being the one, the more difficult it was for me to ignore them. Finally, I made a decision to risk it all by giving her the letter. Again, I have no regrets about approaching her with this letter since I really did believe that she was the one. My only real regret about approaching her with this letter is it led to the loss of my new French Bistro after I gave it to her.

I lost my new French Bistro because I gave her this letter to let her know I thought she was the woman of my dreams. I knew I was moving too fast with her. I knew I was taking a risk by giving her this letter. However, I felt I needed to give her this letter because of all the signs I had been feeling, which had me believing that she was the woman of my dreams. The first sign was when I saw her walking toward me at the fireplace. I saw her walking toward me at the fireplace right after the beautiful brunette freckled angel left as my angel of inspiration. So I was looking for a new angel of inspiration after she left. I knew the beautiful redheaded supervisor was still around. I still thought of her as one of my angels of inspiration. I even thought she might be interested when she sat at a booth right in front of me to study. However, she never said anything to me the entire time I was at my new French Bistro. So I never imagined having a chance with her since I knew the woman of my dreams had to be the initiator. Sadly, I never saw her being the initiator because she was so quiet and reserved. I knew that I could never be the initiator because of my social anxiety. So I was never able to imagine a path to her being the woman of my dreams because I felt we both had a degree of social anxiety. Granted, I felt mine was much worse than hers because she could socialize with people at work.

I could not imagine a path to the beautiful redheaded supervisor ever being the mysterious woman of my dreams. I still thought she was beautiful. I still saw her as my angel of inspiration. However, I could not imagine a path to her anymore because we both had a certain degree of social anxiety. So once I felt the doors close with the beautiful redheaded supervisor, I started to imagine a path to the other supervisor. At first, I never dreamed of being with this beautiful brunette supervisor because of her social confidence. Then as more time passed, it was this same social confidence that drew me to her and had me believing that she might be the woman of my dreams. I knew I could never be the initiator with a beautiful woman. I knew I could spend years at one of my locations of inspiration obsessed over my angels of inspiration without ever saying a word to them. I knew this was something that was probably never going to change after the beautiful blonde library angel. So I knew if the mysterious woman of my dreams existed, she had to be the initiator. Sadly, I doubted their existence until the beautiful brunette freckled angel approached me at my new French Bistro. Then she disappeared, and I started to think this beautiful brunette supervisor might be the one.

Sign after sign had me believing this beautiful brunette supervisor was actually the woman of my dreams. I knew she was out of my league. However, I also believed the idea that opposites attract. I thought if there was ever an angel with the ability to break through all my walls of anxiety, then this beautiful brunette supervisor was the one to do so. Then as I was starting to feel more confident, I started to pay more attention to all these signs. I started to listen more closely to what I felt the universe was telling me about my path to finding the one. I believed it was telling me the beautiful brunette supervisor was the one. Yet I also knew I could not say anything to her because of my social anxiety. Then I decided I had to start listening to the signs more with this angel. I chose to listen to the signs more and to follow them.

The first sign that had me thinking the beautiful brunette supervisor might be the woman of my dreams was going to be a very subtle sign. It was when I saw her walking toward me when I was sitting by the fireplace. I thought she was actually going to say something to me when I saw her approaching. However, I was wearing my headphones. So I will never know if she wanted to say something. Yet this was the first sign that had me thinking she might be the one because this happened right after I lost the beautiful brunette freckled angel. After this, I looked across the fireplace and saw she was sitting across the fireplace as I was writing about my loss. Once I saw her there, this only increased the spiritual energy I was feeling from her. She eventually went back to work and left my new French Bistro. I was thinking this was it of my time with her that day until I saw her return as if she forgot her keys. After she walked back into my new French Bistro, I was thinking she might have slipped out the back or something. So I figured this was it of my time with her at my new French Bistro again. So I returned to writing about the loss of the beautiful brunette freckled angel since I thought she was gone. A few minutes passed, and I decided to go wash my hands to see if she was still around. Then I walked to the other side of the fireplace and saw she was sitting there once again. However, when I saw her sitting across from me this time, I saw she was sitting there also writing. This was such a magical thing to see because I felt we were kindred spirits at that moment. I now knew she also liked writing. Finally, I even found myself starting to imagine that she was writing me a letter to let me know she was interested since it was her only way to let me know.

This was the first sign that had me thinking that she might be the woman of my dreams. I tried telling myself that these were all mere coincidences. I tried telling myself that she was not interested. Eventually, I even started to believe it until I felt another sign that she might be interested and be the woman of my dreams. I am not sure if this second sign was real. So I guess I will let you decide one way or the other. I moved to sit where I could get a better look at this beautiful brunette supervisor when she waved and smiled at me from across the room. Now once again, I was not sure if she was waving at me. So I did not wave back at her.

Maybe I should have waved back at her. Maybe I was being rude by not waving back at her. However, I did not want to risk the embarrassment of looking like a fool by waving if I was wrong. So instead, I sat there and I tried to ignore her as best I could. Yet I could not completely ignore her because she was also the only reason I wanted to move there anyways.

The third sign that she was the woman of my dreams was this real dream I had of her, where she was the manager thanking us for our work at this new French Bistro. I was not sure what this dream was about really. Yet I knew this was not something real with her because it was all a dream. Thus I simply brushed this dream off as nothing more than me thinking of her.

The fourth sign that she might be the one was when she dyed her hair blonde. I was thinking maybe she dyed her hair blonde because she somehow found out about my book. So she wanted me to know that she was interested by dyeing her hair blonde. I was thinking she understood I could not say anything to her. So this was her way of letting me know she was also interested. Sadly, this never led to anything because I could not talk to her. Then she started being really obvious with the signs as she started to smile at me and wave when she left. There was even this one time when she left and started to chase around this receipt. Finally, she stopped chasing it, then smiled at me as she left. I felt as if I was watching this old home movie.

There were these two times when I saw her shopping at Control. The first time was as she was shopping there with her sister. Then the second time was when she was there by herself and waiting for her coffee. The second time she was there, she stopped to talk with the beautiful black haired angel who was now working at Control after she left my new French Bistro. So I was thinking maybe they might be talking about me when they were talking. However, I seriously doubt it. I am sure they were simply talking about what was new since they last saw each other. These were the only times I saw her outside of my new French Bistro. So these signs were quite memorable. These were the signs that reminded me that my spiritual journey with her could continue outside of my new French Bistro. Then I returned to feeling these signs at my new French Bistro when I turned the corner and almost ran into her after getting my food. This time she was not working when I saw her. So she was actually wearing shorts and I got a better look at her beauty. Then when I got back to my seat to do some more writing, she was sitting across the room from me writing in her journal again. So once again, I felt a connection to her. Sadly, I could not talk to her. So I wrote a two-page letter about how I felt.

Some of these signs were much more obvious than others. I was never sure which signs were real because I still could not believe she might be interested. So I kept telling myself these were all mere coincidences because I could never approach her to say anything anyways. However, some of these signs were more clear than others. One of these more obvious signs was when I went to order a French baguette from her and she gave it to me for half the price. I felt this was a clear sign she might be interested. However, I managed to somehow convince myself it meant nothing and that she was simply being friendly. So I thanked her for the discount, and I went back to my seat to try and shrug it off as her simply being a good manager. Then there was this other time when she went to eat at this Mexican restaurant when I started working there.

This beautiful brunette supervisor was eating at this Mexican restaurant with this other guy. I assumed it was a date, which was very discouraging when I first saw her there. Then she did not say anything to me when I took her order. So I thought she did not even know who I was, which was even more discouraging. After this, she was at this Mexican restaurant for the rest of my shift, which was depressing and inspiring. Then I started to think maybe she was there because she knew I was working there. However, I could not talk to her, so this was another missed opportunity with her. So I went to my new French Bistro feeling depressed when I saw that she was starting her shift there, which was great. Yet I was still feeling depressed because I was not able to say anything to her. After this, she started to say hi and asked me about my day. I was able to say hi back, and eventually, I was even able to say hi before she said hello. Once, I even found the courage to ask if she needed help moving a table.

There was one more not-so-obvious sign which had me believing she might be the one before seeing this sign which I could not ignore. The not-so-obvious sign was when she sat with the beautiful red-headed supervisor across the room from me during their break together. They were both laughing and looking at me, which was very encouraging. However, I did not have a clue how to react to this. So I chose to simply try to absorb myself more in my world of isolation because I knew I could not say anything to them. Finally, we get to the sign that changed everything. I call this the ultimate sign and the turning point when I felt I could not ignore the signs anymore because this sign was too obvious.

The ultimate sign was when she literally spun around to smile and wave at me before she left for the day. After this, I could not ignore these signs anymore because I thought she was interested. However, I still did not know how to respond if she was interested. Then I started to find the courage to say hi to her more and more, which led me to start to imagine there may be this path to the beautiful brunette golden angel.

# The Beautiful Brunette Golden Angel

The beautiful brunette golden angel was the beautiful brunette supervisor that was working at my new French Bistro. She turned into the beautiful brunette golden angel during this uninspiring Monday at my new French Bistro. I got to my new French Bistro early that Monday because I was hoping to finally write my second book. I had been struggling to write my second book for about a year now. My first book was never a struggle to write because I always knew it was going to be about my beautiful blonde library angel. I always knew my inspiration for my first book was my beautiful blonde library angel. There was never a doubt because I had never met a beautiful angel like her before. Then she left the library, and my inspiration left with her. I knew I still had my pictures of her to remind me of her angelic beauty. I knew I could still feel her spiritual energy with my passion for writing as I wrote about my spiritual journey to the woman of my dreams. However, after she left the library, I lost the one constant in my life. I lost my go-to angel. She was literally my guiding light out of my pit of darkness, and now she was gone. I knew I was not going to find an angel like her again. Unfortunately, I knew that my time of being inspired by her at the library was now over forever.

My beautiful blonde library angel was gone. I believed I had lost my beautiful blonde library angel forever. I never dreamed she might return to my life after she left the library for the last time. Then my spiritual journey kept bringing me back to her after she left, which only increased my belief that she was the love of my life. Sadly, once she left the library, I was never going to see her in the library again. So my spiritual journey with her at the library was still over. This meant I had to start my search for a new angel of inspiration at my new locations of inspiration. I first thought the fiery redhead at the library was going to be my new angel of inspiration until she left right after her. So I thought it might be the beautiful blonde supervisor until I lost her when I was banned from my original French Bistro. After losing the beautiful blonde supervisor at my new French Bistro, I knew it was time for me to choose between these two beautiful supervisors. I knew that it was now time to select a new angel of inspiration who might carry the torch for my beautiful blonde library angel.

My beautiful blonde library angel was the most inspirational angel of my life. The angelic beauty of this beautiful blonde library angel will never be matched. The inspiration I felt from my beautiful blonde library angel is also something that will never be matched. I felt so inspired by my beautiful blonde library angel because she outlasted all my other library angels. She was at the library for two and a half years. She was at the library for my rebirth as a writer and until I completed my first book and I had it published. Then what added to her power as my angel of inspiration was how she left because I had two weeks to prepare for her loss. This time that I had to prepare for her loss gave me a chance to say goodbye to her. I will never forget how I felt that Tuesday when she unexpectedly appeared to me so I could say goodbye to her. Then I had that Friday to say hello to her as my spiritual angel of inspiration. I thought my spiritual journey with my beautiful blonde library angel was over after she left the library. I never dreamed that I might actually find my way back to her after she stopped working at the library.

I learned my spiritual journey with her was not over when I found out she was the manager at this nearby bakery. I started to feel hope again after I saw that she had not left town. Then when I saw her at Control nearly a year after she left the library, I felt more hopeful because this was not something I could have planned. All the stars had to align perfectly when I saw her at Control because she was there shopping and not as an employee. Then when I saw her at Control again two years after she left the library, I felt even more hopeful. I was now really starting to believe my spiritual journey with her might not be over since she kept returning.

My beautiful blonde library angel is the love of my life. I did not realize this until recently. I know we never said anything to each other. I know I may never see her again. Yet this does not change how I feel about her because I never met anyone like her before. I also doubt I will ever meet anyone like her again. After she left the library, I never dreamed I might find an angel as inspirational as her again. The beautiful blonde supervisor at my original French Bistro was the closest angel to match her spiritual energy. She was the one constant beautiful angel to outlast most other angels of inspiration. Then I lost her when I was banned from my original French Bistro. So I turned to the two beautiful supervisors at my new French Bistro. However, it was not until the beautiful brunette golden angel disappeared that I felt she was my new angel of inspiration. I always knew I was attracted to her, yet I was also attracted to the beautiful redheaded supervisor. Then the beautiful brunette supervisor mysteriously vanished.

The beautiful redheaded supervisor was still there. I tried to see her as my angel of inspiration. Yet I knew something was missing when the beautiful brunette supervisor left for two months. Finally, she reappeared, and I felt alive again. I could not believe how my inspiration returned right after I saw her again. So I knew she was my new angel of inspiration.

My beautiful brunette golden angel was back. I was so excited to see her at my new French Bistro that Saturday. I will never forget that moment when I saw her at my new French Bistro because two great things happened that day. The first thing to happen was that the beautiful blonde from high school accepted my friend request. I sent her a friend request months ago without ever expecting her to accept it. Then for some mysterious reason, she accepted it that Saturday. Thus I was thinking maybe, it might lead to something with her. Then when I walked into my new French Bistro, I saw the return of the beautiful brunette golden angel. I could not believe how great things were going for me because of these two angels of inspiration.

My beautiful brunette golden angel reappeared as unexpectedly as she disappeared. I never thought this beautiful brunette supervisor was going to leave my new French Bistro. She was so dedicated to her work that I knew she liked her work at my new French Bistro. Then several weeks passed, and she was nowhere to be seen. So I thought this was it. I thought she had quit, and I was never going to see her again. I knew my angels of inspiration might one day be gone from my new French Bistro. I knew my angels of inspiration were not going to work there forever. I knew there was a fairly decent turnover rate at my new French Bistro because many of my beautiful angels worked there for only a few weeks before they disappeared. Plus, this work at my new French Bistro was never lazy work. So I knew this was not the greatest place to work, yet it was also not the worst place to work. After all, there were also so many beautiful angels that never left my new French Bistro. However, I never dreamed that one day these two beautiful supervisors might leave my new French Bistro. Then several weeks had passed without me seeing this beautiful brunette supervisor, and I feared she was gone forever.

I will never be able to express how excited I was to see that this beautiful brunette supervisor was back. I knew this beautiful brunette supervisor was still way out of my league. I knew nothing had changed since I still could not say anything to her due to my social anxiety. However, she was back, and there was hope again with her. So I started to find the courage to say hello to her when she passed me occasionally. I was even able to say her name when I said hello to her at times. For me, this took a great deal of courage because it was a way for me to tell her that I knew who she was and that I was interested without taking much risk. Then I overheard her talking to a customer at my new French Bistro. I found out she was leaving again when I overheard her. I was devastated to hear that she was leaving again. Yet I was not that devastated because I thought there was a good chance that she might return after she left. Then one day I walked into my new French Bistro to overhear her talking to an employee there. I overheard her say when she was leaving and when she was returning. After I heard this, I was thinking that this might be the right time for me to take a break from my new French Bistro. About five years had passed since I first saw my beautiful blonde library angel at the library. I had never taken a break from any of my locations of inspiration during these five years. Not even when COVID hit did I take a break from my locations of inspiration. I was still going to my French Bistros to get some tea. However, I felt this was the perfect opportunity to take a break from my new French Bistro since I heard when she was going to be leaving and returning.

I took a three-month break from my new French Bistro. The loss of this beautiful brunette supervisor from my new French Bistro was not my only reason for taking this break. I was also taking this break to work at Bon Gout to finally get the money to buy a car. I was finally back to working at Bon Gout because the manager was not there anymore. This new manager was so much better because she was nicer and much more laid back. She had no problem hiring me back once I applied. I loved my work at Bon Gout. I loved it because my perfect work for writing was now even more perfect. I was now able to work seven days if I wanted to because we were helpers at the store during COVID. We were not giving out food samples because of COVID. Yet the store was willing to pay us to help around the store. Therefore, this break from my new French Bistro was a great opportunity for me to make money.

This break from my new French Bistro was also a great opportunity to finally clean around the house. I never liked cleaning the house because it took time away from my writing. Yet I also felt guilty about not cleaning the house because it was getting so out of control. I started putting off cleaning the house ever since I started my spiritual journey as a writer. However, I knew it was not right because it was not fair to have my mother do all the cleaning. I saw this three-month break from my new French Bistro as a good thing. I saw it as an opportunity to focus upon some of my other responsibilities outside of my world of isolation. Also, I saw this as an opportunity to be a better man for the woman of my dreams. Unfortunately, I was not expecting this break to turn into me never returning after she returned.

Three months passed since I last went to my new French Bistro as my location of inspiration. I spent some of this time at the library to see if I could start to feel some of its magic after my beautiful blonde library angel left the library. Sadly, I was unable to feel that same magic I felt when she was working there. However, I was able to feel some of its magic return my first day back when I learned that she posted a new picture the same day I returned. I was once again reminded of the power of my beautiful blonde library angel that day. I was once again reminded of who started me upon my path to the woman of my dreams. This is not to say I was not missing the beautiful brunette supervisor while she was gone. As a matter of fact, there were these moments when I missed her so much that I felt my heart ache. However, I knew she was not my beautiful blonde library angel because I could live without her. It was not until I returned to my new French Bistro and felt her spiritual energy that I realized what I was missing.

I returned to my new French Bistro hoping my beautiful angels were going to ask me about where I had been. I was hoping that this was going to be one of those times when absence made the heart grow fonder. However, nothing like this ever happened after my absence. I returned to things returning to normal. One of the angels there did ask me where I had been, and I told her I was working because I needed a car. This was all anyone ever really said about my absence. So I was really disappointed when I learned that no one cared that I was gone. Yet I guess I never really expected much from these angels since I never said anything to them. Finally, the beautiful brunette supervisor started to say hello to me again, and I felt things were starting to get back to normal. I was only going to return to my new French Bistro for about a month before I fell into another pit of darkness after I was going to lose my new French Bistro forever.

I was so excited to return to my new French Bistro after this three-month absence. My hope was that my time away might lead to something with this beautiful brunette supervisor. I was hoping that once she returned, she was going to find out I was also gone. I believed that some of the other angels there might have noticed I was also gone and told her. Then she might approach me and ask me where I had been. So I was hoping this break from my new French Bistro might lead to our first conversation other than us simply saying hello. Sadly, this never happened. Instead, I was finding it difficult to find any social confidence to say anything to her. Instead, I felt this time away had taken away any courage I had found with her before she left. So I was losing faith, and I felt I had to do something to let her know how I felt about her. Unfortunately, this was going to be when things were going to start to take a turn for the worse.

I still kept going to my new French Bistro to see this beautiful brunette supervisor because I was still thinking of her as this beautiful brunette golden angel. I still remembered how inspirational she was that uninspiring Monday when I was trying to write my book. I remember sitting at my new French Bistro surrounded by all these uninspiring people. It was so warm and uncomfortable that day that I was unable to do any writing. I was there for about two hours trying to write one page with no luck because I was so uncomfortable. Yet I kept trying because I was hoping to see the beautiful brunette supervisor now that I knew she was back. Then I saw her walk into the restaurant, and it literally felt like a phoenix rising from the fire. I could not believe how everything changed once I saw her. After I saw her walk into my new French Bistro, I started writing my second book, and I knew she was my new angel of inspiration.

I believed this beautiful brunette golden angel was going to be the inspiration for my second book. I remember how I felt when I first saw my beautiful blonde library angel. I still remember how this moment changed my life forever. It led to my rebirth as a writer, and it started me on my spiritual journey to finding the woman of my dreams. Then when she left the library, I lost my angel of inspiration. Thus started my search for a new angel of inspiration to inspire my second book. However, this search for a new angel of inspiration was going to be much more difficult than I expected because I could not find an angel as inspirational as her. The beautiful blonde supervisor at my original French Bistro was the closest thing I found to her because I spent about two years with her as my angel of inspiration. Then I lost her when I was banned from my original French Bistro. I also knew I never had a chance with her because of her boyfriend. Again, they looked so happy together that I never wanted to mess with that because it gave me something to aspire to have someday if I ever met the woman of my dreams.

It was not until I saw this beautiful brunette supervisor at my new French Bistro that I thought I found my new angel of inspiration. All the angels of inspiration who carried the torch for my beautiful blonde library angel were beautiful after she left. Some may have been more beautiful than others; however, they were all beautiful enough to be my inspiration. So what was it about this beautiful brunette supervisor that set her apart from all my other angels? One thing that set her apart was her timing because she outlasted so many other angels. Now she did go away for a few months during my spiritual journey at my new French Bistro. However, every time she returned, this only increased my belief that she might the one. Every time my spiritual journey brought my angels back into my life, I gained new hope with them. I gained new hope with them because I felt the universe was telling me my journey with them was not over. Therefore, timing was going to play a major role in making her my new angel of inspiration.

My beautiful brunette golden angel was very beautiful. Her glowing tan was probably my favorite feature of her. Her timing was also something that made her special. Then there was her dedication to her work, which elevated her above my other angels of inspiration. However, none of these things were what really made her my angel of inspiration. Her social confidence was what really turned her into my angel of inspiration. Not since my beautiful brunette freckled angel had I met an angel as socially confident as her. This social confidence drew me to her because I thought she might break through my walls of social anxiety.

I was so mesmerized by her social confidence that I thought this might be my way of starting my spiritual journey toward her. I am not sure how I got the idea to approach her and try to compliment her. However, I was either sitting at home or at my new French Bistro, and I started to think about telling her how impressed I was by her social confidence. So when I got home, I created a twenty-slide PowerPoint presentation of this compliment. My thinking was that I was going to read this out loud to myself every night until I said it to her. I still did not believe that I was ever going to find the courage to say it to her. However, I felt I had to give it a shot because I felt my chance with her was slipping away if I did not try something.

"Hello, I have to tell you how impressed I am by your energy and your social confidence."

This was the statement I read to myself every night until I found the courage to approach her. I never dreamed that this might lead me to actually approaching her. However, it did when one day I saw her sitting near me eating lunch by herself. I sat there for a good twenty minutes shaking from the anxiety I was feeling because I knew what to say if I could only approach her. I honestly still never really planned to approach her. Then without thinking, I started walking toward her, and I was standing in front of her and I had to compliment her. I could not stop shaking as I was standing there complimenting her. I could not run away fast enough after my compliment. However, I was so proud because I did compliment her. The date when I complimented her will be etched within my brain forever. It was Tuesday, May 18th, 2021.

"Hello, I have to tell you how impressed I am by your cheerful energy and your social confidence."

I finally found the courage to say something to one of my angels of inspiration.

This compliment could have been the start of my path to my beautiful brunette golden angel. It could have been the start of something wonderful if I had stopped there. After all, after complimenting her, she actually said more than she ever said to me before as I was leaving. I honestly do not remember what it was that she said to me as I was leaving. However, I believe it was something like, "You are leaving already?" and "Have a good night!" I wish I had stopped with this compliment. I wish I had seen where things might have led with her after I was able to give her this compliment. Sadly, I did not stop there because I felt it was time to make my grand gesture after this compliment. I felt I had to give her a letter to let her know how I felt about her.

I felt I had to give her this letter because I really did believe my beautiful brunette supervisor was interested. I really did believe that the only thing stopping me from being with my beautiful brunette golden angel was my social anxiety. I thought that she was interested because the day after this compliment, she sat at a booth right in front of me with her friend. She could have sat anywhere else. Yet she decided to sit right in front of me, and she was facing me as well. She must have sat there for a good thirty minutes. I was so anxious when she was sitting there because I thought I needed to say something to her. Yet I could not say a word since I was too scared to say anything to her. I got home that night feeling defeated because I could not approach her. Then when I got home that night, I got the idea to give her the letter since I felt this was my only chance of ever being with her because of my social anxiety. Sadly, this decision was going to be a costly mistake since it led me to my fall into another pit of darkness.

# My Fall Into Another Pit Of Darkness

My fall into another pit of darkness is something I fear I might never recover from because it led me to having an even greater fear of humanity than I ever imagined possible. I always had a fear of humanity. The only time I was not afraid of humanity was during my wonderful French childhood because my social anxiety did not exist back then. I will forever remember these years as being the best years of my life. Even if one day I am able to meet the woman of my dreams, I still believe these years will be the best years of my life. Sadly, I had to say goodbye to my wonderful French childhood once I moved to America. I believe this move was the turning point of my life because it led to the birth of my social anxiety. My social anxiety was born out of my years of being bullied during elementary and middle school. I was bullied for my name, my accent, my sensitivity, and my social anxiety. I could not believe how cruel this world could be after I moved to America. Yet it was, and this cruelty eventually led to my fear of humanity, and to creating the world of my invisible man complex.

My invisible man complex was something that I created during middle school when someone turned around to hit me for no apparent reason. I will probably never know what his reason was for turning around to hit me that day. I do not remember much of this kid from middle school, to be honest. However, I will never forget his actions that day because his actions were what led me to creating my invisible man complex. I remember sitting there waiting for class to start when from out of nowhere, this kid hit me for no apparent reason. I remember how invisible I felt when this happened because no one even cared. There was no laughter. There was no teasing after I was hit. It was as if I did not even exist. I never felt as invisible as I did that day. After I was hit, I felt so invisible that I did everything I could to remain invisible. I was playing word games as I was counting down the minutes until the bell rang. I could not wait to escape the pain I felt from realizing how invisible I was to the world. Then I felt this fear arise within me since I knew to leave class, I had to leave the world of my invisible man complex.

I was able to find the courage to leave class that day. I was somehow able to leave the world of safety where I created my invisible man complex that day. However, I could never find my escape from the pain I felt from realizing I was invisible to humanity. I spent the rest of middle school hoping that the more invisible I was, the less chance I had of being bullied. I tried to see how much time could pass without me saying a word. Hours turned into days. Days turned into weeks. Weeks turned into months. Semesters turned into years. Eventually, my invisible man complex turned into more than a game. It turned into my way of being. I literally felt invisible to the world. It has now been thirty years since this traumatic event, and I still feel invisible to the world. After this traumatic event, I was bullied three more times during middle school. I was literally chased down and attacked at my house by a bully. I was tormented by this one bully who I thought was one of my friends until I stopped letting him borrow things. However, the worst of these was when a rumor was spread through middle school that I was gay.

My invisible man complex was my only way to escape the discomfort I felt around humanity. I treasured my time alone. However, I could not always be alone because I had to work and go to school. So I needed an escape from humanity when I had to work and go to school. At first, I was not able to find this escape from my invisible man complex because the discomfort I felt around all these people was too much to take. So I was skipping school and I was leaving work because I could not deal with humanity. However, I knew avoidance was not the answer because I wanted to find love and I needed to find a way to make money. I was able to somehow stop skipping school enough to graduate high school. As I think back to my motivation for graduating high school, I believe the angels I saw there were my only inspiration.

I lost my way after graduating high school. I could not keep working because of my debilitating social anxiety. Money was never enough motivation for me to keep working because I always had my parents to go to if I needed a place to live. So I kept leaving work because I could not deal with the discomfort of my social anxiety. Eventually, I stopped trying to find work. I tried to find other ways of making money that did not involve socializing. I tried going to community college because my parents were willing to pay for it at the start. Then when they could not afford it anymore, I stopped going since I lacked the passion. I tried the Marines after college. However, this was not the right path because I was surrounded by bullies.

I spent a few years trying to move away from my parents after the military. I tried moving into a few places with my best friend. I even tried to move to Tallahassee, which I loved because I was right near Florida State and all these beautiful angels. I started to make the transition from Florida to Ohio after this because my parents moved to Ohio. Then I felt I had to make one more attempt at moving away. So I moved back to Florida, and I really did try to make this work because my best friend was great support socially and financially. Sadly, I still could not work, and I could not take the guilt of not helping him out. So I moved back home, realizing I was going to live with my parents for the rest of my life unless I met someone. Also, I knew living with my parents was better than being alone. I never did have the greatest relationship with my parents. Yet they were all that I could rely upon until they were also gone.

I lost all hope of ever moving away from my parents. This loss of hope led to me spending a year at home watching television. My parents were disappointed with me because I was not paying them rent during this year of watching television. So we started getting into arguments every night because they did not understand my social anxiety. I had no social support because I lost all my friends once I moved back to Ohio. So television turned into my only escape from this dark reality that was my life. Then I lost this as my escape, and I lost my way again. I had no money to move out. My social anxiety kept me from working. I lost all my social support. I had no hope for the future. So I started to look for some help, and I found my way to therapy at Portage Path. Eventually, therapy led me back to college since work was not working for me because of my social anxiety. So I thought psychology might be the answer because I knew so much about social anxiety from my own life. I also thought that by studying psychology, I might find a way to get over this social anxiety that continued to ruin my life. Unfortunately, once I moved to Alaska to start graduate school, I realized I could not be a counselor because of my social anxiety. Thus I returned to Ohio, and I lost my way once again.

I tried working at a few more places once I got over the depression of having to leave Alaska. I tried to find my way back to Alaska. However, I could not keep working because of my social anxiety. So eventually, I thought truck driving might be the answer since I saw it as an escape from humanity. Then my migraines returned, and I had to let go of my dream of being a truck driver. After I lost my chance to be a truck driver, I fell into my first pit of darkness. I spent two years of my life pursuing my dream of being a truck driver. I could not imagine a life without truck driving. Yet what I was really dreading was the idea of having to socialize with humanity again.

I fell into my first pit of darkness because I knew I had to find the courage to start socializing with people again. I hated the idea of having to do extroverted work again because I hated the idea of having to socialize with people at work because of my social anxiety. However, I also knew I needed money. So I knew I had to work again. I knew there was no way around this if I ever hoped to build a better future for myself. I did not know how I was going to find the courage to return to work, I only knew that I had to find a way. Then I remembered seeing a beautiful blonde librarian at the library, and my spiritual journey was born.

My beautiful blonde library angel was all the inspiration I needed when I started my spiritual journey with her at the library. She was such a perfect angel that she inspired me to write my first book, which was all about my time with her at the library. There were other beautiful angels of inspiration that I had when she was not working. However, none of these angels ever matched the inspiration of my beautiful blonde library angel. Then she left the library, and I had to find a way to continue my spiritual journey without her. So I started searching for other angels of inspiration to carry the torch for her after she left the library. I was really thinking that the fiery redhead was going to be the one to carry the torch for her. However, when she left the library right after her, I knew I had to find a new angel of inspiration.

My search started with the beautiful blonde supervisor working at my original French Bistro. This beautiful blonde supervisor continued to be my source of inspiration at my original French Bistro until I was banned. Also, there was the beautiful Mexican angel working at the nearby gas station, who I was actually socializing with some. Then my spiritual journey briefly led me to this beautiful black-haired angel at the call center. This beautiful black-haired angel was my angel of inspiration at work because she looked so much like the angel who introduced me to my original French Bistro. I rarely got to see this beautiful black-haired angel with glasses at work. However, she still remained my angel of inspiration because she was so beautiful and because of who she looked like. There were all the angels of inspiration working at my new French Bistro. There was the redheaded supervisor who introduced me to my new French Bistro. There was the Asian angel and the black-haired angel who cleaned the dining room. There was the redheaded cashier who looked so much like the fiery redhead from the library that I thought it might be her. All these beautiful angels were beautiful enough to carry the torch for my beautiful blonde library angel. I found each one of these angels inspirational enough to start to carry the torch for her. However, none of these beautiful angels ever matched the inspirational power of my beautiful blonde library angel.

It was not until my search led me to the beautiful brunette freckled angel that I found an angel to match her inspirational power. I also found that this beautiful brunette golden angel was able to match her inspirational power. These two beautiful angels of inspiration were the first angels of inspiration who ever had me thinking I had found the woman of my dreams. Sadly, neither of these angels turned out to be the one. The beautiful brunette freckled angel left during COVID, and I never saw her again after she quit working there. Yet she will never be forgotten because she was the first angel of inspiration to get me to believe that happiness might be possible. Finally, we get to the beautiful brunette golden angel who had me believing I had found the one.

The beautiful brunette golden angel was the first angel of inspiration I ever believed might replace my beautiful blonde library angel as the woman of my dreams. I never met an angel with the social confidence of my beautiful brunette golden angel. She was always socializing with people at work. She was always friendly with people at work. So I truly did believe that if there was a woman with the social confidence to get through my walls, it was her. Then there was the fact that I did not see her wearing a ring at work. So I started to believe that I might have a chance with her because she was available. There was also the fact that she was a part of my spiritual journey for close to two years. This beautiful brunette golden angel was a part of my spiritual journey for almost as much time as my beautiful blonde library angel. However, none of these reasons were the real reason why I thought she was the one. The real reason why I believed that she might be the one was that I felt there were all of these signs leading me to her.

I thought she was the one. My spiritual journey had me believing I finally found the woman of my dreams. So I felt it was time for me to take a risk. I felt I had to approach her to give her the letter to let her know how I felt. I was only going to introduce myself to her. However, as I started to write this letter to tell her how I felt, I felt such strong emotions for her that I felt I had to tell her everything. I felt I had to tell her that I thought she was the one because I was afraid I might never have another chance with her. So I started to write her this two-page letter where I poured out my soul to her. Then I got her this Tigger toy and a card. Finally, all that was left for me to do was to find the courage to give it to her at work on Friday before they closed. I knew she was working that Friday because she always worked Friday nights. So I waited for the right time to give it to her, and I left feeling so proud of myself for finding the courage to give it to her. I was thinking this might be the start of my path to the woman of my dreams. Instead, this grand gesture led me to my fall into another pit of darkness.

My fall into another pit of darkness took about a week because I was still hoping that something might happen with her after I gave her the letter. I was still thinking positively about my grand gesture when I went back to my new French Bistro. My first day back to my new French Bistro after making this grand gesture was that following Sunday. I made only one brief appearance at my new French Bistro that Saturday because I was working all day that day. So Sunday was my official day back to see what her reaction might be after I gave her the letter. However, I saw her drive away as soon as I got there that Sunday even though I knew that she saw me because she drove by me right as I was getting out of my car. I was feeling really anxious about going there that Sunday because I did not know what might happen. I was afraid she might want to start a conversation with me after I gave her the letter, and I was not sure if I was ready to socialize with her. Then I saw her driving away, and I was depressed, yet relieved since I knew I was not going to have to try and socialize with her. Then while eating my food by the window, I saw her drive by where I was normally sitting. Thus I thought she might have returned to thank me for the letter. However, this never did happen since she never stopped as she drove by me that Sunday. So after I was done eating, I started to get back to my writing because I needed an outlet for how I was feeling. I was there for only an hour Sunday because I knew she was not working. They were then closed Monday for Memorial Day.

Tuesday was my first day back at my new French Bistro when this beautiful brunette golden angel was working. I was really feeling anxious when I saw that she was working. She was walking around the dining room peeling off the COVID tags from tables. So she was right there when I first arrived. However, she did not look at me when I arrived. I felt as if she was ignoring me at first. Then she smiled and waved at me, and I felt a sigh of relief. I also felt more anxious because I felt I needed to try to say something after making this grand gesture. However, nothing had changed after making this grand gesture because I still had social anxiety. So instead, I went back to my normal routine of playing musical chairs. I moved to where I could get a better look at her, and this was when I got the first sign that she was uncomfortable. I never expected to make her uncomfortable after I gave her the letter. I saw only two possible reactions from her after I gave her the letter. I thought she might be flattered and it might be what got her to approach me, or she might ignore me because she was never interested. However, I never expected her to be scared and uncomfortable after I gave this letter of interest.

I was feeling very uncomfortable after I moved to get a better look at her. I knew something was different when I made this move. I saw her holding her stomach as she was walking around. So at first, I thought she might be pregnant, which made me feel really uncomfortable because I knew there was no hope with her if this was the case. I also saw her walking around as if she was nervous, which was unusual for her. Finally, I moved back to where I was originally sitting, which was going to be where I was going to stay until closing time.

It was about a half hour before they closed when I started to feel uncomfortable again sitting at my new French Bistro. I started feeling uncomfortable my last half hour there because of this lady who was sitting by me by the fireplace. This lady was not writing or eating. She was simply sitting there doing nothing. At first, I thought nothing of this because I thought she might be waiting for someone or something. Then as I was leaving, she was standing at the counter watching me as I leave. So this was the first time I started to really feel I made this beautiful brunette golden angel uncomfortable. However, I returned that following day since I was still trying to tell myself I was imagining things. Then Wednesday, I thought things were going well until I saw someone hold the door for her and watch her walk to the car. I was so uncomfortable and depressed after seeing this that I did not know how I was ever going to leave.

It took me about two hours to finally leave. I had to do some serious writing before I found the courage to leave after realizing how uncomfortable she was with me being there. This was the moment when I realized she was uncomfortable with me being there. So maybe it might have been best if I never returned after I knew she was uncomfortable with me being there. However, I did not want to leave my new French Bistro because it was still my favorite place to write. So I returned to my new French Bistro Thursday to see that she was not working, which was great because it allowed me to see that I could be inspired by other angels there. Then I returned Friday when she was working, and I felt she was comfortable at work when I was there.

I went into Saturday feeling really good about my last two days of writing at my new French Bistro. I was even feeling hopeful about my chances with the beautiful brunette golden angel. I started to think I might even have a chance with her again someday if I went back to being patient with her. I was done pursuing her. I knew I could never approach her again because I had no moves left to make with her. I knew now that the only way anything was ever going to happen with her was if she was the initiator. So I was feeling really excited about spending time at my new French Bistro after this realization since now I only went there to write.

I did not return to my new French Bistro until Sunday because I had to work all day Saturday. I was ready to start writing my second book from scratch that Sunday. I still believed my beautiful brunette golden angel was the inspiration for my second book. However, I felt I needed to write my story from scratch because I felt my story with her had now changed. So I went to my new French Bistro that Sunday, ready to write my second book from scratch. I found a place to sit at my new French Bistro, where I could see my beautiful brunette golden angel from a distance. I did not want to make her uncomfortable by sitting too close to her. I also was able to see some of the other angels working there. I was only planning to be there for about an hour that Sunday because I had to work at eleven. I was feeling great that hour because I got the first page of my second book written. Then the dark moment that led me into another pit of darkness arrived when I was bullied out of my new French Bistro by these individuals I had never seen before.

I tried telling myself I was imagining things when I first saw these individuals sitting around me as I was writing. I thought about moving. However, I knew I was only going to be there for another five minutes anyways. So there was no point in moving for five minutes. Then one by one I saw more people sitting around me until I could not take it anymore and I had to leave. So finally, I took my headphones off, and the bullying commenced. I was told I was making the beautiful brunette golden angel really uncomfortable by being there. I was also told they read my book and they thought I was a stalker preying upon underaged women. I did try to defend myself. However, there was no point since they were not listening. After this, I never returned to my new French Bistro because I could never feel safe there again. Thus, started my fall into another pit of darkness since this all led to the loss of my new French Bistro.

# The Loss Of My New French Bistro

The loss of my new French Bistro was devastating. I could not believe I could never return to my new French Bistro because I told a beautiful woman how I felt about her. I could not believe how bad I felt all because I told a beautiful woman how I felt about her. I was so proud of myself for finding the courage to give her this letter that Friday night. I was filled with so much hope after I gave her this letter since I thought it was the first step to us being together. I truly did believe with all my heart that once I gave her this letter, she was going to approach me to thank me for letting her know how I felt. Then this might lead us to start socializing more and more as I continued to go there for my writing. Finally, one day she might be comfortable enough to sit down with me during one of her breaks. Then she might start to get to know me better as we talked more. I knew I could never be the initiator with a beautiful woman. So I knew my only chance with her was to write her a letter. My hope was that once I gave her this letter, she might make the first move. Then this might lead her to being the woman of my dreams or to her introducing me to one of her friends as being the woman of my dreams. However, I never thought that giving her a letter might lead to the loss of my new French Bistro.

I lost my new French Bistro because no one at my new French Bistro was willing to understand the weirdness of my anxiety. This was the second time that I was going to lose one of my locations of inspiration because no one was willing to understand my social anxiety. I could not believe how devastated I was to lose my original French Bistro. I could not believe I was told I could never return because of the weirdness of my anxiety. However,

I was, and I could not do a thing to change what had happened. All I could do was wait and hope that this banishment did not mean that I was banned from all my French Bistros. I had to see if this banishment also meant that I was banished from the inspiration I felt at my new French Bistro.

It took so much courage for me to walk into my new French Bistro after I was banned from my original French Bistro. I sat at my spot by the window. Then I went to order myself a drink because I wanted to see if I was still allowed to order things from this establishment. I ordered my drink without a hitch. Then I walked around wondering if anyone might tell me that I had to leave. Luckily, this never happened, and I spent the rest of the day there without anyone saying a word to me about being banned from my original French Bistro. It was such a thrilling relief to learn that I was not banned from my new French Bistro. Once I learned that I was not banned from my new French Bistro, I got over the devastating loss of my original French Bistro.

I loved my time at my original French Bistro when it was my location of inspiration. I still drive by my original French Bistro since I have such fond memories of my time there. Yet I also have painful memories of how I was treated before I was banned from this French Bistro. However, when I think back to my time at my original French Bistro, I mostly remember all the fond memories I have from this place. I mostly remember how inspirational the beautiful black-haired angel with glasses was when she welcomed me into my original French Bistro. Then I also remember how inspirational the beautiful blonde supervisor was to my spiritual journey. These are the memories I cling to when I am writing about my time at my original French Bistro.

The loss of my new French Bistro was much more difficult to get over than the loss of my original French Bistro because I was not ready to leave my new French Bistro. I knew it was time to leave my original French Bistro when I was banned since I was so uncomfortable there. However, I kept going there because I knew the beautiful blonde supervisor was still working there. Sadly, I rarely got to see her because she was working when I was working at Bon Gout. Thus the only time I was able to see her really was when I went there during my breaks. Another reason why I still enjoyed going there was for the random angels that went there to eat and study. Although, I also knew it was time to say goodbye to my original French Bistro because of how uncomfortable all the employees there were making me feel. Plus, it was very warm there, which made it difficult for me to write there. So I was not really too devastated about losing my original French Bistro when it happened; it was more with how it had happened.

The greatest loss from losing my original French Bistro was definitely the loss of the beautiful blonde supervisor. I knew I was never going to be with this beautiful blonde supervisor, which was probably what made her such a perfect angel. I never tried to approach her since I knew I never had a chance with her. So I never really felt socially anxious around her because I never tried to socialize with her. Thus all this beautiful blonde supervisor was to me was this angel of inspiration that I placed upon a pedestal to be my inspiration. Then I lost my original French Bistro, and I knew I was never going to see her again. I still drive by the parking lot occasionally, hoping to see her as she takes an order out to a customer. I know this is stalkerish behavior. Yet I also know this is the only chance I ever have of seeing her again other than seeing the pictures I have of her, which remind me of how beautiful she was at this French Bistro.

My spiritual journey at my original French Bistro was over. I was never allowed to return to my original French Bistro. I hated knowing that I was never allowed back there when I had so many fond memories of being there. Also, it was so close to my work. So I could not stop seeing my original French Bistro as I kept driving by it everyday to go to work. Yet like it or not, I was never allowed back at my original French Bistro. So my new French Bistro was now going to be my only source of inspiration until I took a break from it and got banned. I knew I could always go back to the library if I needed another location of inspiration. Sadly, I also knew my beautiful blonde library angel was not there. So I knew the library had lost its magic. Thus my new French Bistro turned into a powerful location of inspiration after the loss of my original French Bistro. The wells never ran dry at my new French Bistro. There was always an angel of inspiration working there for me to see as my inspiration. Then there were all the beautiful angels who went there to eat and study who were my inspiration. So I never lacked inspiration when I went to my new French Bistro. Thus, I never had to go to the library.

I never imagined there being a day when I could not go to my new French Bistro anymore. I always felt so welcome at my new French Bistro until I gave the beautiful brunette golden angel the letter to let her know how I felt. I never felt uncomfortable at my new French Bistro until my last week there. This was part of the reason why I found the courage and confidence to give her the letter. This beautiful brunette golden angel was so friendly and socially confident that I never dreamed I might be hurt by her. Her social confidence and friendliness were what had me believing that she might be the one. Even now, after everything that happened, I still find it impossible to believe that she was why this all happened. I still believe that she might have been the one if I took a different approach with her. I still believe I might have had a chance with her if I had been more patient with her. After all, things started going really well after I complimented her. Then I felt I grew impatient with my spiritual journey, and I tried to rush things with her, and this was when things took a turn for the worse.

I could not believe I lost my new French Bistro. I could not believe how I felt after leaving my new French Bistro. I thought my years of being bullied were over after middle school. I thought I had found an escape from my invisible man complex. Then I was surrounded by all these bullies at my new French Bistro, and I lost my world of safety. After leaving my new French Bistro, I was not sure how I was going to move forward. I knew I had to go to work that day because I needed the money. So I drove to work, and work was the best remedy for what had happened because it helped me to see that there were other angels out there.

I got to work at eleven. I had no clue how I was going to get through work after this traumatic event that happened at my new French Bistro. I only knew I had to work because I still needed money. Once I got to work, I could not escape my fear of humanity because everywhere I looked, all I saw were bullies. Also, I was afraid that these individuals from my new French Bistro knew where I worked. I had no clue what these individuals might be capable of doing after they surrounded me at my new French Bistro. I also was not sure what they looked like because I was too traumatized to get a look at them at my new French Bistro. So once I got to work, I got my cart ready and got out to the floor as soon as possible. I did not want to say anything to anyone because I was so scared. All I wanted to do after I got to work was get out to the floor so that I could get into the world of my invisible man complex. Eventually, this was exactly what I was able to do as I stood there like a statue for seven hours.

I did not want to go to work. I did not want to deal with my fear of humanity. Unfortunately, I knew I could not go home if I was not working because of my fear of humanity. I was afraid of going home after this traumatizing event because I felt that if I went home, then I might never leave my home again. I was so traumatized by this event that I could not think of a single place where I could go to feel safe again. So the only place I wanted to be after this traumatizing event was work. That's right, work was the only place I wanted to be after I lost my new French Bistro. I wanted to be at work because even after all this happened, I was still hoping to someday find my way to the woman of my dreams. I also still wanted to see some beautiful angels because seeing them was my only escape from this darkness. So after losing my new French Bistro, work was the only place I could go where I could see my angels. Thus, Bon Gout was the only place I wanted to be after I lost my new French Bistro. Unfortunately, I also knew I was going to be surrounded by bullies at work. So I was not going to feel safe at work because I was going to feel threatened every time I looked at an angel. However, I needed to look at angels since seeing my beautiful angels was my reason for living.

I was seriously contemplating suicide after the loss of my new French Bistro. These bullies at my new French Bistro had me believing it was wrong to look at beautiful women. Yet looking at beautiful women was the only reason I wanted to live. So I was in a really dark place after I was surrounded by these bullies at my new French Bistro. I fell into another pit of darkness after this, and it was all because of my love for seeing my beautiful angels. I felt as if these bullies were telling me it was wrong to look at beautiful women. Yet I could not stop looking at beautiful women. I could never stop looking at beautiful women because they were my reason for living. They were the reason why I was a writer. So I felt so wrong for being who I was after I was bullied out of my new French Bistro that I wanted to die. I could not imagine a world where I could not see beautiful women. So I fell into another pit of darkness.

I feared I might never find my way out of my fall into another pit of darkness. I simply could not imagine a world without my new French Bistro. There were so many beautiful angels working and eating at my new French Bistro that I could not imagine never going there again. However, what was worse than losing my new French Bistro was how it happened. These bullies had me so scared of being who I was that I was thinking about not writing anymore. This woman who was the ringleader of these bullies was telling me what I was writing was wrong. She told me she read my book and that she also had social anxiety. However, she was not going around looking at women at work making them uncomfortable. Again, I tried to defend myself and explain that this was never my intention. I knew

I was not a stalker. I knew I was never going to do them any harm. Yet I also knew how inspirational my angels were to me as a writer. Sadly, I lost the angels of inspiration at my new French Bistro after my fall into another pit of darkness. I could not imagine a world without ever being able to see the angels of inspiration from my new French Bistro again. They were such a powerful source of inspiration.

I knew I had already lost the angels of inspiration from my new French Bistro before I was ever even bullied out of my new French Bistro. I knew the beautiful brunette freckled angel disappeared during COVID. I knew the beautiful black-haired angel was working at Control. I knew the beautiful Asian angel was gone. I knew the redheaded cashier who looked like the fiery redhead from the library was gone. I knew that the beautiful redheaded supervisor was gone. I knew that the only angel of inspiration I had left at my new French Bistro was the beautiful brunette golden angel, and she was not interested. So maybe it was a good thing that I lost my new French Bistro as my new location of inspiration. Yet I was still saddened by its loss because its loss also meant I was losing all the random angels who went there to eat and study. There were so many random angels who visited my new French Bistro, and these are the angels who I will miss the most. Sadly, this is a loss that I will need to somehow get over because I do not feel safe or comfortable going back to my new French Bistro.

I was not banned from my new French Bistro. I was bullied out of my new French Bistro. So I know that I am technically allowed to go back to my new French Bistro. However, this is merely a technicality. I do not feel safe or comfortable going back to my new French Bistro now that I know that I am not welcome there anymore. I loved how comfortable these angels made me feel when I was going there before the bullying incident. I could never socialize with these angels, though, which was most likely why they were so uncomfortable. However, I remember there being so many times when they sat facing me as they were taking their breaks. These beautiful angels could have sat anywhere else when they were taking their breaks. However, when they sat facing me at my new French Bistro, it was so inspiring because I started to think that they were actually interested. Unfortunately, I could not say anything to these angels if they were interested. So all I could do was feel their inspiring energy as they sat there.

My beautiful blonde library angel will always be my favorite angel of inspiration. I doubt I will ever find another angel of inspiration as inspirational as her. She was so beautiful with that sweet, angelic face. I will never forget her cute button nose, or those bright white teeth when she smiled and giggled. I could spend book after book writing about how beautiful and inspirational she was without ever getting bored. However, my new French Bistro will always be my favorite location of inspiration because it had so many beautiful angels. It was also nice and cold there when the beautiful brunette golden angel was working. So this only added to her appeal. However, the angels who worked at and visited my new French Bistro were really what made this location of inspiration my favorite location of inspiration. I could not believe how many beautiful angels were working at my new French Bistro. Then there were all these random angels who ate and studied there as well. The well never ran dry of angels of inspiration at my new French Bistro. Sadly, most of these angels of inspiration who visited my new French Bistro made one appearance, then I never saw them again. So I never really remembered these angels after spending the day with them. However, I do remember this one.

This beautiful emerald-eyed angel was a visiting angel that I will never forget. I knew nothing about this angel when I first saw her other than her beauty. She had the most beautiful green eyes that looked like emeralds. She was a brunette with this great figure and a nice tan. After I saw her arrive, I could not stop thinking about her. So I had to move to get a better look. It took me several minutes to move because I did not want to scare her off by moving. Luckily, she remained where she was after I found the courage to move. She was at my new French Bistro for about four hours, and before she left, I somehow found the courage to approach her. I could not sit still anymore because she was too beautiful to not approach her. When this beautiful angel first arrived, I never dreamed of approaching her because she was so beautiful.

I could not believe I was actually approaching this beautiful emerald-eyed angel. I usually could never find the courage to approach a beautiful woman. Yet I was actually going to try and approach this angel that looked like a supermodel. Then what was even more shocking was that I was actually thinking clearly enough to repeat the dialogue I was rehearsing.

I told her I was a writer. I told her that beautiful women were my inspiration. Then I proceeded to tell her that she was one of the most beautiful angels I have ever seen. I even told her she could take a look with her computer to see this was not some line to get women. Then she looked to see that it was real, and I gave her my phone number. I saw her put my number into her phone. Finally, I introduced myself, and she also told me her name. This emerald-eyed angel even told me that this was good timing because she recently got out of a serious relationship. I left after this because I did not want to ruin what I thought was a great first encounter. However, a few minutes later, I did return to tell her I could give her a copy if I saw her again. She then joked with me about carrying around copies of my book to give to random women. I assured her that this was not the case. I am not sure if I was joking or defensive when I responded. However, it did not really matter since she then said she was sure at some point she might return.

This was my first encounter with this beautiful emerald-eyed angel. I never once imagined having another encounter with her after this first encounter. I thought this might be it. Yet I was hoping this was not it because I could not stop thinking about her. Then that following Wednesday, I had a very different and creative day at my new French Bistro. I got sent home early from work that day. So I was going to my new French Bistro to write. Unfortunately, I realized I did not have a computer. Yet I still wanted to go to my new French Bistro to see what angels were working there that day. Then before I got there, I decided to write her a poem. I spent two hours writing this poem about this beautiful emerald-eyed angel.

I never expected to see her again. I was hoping to see her again. However, I never expected to see her again. Yet I was ready if she returned. I had a book and the letter ready to give her if she returned that following Saturday, and then I saw her return. She reappeared around ten that following Saturday, and I approached her as soon as she reappeared. I did not waste any time because I did not want to chicken out. So I approached her as soon she arrived. I started walking toward her. I said hello and gave her my book. Then I also gave her my notepad and told her this was something that I wrote when I was inspired by our first encounter. I also wrote down my phone number. Then she told me that she still had my phone number. She also told me she looked at my book and thought it was very good. This was my second encounter with her, and I thought it went well until I knew she had my number and never called.

I saw this beautiful brunette emerald-eyed angel two more times at my new French Bistro. I felt more heartbroken each time I saw her at my new French Bistro because she ignored me every time she was there. So I knew nothing was ever going to happen with her because it was obvious she was not interested. Eventually, I got past this heartbreak and returned to thinking the beautiful brunette golden angel might be the one. However, I do still think about what might have been with this beautiful brunette emerald-eyed angel. I so thought I had a chance with her because she was joking with me and she also told me she was actually available.

These are the memories I have of my time at my new French Bistro. These are the memories I want to think about when I think of my time at my new French Bistro. So I will treasure my time at my new French Bistro even after my fall into another pit of darkness. Unfortunately, I do not have many fond memories of my time at the coffee shop of inspiration.

# The Coffee Shop
# Of Inspiration

The coffee shop of inspiration was slowly starting to turn into my new location of inspiration. This coffee shop of inspiration was located right across the street from where my beautiful blonde library angel was working. I always knew of this coffee shop's existence. However, I never went there before because I had other locations of inspiration to go to for inspiration. Then I lost my new French Bistro as my location of inspiration, and I knew it was time for me to start looking for a new location of inspiration. However, before I could find a new location of inspiration, I had to find the courage to keep writing. Luckily, this happened very quickly since I knew how important it was for me to keep writing. Now I was not sure if I was going to be able to publish my books once I wrote them. However, I knew I had to keep writing. I could not live life any other way then as a writer. I knew how my passion for writing inspired me and filled me with confidence. So I knew I had to keep writing because it was my only path to salvation. I was never going to find my salvation through work or sports. I was never going to be the best-looking person since I hated to exercise and I loved food and soda too much. I was never going to be the most outgoing person because of my social anxiety. So I knew of only one path to success, and this one and only path was my passion for writing. Thus I had to keep writing.

I had to keep writing to escape my fall into another pit of darkness. I was afraid I was never going to be able to escape my fall into another pit of darkness since I had lost my inspiration. My new French Bistro had been such a powerful source of inspiration for well over two years now, and it was gone. So I was not sure how I was going to find my way back to the path of my spiritual journey to the one now that it was gone. However, I knew I had to find a way because I was not ready to stop my search for the one. I knew the path to finding the one was looking quite gloomy and dark, yet I was still feeling some hope that she existed. Why was I still feeling hopeful that she existed after losing all my angels of inspiration from my new French Bistro. Well, it was really quite simple. I still felt hopeful because of my beautiful blonde library angel.

My beautiful blonde library angel was the only angel of inspiration I had left after the loss of my new French Bistro. I knew she was not at the library anymore. However, I knew she was still around because I knew she was now working at this bakery near the library. So my search for a new angel of inspiration led me back to my original angel of inspiration. I knew when all hope was lost I could always go back to my beautiful blonde library angel. I knew I could always go back to her because I was never hurt by her because I never approached her. I was so grateful to have never approached her after my fall into another pit of darkness. My inability to approach her and knowing she never left was why I was able to go back to my angel. So once again, my beautiful blonde library angel was going to be the angel of inspiration for my second book. However, I was going to see her as a different source of inspiration for my second book because I could not see her that much for my second book. I started out writing my second book, hoping to see her everyday. Then I lost this coffee shop as my location of inspiration, and the bakery was closed for maintenance. Sadly, she disappeared once again. However, I still knew she was out there somewhere because I saw her at Control a year after she left the library.

It had now been over two years since I last saw my beautiful blonde library angel at the library. I never imagined my spiritual journey with her might not be over as she left the library for the last time. However, my spiritual journey with her was not over after she left the library. She kept magically reappearing to me at times when I was not even thinking of her. First, there was the time when I learned she was working at this bakery near the library. Later I learned she was the manager of this bakery. Thus I knew she was not going anywhere. Then she reappeared to me at Control a year after she left the library. I could not believe it when I saw her at Control that day. I had to walk into Control at that exact moment to see her with that bright white smile. Then she was gone as quickly as she appeared. After this, I never dreamed of finding my way back to her. Then I fell into another pit of darkness, and she was the only angel of inspiration left for me to turn to for inspiration since she was still working at the bakery.

I started to go there for an unsweetened tea to start my day, hoping to see her at the bakery. This was the first time I went to the bakery since I found out she was working at the bakery since I did not want her thinking I was stalking her. I always knew she was at this bakery. Yet I knew that I could not say anything to her if I went there to see her. So I decided it might be best to leave things to my spiritual journey with her. I decided it was enough to simply know she never left town after learning she was at this bakery. Then I fell into another pit of darkness, and I lost all my angels of inspiration. After losing all my angels of inspiration, I decided it was time to try to see her again at the bakery. So I started a new routine of going there for my unsweetened tea everyday before I went to the coffee shop right across the street to start writing.

I believed this was going to be my new routine as I wrote my second book. I believed this coffee shop was going to be my coffee shop of inspiration. Then the unthinkable happened. I was banned from my coffee shop of inspiration. I was afraid I might never find another location of inspiration after the loss of my new French Bistro. After the loss of my new French Bistro, I had found ten locations of inspiration. However, none of these locations of inspiration were inspiring enough to be my new location of inspiration. It was either too warm at my locations of inspiration, or there were no beautiful angels of inspiration working there. So I started to fear I might lose my way as a writer since I could not find my inspiration to write. Then this coffee shop of inspiration started to be a great place to write until around two. Therefore I thought I found my location of inspiration until two, until the unthinkable happened.

I was starting to find my way out of my fall into another pit of darkness when the unthinkable happened. I had only been going to this coffee shop for about two months before I was banned. So I had no time to build any real memories at this coffee shop. My only real memory of this coffee shop of inspiration was being banned from it. I will never forget how I felt when the manager approached me to tell me that I was banned from this coffee shop. I remember I was sitting by the window to see the bakery where my angel was working. Then I saw this beautiful blonde coffee shop angel sit where I could see her during her break. I thought things were going great because I thought these angels were comfortable with me being there. Then I looked over at the cash register, and this other angel made me really uncomfortable. She was making me uncomfortable because she was looking at me look at the coffee shop angel. However, I tried to tell myself I was imagining things. Then the beautiful blonde coffee shop angel went back to work, and I was feeling great about finding a new location of inspiration. Then the unthinkable happened as the manager banned me from the coffee shop of inspiration.

The manager started walking toward me at my coffee shop of inspiration. I somehow knew why he was walking toward me because of my original French Bistro. I somehow knew he was approaching me to tell me I was banned from this coffee shop of inspiration. Then he proceeded to ask me to pack my things because he wanted to talk with me outside. So I packed my things, and I took the slow, embarrassing walk outside. I could not believe what was happening. I could not believe how cruel this world could be to me, all because they did not understand the weirdness of my anxiety. Then I went outside, and he explained that he looked at my book and did not want my kind there. He may not have said "my kind." However, it felt as if this was what he said because I felt I was being discriminated against for being different. He also said something about me never buying anything there, and I knew it was always busy there. So this may have also had something to do with it. Yet I felt it was more discrimination because the beautiful coffee shop angels working there banned against me to get me out of there.

I was so angry about being banned from this coffee shop of inspiration. I could not believe I was getting banned from a third location of inspiration. I tried to explain myself to him, and I asked him what I was doing wrong. However, I did not really care what he had to say because I was still banned no matter what he said. After this, I started walking toward my car feeling so hurt that I wanted to commit suicide. I simply could not live in a world where it felt so wrong for liking beautiful women. I knew I could never stop liking beautiful women. I knew how I felt when I saw a beautiful woman. I knew how inspiring it was to see one of my angels. So I knew I was never going to stop wanting to see these beautiful angels. However, I felt the world was telling me I was wrong for wanting to look at beautiful women. I felt the world was telling me I was evil for wanting to see beautiful women. Unfortunately, I could not stop being who I was no matter how much the world felt it was wrong.

I knew there was nothing I could say to the manager to get him to change his mind. I knew this coffee shop of inspiration was lost to me forever. So I started to defend myself to him before I left. I asked him what I was doing wrong because I was not approaching these angels because of my social anxiety. Then he said the words I was starting to hate hearing. He said he understood because he also had social anxiety. Hearing people say these words was like hearing fingernails scratch a chalkboard. I am not saying that none of these people have never had social anxiety. However, they do not understand the extremities of my social anxiety. They got over their social anxiety somehow by talking. They do not understand what it is like to truly be me because if they did, they knew I was not a threat because I could never approach my angels. Finally, I stopped defending myself because I could tell it was not helping because I really did not care what he had to say since I was still banned from my coffee shop of inspiration. So finally, I left this coffee shop of inspiration with this memory of being banned and a few angels.

I do not have many fond memories of my time at this coffee shop of inspiration since I was only there for about two months. I do remember this one beautiful blonde coffee shop angel that worked there because she was so beautiful. Then I also remember this one visiting blonde angel because she literally moved to face me one time when I was there writing. I also remember these angels who helped me find my way after I fell into a really dark pit of darkness.

It was the fourth of July, and I was working at a convenience store near my house for extra money. I had to work with this guy who made me really uncomfortable because he was such a bully. However, I knew this was the last time I was ever going to work with him. Therefore, I tried to keep to myself as best I could. My plan was to stay hidden away at the cooler until it was time to go home. Then the shift started with me talking to one of the most beautiful blonde angels I have ever seen. So I thought the night was going to be all right because I was even able to joke with this Bluto at work some. Then some more angels were at the convenience store. So I decided to leave the cooler and help out at the registers. However, this was a mistake because this was when I fell into my darkest pit of darkness.

It started to get really busy. I mean really busy. The convenience store was filled with people, and this bully kept insulting me and provoking me into a fight. I tried to ignore him for about two hours. Then he walked toward me as though he was going to attack me, and I was done because this work was not worth me losing my life. So I went to clock out, and I left him with all the customers. This did not sit well with him or the customers because they did not care about anything that was happening other than getting their alcohol. However, I was able to get out of the store safely and I made my way to my car when I realized I forgot my phone. I could have left my phone there, and maybe this was the smart move because things got much worse after I returned.

I walked into the convenience store ignoring everyone. I got my phone without this Bluto doing anything. I am honestly shocked that nothing happened when I walked by him to get my phone. However, luckily, nothing did happen with this Bluto at the convenience store. Then I got to the door and I was about to leave when everything hit the fan. I heard this woman ask my name, and she told everyone at the store that I was this stalker of young women. She was spreading all these lies about me and about all the contents of my book. All I could say was that they were lies. Then I left the store and literally felt as though I had walked into a warzone because I was surrounded by people and cars due to the fireworks at the airfield across the street.

I had never been more scared than I was that Fourth of July. I was literally afraid someone was going to follow me home that night. So I could not go home because I did not want anyone to know where I lived. Also, I was not thinking clearly after all this happened because of my fear of humanity. All I could do for about an hour after this happened was drive around town looking for a place to get a Pepsi since I did not get one at the convenience store. Finally, I did get home to tell my mom about what had happened. However, she did not know what to tell me other than to not go back to work there, which I never planned to do anyways. I could not stay home the first time I got home, though, because I still wanted my Pepsi. Plus, I could not sit around the house dwelling upon what had happened. So I went back out to find a place to get a soda. I finally got my soda and returned home for the night. Although, I was so traumatized by what had happened that night that I could not eat or calm down enough to sleep.

All I could do was think about one of the most traumatic bullying events of my life. I could not turn to my best friends for support since I signed off on all social media sites. I decided to sign off on all social media sites after I lost my new French Bistro since they were no help. Everyone I communicated with was telling me I was a stalker. Nobody understood my side of the story, and I could not find the tolerance to defend myself to humanity. So I told my best friends goodbye until I wrote my second book. I decided to pour everything into my book since I felt I was the only one who could understand the weirdness of my anxiety. Finally, I went to sleep and a new day started. I was not feeling any better when I first got out of bed. Honestly, I am not even sure how I got out of bed. Yet I did manage to somehow get out of bed. I took a shower. I got dressed. Then I got into my car, not sure where I was going to go that day. I only knew I could not stay home because I might never leave my house if I stayed home. My first stop was at the convenience store to tell the manager about what happened. I said I was done working there. After I explained what happened, she said she understood and hoped I might feel safe again. Later, she looked at the tape and apologized since it was the bullies' fault.

I was not expecting to have a very inspirational day at the coffee shop once I finally arrived. Then when I got to the coffee shop, there were these two beautiful blonde angels who I first tried to avoid. I remember walking by them to sit somewhere where I could not see them because I feared making them uncomfortable if I sat too close to them. Then I changed my mind, and I went back to where they were sitting, and I sat beside the most beautiful of the two.

I was feeling so proud of myself for finding the courage to sit beside these two very beautiful blonde coffee shop angels. I knew that they could have left once I finally decided to sit beside them. However, I was hoping they did not leave because these angels were so beautiful. So I knew this was a risk I had to take because I felt the risk of them leaving was worth the reward of them staying. Luckily, once I finally sat by them, they did not leave. Instead, both the angels remained at the coffee shop until right before I was about ready to leave. Thus I knew sitting by them was one of the best decisions that I could have ever made after the Fourth of July.

What made me sitting by these two beautiful blonde coffee angels an even better experience was that I forgot my headphones. I thought this meant I was going to have to leave these two coffee shop angels because I could not listen to my music to feel a sense of safety. However, I decided to stay because I felt so inspired by the beauty of these two beautiful blonde coffee shop angels. Then I heard them start socializing, and I felt even more safe because they felt safe talking with me right there beside them. This probably meant nothing to them. However, to me this meant the world. I loved that these two angels felt a sense of safety while I was there after what happened at the convenience store. Finally, I even heard one of these angels say she was single, which had me thinking I might have a chance with her. However, I had no plans to do anything about this after the Fourth of July. I doubted I was ever going to find the courage to approach one of my angels again after the beautiful brunette golden angel. However, this pain I was feeling did not mean that I was ready to let go of my love for beautiful women. After sitting near these two beautiful blonde angels at the coffee shop of inspiration, I knew beautiful women were always going to be my inspiration no matter how dark my existence got.

I will never forget how sitting beside these two beautiful blonde coffee shop angels comforted me after the traumatic experience I had at the convenience store. I do not remember what these two beautiful angels looked like. I only remember they were so beautiful that they helped me to forget about the Fourth of July those few hours I was sitting beside them that day.

These two random coffee shop angels were so inspiring that I did not care that I could not listen to my music because of their voices. I also did not care about the discomfort I was feeling because I was sitting so close to them. I simply loved knowing that they felt comfortable enough to have me sitting so close to them. All I cared about was feeling their spiritual energy while they were sitting there. I literally felt like Superman when he is being energized by the yellow rays of the sun. I will always remember these two beautiful coffee shop angels because their beauty and comfort were the start of my rise from my fall into another pit of darkness. After seeing these coffee shop angels, I was reminded of the spiritual energy that I felt from my angels.

I am purposely saying angels rather than angel because I was now finding I valued variety over the one. I was not ready to return to my search for the one after what had happened with the beautiful brunette golden angel. I truly did believe I had a chance with the beautiful brunette golden angel before I gave her the love letter. I felt there were all these signs of interest I was feeling from her that had me believing that she might be the one. I had been going to my new French Bistro for two years. I never could talk to this beautiful brunette golden angel, and she never approached me to start a conversation with me either. So maybe this should have been a sign that she was not interested. Yet I felt there were these signs telling me she was the one.

I never dreamed I might feel worse than I did after the loss of my new French Bistro. The loss of my new French Bistro was so devastating because I lost my favorite place to write. I never thought I was going to get past the loss of my new French Bistro. Until I was slowly finding my way out of my fall into another pit of darkness at the coffee shop of inspiration. Then I got banned from my coffee shop of inspiration after the Fourth of July, and I fell into the darkest pit of darkness of my life. I was not sure if I was ever going to find my way out of this pit of darkness since I had lost all hope of ever finding the one after being banned again. I lost any confidence in approaching my beautiful angels after the beautiful brunette golden angel. Thus I felt all hope of finding the woman of my dreams was lost since I knew I could not approach an angel. So I lost all hope until the reappearance of the beautiful blonde sales angel.

# THE BEAUTIFUL BLONDE
# SALES ANGEL

The beautiful blonde sales angel was the first angel since high school who I really believed might be interested. The beautiful blonde from high school was this beautiful blonde angel who wrote me a letter to let me know she was actually interested. I may not remember exactly what this letter said since it was about thirty years ago now since she wrote me the letter. However, I know she was interested because she took the time to actually write me this letter. Sadly, I could never do anything to reciprocate her interest after she wrote me the letter because my social anxiety was always impeding my ability to socialize with her. Although, she did give me four chances to be with her, which is why I always think of her as my American soulmate. After I had lost all chances of ever being with this beautiful blonde angel from high school, I never dreamed I might find another angel as courageous or as forward as her. Then while working as a helper at Bon Gout, I met three of these socially confident angels one after another.

The first of these three beautiful sales angels I met at Bon Gout was only going to be at Bon Gout for one day. She was there for only one day because she was this traveling cell phone angel from Missouri. However, my day with her at Bon Gout was such a perfect day that it is a day I will never forget. This day started out like any other day. It started out with me standing at the entrance, helping my coworker with carts and talking to her about my angels of inspiration. I loved spending this time talking to her because she never judged me for my obsessions. She was one of the few people who actually understood me, and even supported my love for these angels. This was such a rare thing to find. So, I truly did treasure my time spent talking to her. Then as I was talking to her that Tuesday, one of the most beautiful blonde angels I ever saw arrived. After I saw this blonde angel enter the store, I could not stop thinking about her. Partly, this was because she was standing only a few feet away from the entrance selling cell phones. So I spent the following two hours at Bon Gout, thinking about this beautiful blonde sales angel. I could not stop talking to my coworker about how much I wished I could say something to her. Then she approached me to get a cart, and I was actually able to say something to her. I did not say much to her. I was simply responding to her calling me a gentleman after giving her a cart. However, this was enough to give me some hope. Then I had the best lunch of my life with her.

The best lunch of my life with her started with me going to the back room to sit by myself because I was feeling so depressed about not being able to socialize with this angel more. I was thinking about how much I wished I could be different. I thought about how much I wished I could be that person who could spend hours socializing with her. Sadly, I knew that this was not me because of my social anxiety. So I went to the back feeling sorry for myself. Then I decided to write a script of what I wished I could say to her if I had the courage. I never dreamed of actually reading this script to her after writing it. However, I was thinking I was prepared with what to say to her if I was ever able to get the courage to actually talk to her again.

It was finally time for me to eat lunch. I had all intentions of eating lunch by myself. Then something was telling me to go to the break room to eat lunch with everyone. I did not normally eat lunch with everyone because it was so quiet there you could hear a pin drop. However, this time my gut was telling me to go to the break room, and I was so glad I listened, because this was what was going to make this the best lunch of my life. After getting to the break room, I saw my coworker before she left for the day and told her about the script I wrote. Then I went to the microwave to heat my food. Finally, I spun around to sit down and eat. Then to my disbelieving eyes, I saw this beautiful blonde sales angel sitting right there.

This beautiful blonde sales angel was one of the most beautiful women I ever saw. I could not believe she was sitting right beside me during lunch. Then after she sat beside me the most unbelievable thing happened, I actually started to say something to her. I not only said something to her, I had one of the greatest conversations I ever had with a beautiful woman. I learned more about this angel during that lunch, than any of my other angels of inspiration. I learned what motivated her to be a sales agent for cell phones. I learned about where she lived. I learned about some of her likes and dislikes. Sadly, I also learned that she was only going to be at the store for one day since I made the mistake of telling her another store was much busier. We also spent some time talking about football and the Chiefs since she was from Missouri. Then I started to make her laugh, and she said that I was funny. After this, I started to tell her I was a writer, which led her to look for my book and joke about promoting my book. This lunch was literally the best lunch of my life since there was rarely an awkward silence. Honestly, I even felt as if my father was my inspiration since I felt I was him as I talked to her.

I knew I was eventually going to have to return to reality. I knew I could not sit there with her forever. Although, I did not want this lunch to be over since I was doing something I had literally never done before. Annabelle was the only other beautiful angel I had ever felt comfortable talking to before, and this was more than twenty years ago. Thus I knew that I rarely had an opportunity like this with these angels, and it was about to be over after this lunch.

I watched her close the lid to her snack. I watched her walk out of the break room. I knew that the best lunch of my life was over. I was proud of myself for having this conversation with this beautiful blonde sales angel. However, lunch was now over, and I had to return to the dark reality of knowing that this was an aberration that I doubted I could ever repeat. After the best lunch of my life was over, I could not say much to her after she returned to work. I was able to say hello to her a few times as I passed by her to admire her beauty. Also, there was a time when she told her coworker about my book. Finally, it was time for me to go home. So I had to say goodbye to her. As I said goodbye to her, she said she might buy my book, which I never really expected. After this, I never saw this beautiful blonde sales angel, or talked to her again.

This perfect day I had with this beautiful blonde sales angel is a day that I will never forget. I did not know why she only entered my life for this one perfect day. However, as much as I was devastated by her loss after that perfect day, I was still grateful I had this day with her. Unfortunately, I was never able to mimic this day again after she left. Sadly, I was never going to be able to find the courage I found that day to talk with another beautiful angel. However, after this perfect day, I was hopeful that I might find this chemistry again with another angel. The woman of my dreams was still a mystery, yet this experience increased my belief that she might exist.

I never thought I might find another angel as inspiring as this beautiful blonde sales angel. I was not sure how to move forward after I had this perfect day with her. Unfortunately, I also knew I had to find a way to move forward without her because she was gone. Yet I was still holding out hope that maybe a miracle might happen and she might return to my life. After all, I knew she was a traveling sales agent. So I knew there was a chance that she could one day reappear in my life. Yet I also believed that if I ever hoped to see her again, I had to keep working at Bon Gout. Thus I knew I could never lose my work at Bon Gout if I ever hoped to see her again. Sadly, days turned to weeks, and weeks turned to months, and I never saw her miraculous return to Bon Gout. Eventually, I started to forget about her. However, occasionally, I do still find myself hoping that this beautiful blonde sales angel might reappear.

I knew the chances of me seeing this beautiful blonde sales angel again were growing dimmer. I knew I had to find a way to forget about her because I was probably never going to see her again. Then as I was waiting for her return, another beautiful sales angel made her return. This angel was this beautiful black-haired sales angel who I was obsessed with seeing the week prior to seeing this beautiful blonde sales angel. I knew that this angel was not the beautiful blonde sales angel. However, she was still this beautiful angel with social confidence, and I was thrilled to have her back. Then she started talking to me as I walked by her, and I was inspired to try to approach her to say something. I knew that she was probably only talking to me to sell a phone. However, I was still inspired to try and approach her because she was being the initiator. Eventually, I felt so courageous around her that I approached her to let her know how impressed I was by her social confidence. She then said thank you, and I was feeling so much confidence from this interaction that I was starting to believe that I had a chance with her.

Her social confidence was so contagious. I could not help myself from feeling more socially confident when she was working. I never really did believe that she might be interested because I knew this social confidence was all merely a part of her personality. However, her social confidence had me believing I might actually have a chance with her. Then one day during lunch, I was at the mall nearby having lunch when I thought about giving her this gift.

I first got the idea to give her a gift when I saw a stuffed animal that made me think of her. This stuffed animal was a lion with a unicorn's horn. It also had this purple streak running through its mane of hair. After seeing this lion, I started to think about giving it to her. However, I knew I was not going to give it to her since I knew this was way too much too soon.

I knew I had to try to talk to her more to see if there was a connection before making such a grand gesture. I knew this was the normal way of doing things. Sadly, I also knew I had social anxiety. So I was afraid I might never be able to socialize with her. So I could not stop thinking about giving her this gift since I knew socializing was not my path to her. I knew my only path to her, if there was one, was to tell her how I felt with letters and cards. So I kept thinking about giving her this stuffed animal with a card. Yet I still thought this was too much until I talked to my coworker. Shockingly, my coworker encouraged me to give her this gift, which only enticed me more to make this grand gesture. So finally, I decided I had to at least get the stuffed animal to give it to her if I was ever able to find the courage to do so. The following day during lunch, I went to the mall to get her this stuffed animal and get her a card.

It took no time at all for me to find her a card to go with the stuffed animal because as soon as I started looking for a card, I found this blank card that was shaped like a cat. I knew that this card was what I was looking for because of what I was going to write on this card. I wanted to write, "This is for the beautiful black-haired angel with the pride of social confidence." I felt this was the perfect thing to write because this was exactly how I felt about her. I felt I was telling her exactly how I felt about her without scaring her. So I had the stuffed animal to give to her, and I had the perfect card to give to her. Now all that was left for me to do was to somehow find the courage to give her everything. However, this was also the most difficult thing to do because I was so scared she might not accept it if I approached her. I knew I was taking a chance of her saying no if I gave it to her. I knew that she might not be receptive of my grand gesture. I was also not sure if I was ever going to find the courage I needed to approach her to make this grand gesture. Finally, I got the idea to give it to her when she was not looking.

I knew that this was the cowardly way to do things. I knew I might never know if she even accepted it by giving it to her this way. However, I also believed that it was the cowardly way or no way. So I decided to go the cowardly way. I decided to approach her desk while she was with a customer and drop it off when she was not looking. I decided to do this right before I left for the day because I did not want to see her again after I gave it to her. Then I knew I was off that following day. This meant she was going to have a day to absorb it all before we saw each other again. Then I was going to see her again and find out her response. So I knew once I gave her everything, the difficult part was over. At least I thought giving it to her was the difficult part. However, then I realized that finding out her response was the real difficult part.

A day had passed since I gave her the card with the lion. It was now time to return to work to find out what she thought about my grand gesture. I was feeling so anxious about seeing her at work after making this grand gesture because I had no clue what might happen. At first, when she got to work, she did not see me, which was really disheartening. Then when she did see me, she approached me to thank me for the card and the lion, and she told me it made her day. So I was relieved to learn she appreciated it. Unfortunately, once I made this gesture, I still could not say anything to her due to my social anxiety. So after giving her the card and the lion, I started to think about giving her a letter to introduce myself and explain my social anxiety. I wanted her to understand that I was not trying to be rude to her. I wanted her to know I was still interested. However, my social anxiety was keeping me from telling her all these things. So I started to write her a letter. I wanted to introduce myself while also not scaring her by telling her that I thought she might be the one. Finally, I wrote the letter and gave it to her the same cowardly way I gave her the card with the lion. I again waited a day to see her again. Then when I saw her at work, she told me she liked the confidence that I showed with the letter. Sadly, once again, after I gave her the letter, I could not socialize, so nothing happened with her. So this was when I realized that she was never actually interested and she was merely being polite and kind. I was disappointed until I was introduced to a third beautiful blonde sales angel.

The third beautiful blonde sales angel was the most inspirational angel of all three beautiful sales angels because I did not even notice her at first. I was so involved with trying to see if anything might happen with the black-haired angel when she arrived. Also, I did not believe I had any shot with this blonde angel when she first arrived because she was so beautiful. Then after I gave the black-haired angel the letter, the most unbelievable thing started happening. This beautiful blonde sales angel started to approach me at work, and I thought she might actually be interested. However, I still could not believe this gorgeous supermodel was interested. So I kept telling myself she was not interested until I felt there were too many signs of interest to ignore anymore. Yet even though I felt she might be interested, I still could not believe that this beautiful blonde sales angel might be interested because she was so beautiful. I never imagined having a chance with this beautiful blonde sales angel. So when she started showing me all these signs of interest, I was not sure how to react due to my social anxiety.

I felt such mixed emotions when she was showing me these signs of interest. I was feeling excited because I thought I might have a real chance with her. Then I was also feeling such fear because if she was actually interested, this meant I had to socialize with her. Yet I knew that my social anxiety was not going to disappear because she was interested. Then as I felt things get more real with her, I started to feel more anxious because I liked her so much. Then she was standing so close to me at the entrance that I was confused about all these mixed emotions. I finally left for the day, and when I returned the following day, she was gone.

Days passed! Weeks passed! My beautiful blonde sales angel was gone. I never felt more heartbroken than I did after she disappeared. I felt so heartbroken after she left because I felt something real was happening with her. Then she disappeared, and I was not sure how to deal with her loss because she was so special. I was not sure if my beautiful blonde sales angel was ever going to return to Bon Gout after she left. However, I was hoping that she might return. So I knew I could not lose my work at Bon Gout since I was so hoping to see her again.

Could this beautiful blonde sales angel be the woman of my dreams? Who knows? I only know that I never met an angel as special as this beautiful blonde sales angel before. I had never met an angel with the social confidence and compassion that she had before. Plus, this beautiful blonde sales angel was one of the most beautiful angels I ever saw before. As a matter of fact, this beautiful angel was so beautiful that I could not imagine having a chance with her. This was why I approached the beautiful black-haired angel. Then after I approached the beautiful black-haired angel, this beautiful blonde sales angel showed me these signs of interest.

The first sign that had me believing this beautiful blonde sales angel was actually interested was when she said hello to me as I was helping a customer. Sadly, I did not really hear her when she said hello to me because I was helping this customer. Thus I decided to ignore her because I could not believe this gorgeous supermodel went out of her way to say hi.

The second sign of interest happened when she went across the store to ask me a question about televisions for a customer. She could have asked anyone else for help because there were so many other employees working there that Wednesday. Yet she chose to walk across the store to ask me a question out of everyone else, which really made me feel special. After this, I could not ignore her anymore.

I was confused about which sales angel I really wanted. Honestly, I was never really that confused though because I knew the beautiful blonde sales angel was the one I really wanted. However, I still could not believe she was interested until I felt so many more signs that this gorgeous supermodel may actually BE INTERESTED!

The third sign of interest I felt from this beautiful blonde sales angel was not any one sign. It was more about all the times she was smiling and waving at me at Bon Gout. I mean, she never ignored me as we worked together at Bon Gout. Every single time she saw me looking at her, which was all the time really, she smiled at me and waved. So she must have been interested. Maybe not physically. However, I really do believe that she wanted to be friends. Unfortunately, my social anxiety kept making it so difficult for me to socialize with her.

The fourth sign of interest was when I really believed that she was interested. I believed that she might be interested when she approached me about a rude customer one day. I was standing at the entrance when she was returning from lunch. I was trying to act like I was not staring at how beautiful she was, which was quite difficult. Then she pulled me to the side to tell me how bad she felt when I had to deal with a rude customer since she also dealt with a rude customer. After this, there were a few more signs that she might be interested. However, none were as clear as this one. There was a time she said she liked my haircut after giving the letter to the beautiful black-haired angel. Finally, there was how she was so close to me at the entrance as she greeted customers. I could not ignore how close she was to the entrance because there was no need for her to be that close. Her station was much farther from the entrance than this, and none of the other angels were ever that close to the entrance. So I felt she wanted me to see her.

A Friday was the last day I thought I was ever going to see her at Bon Gout. I was really starting to believe that she was the woman of my dreams that Friday. I was so flustered as she was standing so close to me that Friday that I could not compose myself. I could not think clearly, and

I knew then that she was interested. So I thought I had to start thinking about how to make a move. Then she disappeared from Bon Gout forever that following Saturday. So the beautiful black-haired angel was the only one left until she also disappeared that Monday. So now all three of these beautiful sales angels were gone. I was hoping that someday I might see my beautiful blonde sales angel again. Then as the weeks passed, I was starting to lose all hope of ever seeing her again. Then she magically reappeared to me after my fall into another pit of darkness. So I thought my spiritual journey might have been leading me to her until my social anxiety impeded my ability to be with her once again. After the loss of this beautiful blonde sales angel, I lost all hope of finding the one until the return of my beautiful blonde library angel.

# THE RETURN OF MY
# BEAUTIFUL BLONDE
# LIBRARY ANGEL

The return of my beautiful blonde library angel was something I never expected. It was kismet all over again. I was having a very dark day when I walked into Control that day because I was unable to say much to these two angels I was attracted to at work. Before leaving work that Friday, these two beautiful angels were angels that I was starting to socialize with at work. I could not believe that I was actually starting to socialize with these two new angels at work. However, I was able to, and one of the main reasons why I was able to was because they were the initiators. The first angel to initiate a conversation with me was this beautiful Latin angel working at Bon Gout. I could not believe how friendly and socially outgoing this beautiful Latin angel was with people. She was this bubbly shot of energy at work and I could not stop being drawn to her beauty because she was also very beautiful. Then she started to say hi to me at work, which felt wonderful because she entered my life after I'd lost all hope of finding the one.

So this beautiful Latin angel at Bon Gout was starting to turn into my new angel of inspiration. Then she disappeared for about two weeks, and I was truly devastated because she was so inspirational. I literally felt the atmosphere at Bon Gout darken until her return two weeks later.

This beautiful brunette Latin angel working at Bon Gout was my glimmer of hope after losing all hope of ever finding the woman of my dreams. I lost all hope of finding the woman of my dreams because I felt all hope was lost with the beautiful blonde sales angel. I never imagined I might see this beautiful blonde sales angel again after she left Bon Gout the first time. I was hoping to see her again. However, I was hoping to see the first beautiful blonde sales angel again too, and she never returned. So, I never imagined I might see this beautiful blonde sales angel again until I saw this beautiful blonde angel cross my path at Bon Gout. At first, I did not know that this was her because she was even more beautiful than I remembered. Then, I saw her smile and vibrant energy as she waved and said hello, and I thought it might be her. After leaving Bon Gout, I thought about going back to find out for sure if it was her. Yet I chose not to because I did not want to know the truth. I wanted to keep the hope alive that it might be her. Then I returned that following day, and she was not there. So I thought I was wrong about her return until I did see her again two days later. However, I was not sure what to do with her being back. I knew I could not approach her after my fall into another pit of darkness. I lost any courage or confidence I had found to approach my angels after the beautiful brunette golden angel. I knew I was not ready to pursue her after getting hurt by the beautiful brunette golden angel. Yet I did not want her to think I was not interested if I did not talk to her.

I did not have to worry about how to approach her. She was going to be the one to initiate the conversation with me on her first day back at Bon Gout. I saw her walking toward me at Bon Gout. I was not sure what to do when I saw her walking toward me because she was so beautiful that I wanted to keep staring at her. Yet I knew it was not right to stare at her. So I tried to get back to folding clothes when I saw her getting closer and closer. Then, she finally walked toward me and asked me if I missed her. I said, of course, I missed her, and stopped there.

I wanted to say, "What a dumb question, of course I missed you! You are one of the most beautiful women I ever saw! You could be the woman of my dreams! You could be the angel I had been waiting for all my life, and you are back! So of course, I missed you!"

However, I stopped myself from saying all these things since I knew this was way too much too soon. So after telling her that I missed her, she voluntarily told me where she was working now. Sadly, she also told me that she was back for only one day. Finally, she left to get back to work, and I returned to folding clothes. As I was folding clothes, I started thinking how great it felt to see her again. I knew that she was only back at Bon Gout for a day. However, after talking to her, I now knew where she was working. So I was thinking I might be able to go and see her everyday after work. So I started to think of her as being the woman of my dreams again. However, I was not sure how to pursue her because of my social anxiety. I still knew my social anxiety was going to make it difficult for me to socialize with her. I still knew that I had to socialize with her to have a relationship with her. Sadly, this was still something I was unable to do because of my social anxiety. So my dreams of being with her started to unravel after her return since I was unable to socialize with her. Yet I still tried to pursue her since I believed she might be the one.

I approached her during lunch that same day. We were able to have our first brief conversation. I told her I was a writer. Then I told her that I was really excited about investing money into my book because they wanted to try to turn it into a movie. We talked about my wanting to be a traveling writer. She said that she also liked to travel. Then I said I wanted to move where it was cold, and she told me that she also liked the cold. Finally, we were even starting to talk about how Colorado was a great place to live because of the cold and the people.

This was our first real conversation. I felt really uncomfortable when I was talking to her. I learned about her when we talked, and it was really great to learn so much about her. I learned almost as much about her as I did about the first blonde sales angel. However, I knew the comfort I felt with her was not there. This was really disappointing because before our first conversation, I thought there were all these signs that she was interested. Then during our conversation, I was starting to realize that this may have only been her personality. This was a painful thing to realize because I so wanted her to be the one because she was so beautiful. Sadly, I started to realize the chemistry was not there with her as it was with the other blonde. I still tried to pursue her after this because I was hoping I was wrong. I started driving out to where she told me she was working to try to socialize with her, which was very uncomfortable.

Our conversations never went anywhere. I could never feel socially comfortable with her. I wanted it to work because I remembered my time with her at Bon Gout before she left the first time. Sadly, I could never feel socially comfortable with her. However, I was able to somehow give her my book and a card, which she appreciated. Also, I still hope to one day find my way back to her. However, I know I have to learn how to socialize with beautiful women better before this ever happens. After all, I still believe she was interested. I still believe that those signs of interest were real. Sadly,

I was unable to take advantage of the chance she offered me because of my social anxiety. So I do not blame her at all for things not working out because I believe she gave me these chances to be with her. Sadly, I could not do anything with those chances because of my social anxiety. So for now, my spiritual journey with her is over. However, I hope someday I will be able to find my way back to my beautiful blonde sales angel.

I'd lost all hope of ever finding the woman of my dreams after the loss of this beautiful blonde sales angel. I knew I was done pursuing one of my angels because of my social anxiety. I now knew my only chance of being with the woman of my dreams was if she had the social confidence to be the initiator. I knew I was never going to be socially comfortable with a woman unless she started to socialize with me first. I did not care if this was fair. I did not care if this meant that I was going to be alone for the rest of my life. This was who I was, and this was never going to change, especially after my fall into another pit of darkness.

Sadly, I knew how rare it was to find beautiful women with the social confidence to be the initiators. I knew there were beautiful angels out there because I still saw them at Bon Gout. I knew there were women out there who could make me feel socially comfortable because of the wise old grandmothers at Bon Gout. However, the three beautiful sales angels were the only angels of inspiration I met who were both beautiful and socially confident enough to make me feel socially comfortable around them. So after the beautiful blonde sales angel disappeared again, I lost any hope that I had of ever finding the woman of my dreams. Then I met these two beautiful brunette angels at Bon Gout.

The beautiful brunette Latin angel working at Bon Gout was gone for two weeks. I thought she might be the woman of my dreams. So I was devastated to learn that she might be gone before my spiritual journey with her went anywhere. Then I met this other beautiful brunette angel at Bon Gout, who gave me hope while she was gone. I knew from the start that this beautiful brunette angel had a boyfriend. So I knew that nothing could happen with her. Yet she kept saying hi, and we kept talking to each other anyways. So I started to believe that maybe someday there might be a path to her if we kept talking to each other. However, if anything was ever going to happen with her then she had to first be single.

I never wanted to be the other man. I never wanted to be the man to take a beautiful woman away from another man. I knew how difficult it was to find a beautiful woman. I knew how hurt I would be if a man ever took away the woman of my dreams. So I knew I never wanted to be that man because I could not live with myself if I was that man. Yet after saying all this, if the man is truly hurtful and a bad man, this is a different story. Also, if the woman is not with the man anymore, then this is a different story. Sadly, this was not the case for this beautiful brunette angel I was talking to at work. She was with the son of someone I liked from work, who was having a difficult time because of injuries, and the son was helping her. So I believed him to be a good person. So I could not do anything to try to be with her. Yet we were socializing, and I liked talking to her. I liked that she was always the initiator of these conversations. So I had to take this as an opportunity to learn how to socialize with a beautiful woman. This was difficult to do because I hated being alone. I never felt the need to socialize with beautiful women if I had no chance of ever being with them. I knew what I was looking for from a beautiful woman. I knew I wanted a relationship with a beautiful woman. I knew I wanted someone who liked me as much as I liked them. I knew I was never going to find someone who liked me as much as I liked them if they were not available. So I never saw the point of socializing with a beautiful woman if they were unavailable. Then this beautiful brunette angel started talking to me, and I felt different about her because she was so friendly.

These were not the only beautiful angels at Bon Gout who were unavailable. Most beautiful angels working at Bon Gout were unavailable. There was a beautiful blonde pharmacy angel who was unavailable and way out of my league. She was way out of everyone's league. She was way too beautiful, friendly, married, and rich to be working at Bon Gout. However, she was working there, and I saw no signs of her ever leaving. This beautiful blonde pharmacy angel had been at Bon Gout ever since I started to work there. However, it was not until I made my return to Bon Gout that she turned into this beautiful blonde pharmacy angel. Sadly, I always knew I was never going to have a chance with her because she was married. She was wearing this bright, glowing diamond ring, and I also knew that she had four children. Plus, she was so happy all the time. So I knew the guy had to be a really respectable and good man. I honestly could not see her settling for anything less. Thus this beautiful blonde pharmacy angel was someone at work I was very attracted to, yet I knew I could never be with her. However, this never stopped me from passing by the pharmacy everyday to see her. Everyday, whether I was off or working, I went to Bon Gout to get a soda. Then I walked by the pharmacy to see this beautiful blonde pharmacy angel. Afterward, I made my rounds to see if any of these other beautiful angels were working before passing the pharmacy once again to see this beautiful blonde angel.

This beautiful blonde pharmacy angel was not the only angel at work I was obsessing over who I never really had a chance with since I knew they were involved with someone else.

There was this beautiful brunette tattooed angel from the bakery who I was attracted to ever since my return to Bon Gout. This beautiful brunette tattooed angel was very quiet. She liked to stay hidden and invisible when she was at work, and she was very good at it. However, this never stopped me from seeing her everyday if she was working. This beautiful brunette tattooed angel was my second stop after seeing if the beautiful blonde pharmacy angel was working. I was never really a fan of tattoos before this beautiful brunette tattooed angel. I never really cared for tattoos because when I saw someone with a tattoo, I automatically saw them as a bully. However, I never really cared that this beautiful brunette tattooed angel had tattoos because she was so darn beautiful. Sadly, she was also so quiet that I could never dream of saying anything to her because of my social anxiety. Although, I do remember being there this one time when I was able to say good night to her because it was so quiet, and I was feeling so calm and brave. Regrettably, this was the only time I ever said anything to this beautiful brunette tattooed angel.

This beautiful brunette intimidating angel was another beautiful angel at Bon Gout I could never be with since she was unavailable. This beautiful brunette intimidating angel was very intimidating because she also looked like a bodybuilder. Plus, she always looked so serious. She was also very dedicated to her work at Bon Gout. So I never really felt comfortable looking at her at work because I was afraid she might confront me about it. Also, I knew I could not be with someone who looked so intimidating because of my social anxiety. Then I started to see this angel at work more and more, and I started to realize she was really beautiful and actually very friendly. So while her confidence was intimidating at first, I eventually started to believe that this same confidence might actually give me a chance with her.

I still believed she was unavailable and I still could not talk to her. Yet I was able to somehow find the courage to say hi to her a few times. Then, I lost my courage and she returned to being the beautiful brunette intimidating angel. So I kept trying to bring myself back down to earth when I saw her. Yet I could not stop thinking I might one day have a chance with her. Then I was stationed to work right where I could watch her cut meat for about five hours. This was like heaven because I was paid to watch this angel work. I did have moments when I was uncomfortable. Mostly, though, these moments were heavenly because she was so beautiful. I still do not believe she is the one. However, it was great to imagine that my spiritual journey might have been leading me to the beautiful brunette intimidating angel.

I was devastated to learn that the beautiful brunette Latin angel was gone. Two weeks passed since the last time I saw her at Bon Gout. I never imagined she might return because her brother was also gone. Then to my delightful surprise, I saw this beautiful brunette Latin angel return. I could not believe my eyes when I saw the return of this Latin angel. So I said hi and told her I thought she quit. Then she said she was gone because of COVID. I told her how thrilled I was to have her back, and she said thanks. Unfortunately, I rarely saw her at work after this because she worked nights and I worked during the middle of the day. So we worked together for only about two hours and she was all over the store when I had to stand at one spot. Thus all I was able to do was say hi to her. Although, I did try to seek her out before going home to say goodbye. Unfortunately, I felt uncomfortable doing this because of my past of being banned from places for being seen as a stalker and because of my social anxiety. So I was putting less and less effort into finding her because I did not want to scare her. Yet I also wanted to see her because she was so beautiful. Also, what I loved about her was she might be available. I was not sure if she was single. Yet I believed that I had a chance with her because she was young and not wearing a ring. Sadly, I also felt uncomfortable talking to her. So I knew if I was ever going to have a chance with her, then I was going to take it very slow with her.

I was done pursuing one of my beautiful angels. I was prepared to spend a life alone without love because I could not be hurt by another one of my angels. I had to know for certain if this angel liked me before I tried to be with her again. The beautiful blonde sales angel was the last beautiful angel I was ever going to pursue again. At least, this was how I felt when I was writing my second book. I had lost all hope of ever finding love after the loss of the beautiful brunette golden angel and my beautiful blonde sales angel. I know a man is supposed to be the initiator. I know they say that this is the only way for a man to ever be with a beautiful woman. So if this is the case, then I guess I will be alone forever since I fear I will never find the courage to approach one of my angels ever again. Then if I am somehow able to find the courage, I have no clue how to talk to them when it is time to talk to them. This was how I felt after being banned from my French Bistro and the coffee shop of inspiration. This was how I felt after I was hurt by the beautiful brunette golden angel. This was how I felt after the second disappearance of the beautiful blonde sales angel. This was how I felt after I realized how uncomfortable I was when I tried to socialize with the two beautiful brunette angels. I realized how I might not find love due to my debilitating social anxiety and my fear of humanity.

This was how I felt when I left work that Friday. This was the cloud of darkness I had hovering over me when I left work that Friday. I saw no hope for my future. I did not see this as a belief anymore. I felt I knew I was going to die alone. I saw no way around it. I felt my fear of humanity was something that I was never going to be able to get over to be with someone. I believed that everyone saw me as a criminal because I loved to look at beautiful women. I believed that all beautiful women were uncomfortable with me looking at them. Yet I could not stop looking at them because I loved seeing their beauty. I felt I knew that I could not talk to beautiful women. Then even if I somehow found the courage to say something to them once, I could never continue to talk to them. Finally, there was the belief I had that I was always inferior to other men because of all my inadequacies. Thus I left work feeling that all hope was lost.

I started my routine of walking around Bon Gout to see my beautiful angels before leaving for the day. I was feeling dark. However, I was not dead. I still had to see the beauty of my angels of inspiration at work before I left for the day. I did not care how dark things got—I still wanted to see the beauty of my angels. So I walked by the bakery to see if my beautiful brunette, tattooed angel was working. I knew the beautiful brunette intimidating angel was not working because she was always off before I left work. Then I walked around Bon Gout to search for the beautiful brunette angels since they did not have a station where they worked. Sadly, I got only a quick glance at the beautiful brunette Latin angel and the other beautiful brunette angel. Finally, I walked by the pharmacy to see the beautiful blonde pharmacy angel.

I got my soda. I was ready to leave Bon Gout. Then I walked over to the entrance before I left because I was hoping to tell my coworker about this darkness that I was feeling. However, I saw that she was talking to someone, and I knew that I was not going to be comfortable talking to her with him there. So, I literally did a U-turn after I saw him there, and I left the store for the day feeling that all hope was lost. I was not sure if I wanted to go to Control when I felt all hope was lost. I was not sure if I wanted to deal with humanity and everyone knowing that I was there to see the beautiful angels that worked and shopped there.

Honestly, though, I knew I had to go there to see these angels to be lifted out of this darkness. I was unsure of what to expect as I walked into Control Friday, October 1st, 2021. I was hoping to see either the beautiful blonde security guard or the beautiful brunette clothing angel. Instead, who I saw was a blonde angel with a bright, white smile and the face of an angel.

Thus, once again, my spiritual journey led me back to my beautiful blonde library angel.